I0719053

The Platinum-Level Transluminal Vacation Package of
Your Dreams

Creative Writer PRO
Chicago

Produced in the United States of America.

Library of Congress Cataloging-in-Publication Data
Garlington, Bull.
The Platinum-Level Transluminal Vacation Package of Your Dreams
ISBN 978-1-943333-16-5

www. creativewriter.pro
www.bullgarlington.com

For son, for my daughter, for the noble tardigrae wherever they may be, and of course forever and always for [My Attorney].

Contents

Chapter 0

"Agent Number 1134. Please, take a seat." The Human Resources Manager of Transluminal Vacations, Inc. shuts the door to her office behind Agent 1134. She sits down at her desk. She picks up a pen and clicks it once.

Click.

"Why're you using my employee I.D. Number?"

"Anonymity assures impartiality," She clicks the pen two times. "The nature of our services requires us to take every precaution against favoritism."

"Specknacular." 1134 looks around. "I've never been called into H.R."

She opens a folder. Looks down.

Click. Click. Click.

"Twenty years on the job, 1134. Not a single incident. Not only that, you've written a number of our protocols."

"I didn't know about the impartiality thing."

"It's need-to-know."

"Why do I need to know now?"

She leans back into her expensive office chair.

Clickety click.

"You're about to make your 100th sale."

"Am I? I hadn't noticed."

"Despite how you've decorated the last square on the closing board?" She almost grins.

Click clickety ckick.

1134 sees that whiteboard in his mind. It's divided into rows of salesmen's names and a hundred columns for their sales. He can see the final box of his row—his last sale. It's filled-in with a cartoon palm tree drawn in dry-erase green.

"I may have thought about it once."

Clickety clickety clickety click.

"Not all salesmen have a Fuck You Money Timeline, 1134."

"Language," 1134 deadpans.

"How, in twenty years, have you managed to avoid it?"

"Deep in my heart, I'm a rules guy."

"The pain of withholding explosive sardonic laughter is excruciating."

1134 folds his arms and looks at a poster on the wall.

"I may have peeked. Once," 1134 inspects the bookshelves, the furniture. "Twice."

"Fourteen instances of unauthorized access to alternate timelines."

"Or fourteen. Am I in trouble?"

She slaps the folder closed.

"No. We're in weird territory, ethically. I mean we as a company. We sell vacations into alternate timelines to greedy billionaires. What we do isn't what a lawyer would describe as legal. However, no lawyer can describe it as *illegal*. It is, in the finest definition of the term, *unlegal*.

Which puts people in my position in a tight spot, ethically speaking. The thing is, twelve of the unauthorized access incidents occurred in the last three years."

"That's weird."

"And in none of them did you actually access your financial derivative stream, your FMYT. You visited the same baseline adjacent downstream thread every time. Statistically, it is indistinguishable from your base timeline."

1134 looks at her thumb on the top of the pen.

Click click. Click click.

He looks into her eyes.

"Look, I never accessed my FYMT, and I never took anything, and I never changed anything. It was...It was personal training. That's why it's the same one."

Click. Click. Click.

"You gotta stay honed in this game," 1134 says nervously.

Click. Click.

"I mean, there's a whole generation of grinders coming up on my tail. I'm forty-eight years old. I have to stay sharp."

Click.

"They make a great chardog."

"There's no protocol against visiting adjacent timelines. It would be hard for you to sell alternate timeline vacation packages if there were. And your track record–ninety-nine platinum-level packages," she lays the pen down. "Well, it carries a lot of weight." She slips out a paperclipped document with yellow signature tabs feathering the edges. She plops it down in front of 1134 and spins it right side up. 1134 is carefully avoiding looking down at the document, keeping his eyes blank and steady on hers. "You've earned this."

Then he looks down. He sees what he knew was already there, the reward of 20 years of hard work, 20 years of jumping timelines to run down leads and play them out like it's a long con in some crime movie. His gold watch. His retirement package. He'd dreamed about this moment for 20 years, waited and grinded endlessly just to look down and see, on company letterhead, a Platinum-Level Vacation Package with his name at the top.

"Goddam," he whispers.

"Just sign where it says to and be aware this is contingent on you closing your 100th sale. But that's kind of a foregone conclusion,"

Clicketyclicketyclicketyclicketyclicketyclickety clickety clickety clickety clickety click.

"You are, undoubtably, the best salesman in the biz. This is almost a formality."

He signs. Turns a page and signs again. Turns to the last page but before he signs his final signature, 1134 asks.

"What happens if I don't close?"

"You're in the sales funnel already, aren't you?"

"Actually, I don't have a lead."

"1134, you're retiring in two days. We had you down as being in the close phase of a pitch."

"Guy backed out." He signs his name.

"Oh," she carefully slides the clip back onto the papers, places them in the folder, then drops the folder into a vertical file. "Well, your package is only viable while you are employed. If you don't close by the time your retirement kicks in, you lose access."

1134 looks back at the poster. It says, "Hang in there Baby".

It is not encouraging.

Chapter 1

"Don't freak out!"

"AAAAAAAAAAAAAAAAAAAAAAAAAAAAAAAAAAAAAAAAA
AAAAAAAAAAAAAAAAAAAAAAAAAAAAAAAAAAAAAAAAA
AAAAAAAAAAAAAAAAAAAAAAAAAAAAAAAAAAAAAAAAA
AAAAAAAAAAAAAAAAAAAAAAAAA—"

"Dude, stop fre—"

"AAAAAAAAAAAAAAAAAAAAAAAAAAAAAAAAAAAAAAAA
AAAAAAAAAAAAAAAAAAAAAAAAAAAAAAAAAAAAAAAAA
AAAAAAAAAAAAAAAAAAAAAAAAAAAAAAAAAAAAAAAAA
AAAAAAAAAAAAAAAAAAAAAAAAA—"

It's a beautiful day in Chicago. In Millennial Park, not far from the magnificent jets of Buckingham Fountain, barely a stone's throw from the Cloud Gate sculpture whose legumish chromium corpse reflects the stately early 20th-century high-rises from across the Magnificent Mile, in full view of Lake Michigan whose jade waves sweep lazily into shore, crashing onto the beach where they fall into a quiet pelagic slumber before receding, half-awake, back into the inland sea; Chicago in the shadowless afternoon light, under the protective gaze of the Bowman and the Spearman, native American warrior statues with their fierce headdresses and skin aged to emerald over a century as Millennial Park's bronze sentinels; Chicago, a city that does summer right, the air so tempered by the lake breezes you have to wear a light sweater in June, there in a metropolitan oasis of charm Dilbert Sykes is begging a client to please, please, *please* stop freaking out, which is ridiculous.

Anyone at the uncontrollable screaming stage has gone way past mere alarm. They're in the losing-one's-mind-phase. Saying don't freak out only makes everything worse, but there's Sykes, whisper-shouting with his hand cupped over his phone desperately trying to get through to the tech department at Transluminal Vacations, Inc. where he's been employed as a passably gifted salesman for eleven years.

He is stark naked.

"Tech department—"

"It's Sykes. I need a ticket. Bounced a client into a bad timeline."

"Can you describe—"

"AAAAAAAAAAAAAAAAAAAAAAAAAAAAAAAAAAAAAAAAAAAAA AAAAAAAAAAAAAAAAAAAAAAAAAAAAAAAAAAAAAAAAAAAAAA AAAAAAAAAAAAAAAAAAAAAAAAAAAAAAAAAAAAAAAAAAAAAA AAAAAAAAAAAAAAAAAA!"

There is a beat of silence.

"I have another agent on his way. He's two minutes out."

"*Who is it?* Man don't send me a new guy! This is bad. Worst I've ever seen. I need experience, I need savvy—"

"It's Heller."

"Holy crap! Heller? Really?"

"Two minutes."

Sykes pockets his phone and looks down at the screamer. "Heller's a legend."

"AAAAAAAAAAAAAAAAAAAAAAAAAAAAAAAAAAAAAAAAAAAA AAAAAAAAAAAAAAAAAAAAAAAAAAAAAAAAAAAAAAAAAAAAAA AAAAAAAAAAAAAAAAAAAAAAAAAAAAAAAAAAAAAAAAAAAAAA AAAAAAAAAAAAAAAAAAAAAAAAA—"

Sykes' howling companion is also stark naked, but he is not a passably gifted salesman from Transluminal Vacations, Inc.

He is a hot lead. That's sales talk for a person who fits to a "T" the target demo of recently graduated frat bros just starting out in their profession. They are suffused with desperation to make bank and they've expressed strong interest in purchasing a vacation package. Such men are the bread and butter of Transluminal Vacations, Inc. This one is Steve.

Steve is a mid-level freelance data analyst with debilitating arachnophobia surrounded by a hundred or so people strolling around Buckingham fountain who are also *en flagrant*. It's wildly unsettling to find oneself publicly unclothed amid so many other people also unclothed in public, people of all ages, people whose bodies demonstrate the full taxonomy of the degrees and dependencies of sag in all the places where sagging might be taxonomized.

Mere moments before, just prior to the howling, a naked septuagenarian was smiling at Steve as her schnauzer-sized pet spider furiously humped his leg.

"Rodney! Stop!"

"AAAAAAAAAAAAAAAAAAAAAAAAAAAAAAAAAAAAAAAAAAAAA AAAAAAAAAAAAAAAAAAAAAAAAAAAAAAAAAAAAAAAAAAAAA AAAAAAAAAAAAAAAAAAAAAAAAAAAAAAAAAAAAAAAAAAAAA AAAAAAAAAAAAAAAAAAAAAAAAAAAAAAAAAAAAAAAAAA!"

But that's not why he's screaming.

She jerked Rodney's lead. Rodney detached himself from Steve's leg, skittered behind the naked septuagenarian, scuttled up her back, perched on the flossy summit of her extraordinarily lavender pompadour then pointed his posterior at the previously employed Analyst, clearly aiming his trembling hexagon of spinnerets to squirt hot ropes of glutinous silk up Steve's nose.

Which prompted our little old lady, her breasts pendulous and dour, her lips pursed into a curt coral-colored dash, her pubes sheared into an adorable magenta lightning bolt that complements her spider-sporting-pompadour to say:

"That just means he likes you," before she tottered off to see the fountain.

As she walked away, Rodney scuttled around to eyeball Steve, his forelegs spreading slowly out to either side, chittering what is surely the arachnoid version of *come at me, bruh.*

Sarcastically.

That's why Steve is screaming.

"We gotta get out of here," Sykes says to himself.

Sykes glares at his watch, grabs its brass bezel with his thumb and his middle finger, then twisted it anti-clockwise.

It's essential for me, your humble author, get this next part right.

Imagine me at my desk, hunkered over my laptop, cracking my knuckles and rolling my neck around like a wrestler psyching himself up before he enters the ring because herein lies a peculiar weirdness you'll need firmly lodged into your gray matter since it's going to happen a lot as the story unfolds and I want to get it right.

What's about to happen is that when our guy Sykes spins the bezel on his watch, he will shift instantly from his current timeline into an entirely different, adjacent, timeline. It is a lateral move. Same day. Same hour. Separate thread in the undulating fabric of temporal potentialities. And he will take Steve with him.

Imagine you're holding fifty green glowsticks. You can barely get your hands around them. These are all the adjacent–but duplicate–except not exactly–timelines. One of them is red. That's THIS timeline, the one you're in now, reading this story, comfortable and happy.

When Sykes spins the dial on his watch, he will jump from the red glowstick into one of the green glowsticks. Now *that* one glows red and the *old one* glows green. Because he jumped there. Now he's in that reality, not this one.

The red one is his new timeline. His new now.

However, the new timeline is not a new day. This isn't time travel. It is time slithering. Time scooching. Time wanging? It's leaping sideways into an adjoined temporal thread, a unique version of this very same day, of this very same hour, in the exact place where Steve is screaming.

"Oh shit, no!" Dilbert darts in front of Steve to block his view because Steve is still screaming and because the visual ambience of this entirely new and distinct version of reality (that is the same) remains distressingly insectoid.

He's still naked.

Everyone is naked.

Only now they're walking scorpions. One of these segmented creatures–probably named Rodney–skitters up to Steve's knee, led on a leash by the same denuded old lady with the same pendulous accoutrements.

"Did we wuv the fountain wountain?" She burbles to her pet.

Only this time the incredible architecture of her hair is held aloft by, and is indeed apparently home to, a swarm of bees.

Still screaming, a poodle-sized scorpion sniffing his foot and probing his kneecap with its needle-sharp stinger, Steve howls in horror at the septuagenarian's buzzing beehive, unconsciously reaching up to his own hairline.

"Don't!" Dilbert lashes out to snatch Steve's hand away, but it's too late. Steve jams his fingers deep into his vibrating *pella apis.*

His scream, which so far has reached but not truly explored its limits, decides this is the perfect time to really go for it, to really leave everything on the table, so it digs deep into its sonic tool chest and uncurls a raw, savage wail that had been wrapped around Steve's spleen since birth, stored carefully by evolution to be used exclusively for near-death experiences. Dilbert winces. Steve's face turns purple. Dilbert looks at the denuded elderly woman who is wildly confused.

"That just means he likes you."

He looks at his watch, daintily grasps the dial, then slowly rotates it clockwise, feeling for faint bumps under his fingertips as the bezel makes its way over invisible mechanisms until he's turned past three of them, which will bring them back to their starting point.

Reality melts. Recursive Chicagos flicker through previous iterations. The Chicago of spider dogs; the Chicago where Hitler won; the Chicago where they're lizards; the Chicago where 1920s gangster culture's a thing. They land in the Chicago from which they had recently disembarked before getting a facial from Rodney.

"Heller better hurry," Dilbert says, guiding Steve, now reclothed since he's in his original timeline, to a bench by the fountain. Dilbert rubs Steve's back as Steve, still bawling, still bug-eyed, stares in utter bewilderment, in absolute unhinged endless terror, wondering what in the hell just happened.

Chapter 2

Which is understandable. When Sykes first approached our wailing Analyst, he gently, carefully, and systematically led the man to the idea that there are infinite simultaneous timelines. He led him to understand reality as a nested, interleaved multiverse, and that he, Dilbert Sykes, a representative of Transluminal Vacations, Inc., had discovered an adjoining timeline wherein Steve had formed a multibillion-dollar start-up and lived Elon Muskishly in gilded splendor.

Further, he carefully, gently, and systematically informed Steve that he, Dilbert Sykes, using his magic watch, could take him there and let him enjoy that brilliant existence for a few weeks at a time. Like a vacation.

Sykes didn't tell Steve that jumping timelines is a crapshoot and (note the screams) rather alarming.

A small crowd has gathered, drawn by Steve's racket. They have their phones out. They have concerned looks on their faces. They're wondering if perhaps Dilbert might require their expertise in dealing with howling arachnophobic data analysts. They're wondering what's going to happen next when a tall man cuts effortlessly through them and kneels in front of Steve. The man studies Steve's exceedingly dilated pupils.

"You got a screamer."

Lloyd Heller: impeccable; peerless; self-proclaimed and widely acknowledged greatest salesmen Transluminal Vacations, Inc. has produced from its long history of selling transluminal vacation packages; a man who carries more swagger in any one of his perfectly pedicured toenails than most men have in their lifetime–swagger he's earned by closing more of Transluminal's vacation packages than anyone else, added up; a guy who is, to be diplomatic, confident.

Heller is decked out for the weather in a perfectly pressed short-sleeved white Tommy Bahama Cubavera shirt unbuttoned and loose over a sky-blue Henley tucked into vintage military khakis that cost him a week's pay. He looks like Denzel Washington on vacation.

Heller's grinning at Dilbert and Dilbert's loudly shrieking client through flawless Ray-Bans flashing out from beneath a short-brim straw fedora with an old concert ticket in the brim. He wears a watch exactly like Dilbert's. They greet each other with a complicated handshake which is actually a protocol for passably gifted salesmen of Transluminal Vacations, Inc., so that their timepieces are close enough for the signals to synch.

Heller reaches out a fatherly hand to pat Steve's trembling knee. He stands up, suddenly there, suddenly and clearly in charge.

"Scorpions?" Heller fishes a matchbox out of his shirt pocket and pops an Ohio Blue Tip matchstick between his teeth. He props one foot on the bench and grins.

"Nudity. Spiders. Scorpions."

"Spiders *and* scorpions," Heller takes the match out of his mouth. He gives the screamer an appraising nod.

"No," Dilbert says. "Spiders then scorpions. Everyone naked." Dilbert rubs Steve's back to comfort him.

Two bike cops are standing near the bench with their arms crossed looking like they don't believe Dilbert's got the situation under control even though he's clearly told them 'I have the situation under control!'

"Sounds like a party," Heller pops the match back into his circus barker grin then addresses the crowd by addressing the officers. "Officers, our friend has a habit of forgetting his medication. Then he runs away from the facility and so forth and sordid details to follow with the yadda yadda yadda and the hey hey hey." He shakes their hands. "We'll take it from here."

The cops pedal off. The crowd follows. Heller shoos Dilbert off the bench and sits down with Steve, whose exhortations have finally scaled back to merely uncontrollable sobs. Heller takes the man's hand. As he talks, he gently rubs his thumb along the man's palm, a technique he learned in his advanced sales training to calm down howling clients after they've been dialed into a terrifying alternate timeline. The sobbing ebbs into sniffling.

"I remember the first time I landed in a spider thread," the guy glances up at Heller. Wipes snot off his nose. Shudders. "There's a lot of uncategorized parameters when we slide. We never know exactly where we're gonna end up. But we look for markers, you know, indicia. Naked pedestrians are a huge red flag. Any timeline where they didn't invent clothes is guaranteed to be a problem." He snorts. Heller lets go of his hand. "Dil tell you not to freak out?"

"I want to go home." Quiver.

"See, that's the thing," Heller cranes around to berate Dilbert. "What were you thinking, Dil? You see nudity, you clock out. That's protocol. You can't keep glitching, Dil. The front office is fed up with your mendacious blundering. Why's it always nudity with you?"

"I'm not interested in your vacation package anymore." Steve gets up. So does Heller.

"I don't blame you. Unforgivably amateurish. It would be different if I was your handler, but, no, I get it." Heller claps Steve on his shoulder. "Let's just go back to the office so we can deplane your short-term memory. We'll take you off our mailing list. I suppose I can get promotions to send you a couple of gift cards to take the sting out of the scorpion world." Heller whips around, glaring at Dil.

"You, Dilbert Whitfield Sykes, are a subnacular gleet-filled torpid polyp. You are a half-mounted mannequin. You–" He looms closer, nose to nose in Dilbert's face. "I was in the middle of a level six deal when I had to dial into this faltering parade to deprogram this poor civilian because you took him to a nude beach scenario. With spider dogs! We've talked about this." Heller holds a long pause. "I'm afraid we'll have to let you go."

"But Heller," you can see Dil's high school role in *Death of a Salesman* acting skills from a mile away. "I got a wife and kids."

"Hey," Steve grabs Heller's arm. "He was just trying to show me the timelines. I mean, you said you never know. Don't fire him."

Staring right into Heller's face which is half-hidden from Steve, Dil tries not to grin. Heller isn't his boss by a long shot, and besides, spider dogs are a hazard of the trade. Heller is smooth. The Analyst got canned a week ago. He's sensitive to job loss.

"Yeah, well. I suppose," Heller turns back to Steve. "Whattaya think? Want to hop back on the horse? Your odds of entomologically etiolated endpoints are pretty much naught. Hell, the next slide could rotate us right into your FYMT timeline."

"My what?"

"Sorry, industry lingo. Your Fuck You Money Timeline."

"I don't know." The Analyst probes his cheeks for silk. "Maybe."

"Let's play it safe," Heller switches places with Steve–which accomplishes absolutely squat, but it makes Steve believe everything will be different this time because he's been physically moved–another artifact of Heller's years of experience.

"Ready?" Heller spins his bezel with a flourish. A kaleidoscope of Chicagos blurs over their heads. Suddenly the bench is in an ornate garden. There are pea gravel paths and an absolute madness of flowers. The analyst stares. Heller looks over him at Dil. He flicks the bezel.

Oscillating Chicagos. A Chicago where everyone is three feet taller. A Chicago underwater. A Chicago that looks exactly like their original city but replete with lurid graffiti and populated with fierce street punks. A Chicago where everyone is French, and the city is called LaSalle.

They land *mise en scene* in a Chicago where they're dressed in Brioni suits. Two well-heeled guys are mid-conversation with Steve, who looks over at Heller with a question.

"In any case, we've got your reports prepared, and your jet fueled up for the Paris meeting," says one of the well-heeled guys. "So, if you'd like to wrap up your meeting with your vacation planners–"

"My jet?"

"One of them."

Heller grins lasciviously around his match. "Listen, Harold."

"It's Franklin, sir."

"Franklin, can we just real quick ballpark our friend's net worth?"

"Mr. Heller, it's widely published. A simple Google search–"

"Just spill it, Jeeves."

"Thirteen billion, presently. It fluctuates. The market is soft right now," Franklin sniffs. "We'll recover."

"And what's your job again?"

"Honestly, Mr. Heller," Franklin does a quick breathing exercise. "I am something between a butler and an executive assistant." He turns to Steve. "Your wife suggested–"

"My wife?"

"Are you well, sir?"

"Yeah–my wife?"

Franklin nods discreetly past the men toward the vintage ice cream stand where they behold a woman so breathtakingly beautiful, they collectively hold their breath. Without taking his eyes off her, Steve asks, "Franklin, do I have any pets?"

"Am I under review?" Franklin takes a breath, then as if he's reciting a bio, "You detest pets. You consider owning a dog like slavery, you even–"

"How big is the biggest scorpion?"

"In the world? Well, I guess a really big one would just barely rest across your open hand–"

"Mr. Sykes–"

Steve stops talking because his wife has caught his eye. She saunters across the square right up to Franklin.

"We are not taking the Beechcraft, Franklin. I swear to God if you've even fueled that fucker up, I will shave your balls with a broken teacup, you bloodless limey tumor." She turns to Steve. Her neck is laced with glistening freshwater pearls. A drop of chocolate chip mint ice cream is jiggling on the precipice of her bottom lip, considering suicide. "Besides, the Beechcraft is the only one with a bed." She levels her gaze at Steve, a bouquet of daggers blooming from each eye, "We won't be needing that."

"Get me out of here."

Dil shoves his hands into his pockets. Heller spins the bezel. Chicago churns.

Same park. Same day. Everyone is reading a book. Steve's wife is sitting on a bench across the pea gravel path from him, a massive hydrangea laden with enormous white blossoms practically embraces her from behind the bench. As he stares, she slowly turns a page, utterly absorbed, her face slack with wonder, the light beaming up from the story, bathing her in a luminous ivory haze. She glances over at Steve. She cocks an eyebrow, smiles, then goes back to reading.

"Ready?" Heller takes the bezel between his fingers.

"Wait," The Analyst looks over at the salesmen. "I'm in."

"Well, ok, but look, this is not a very lucrative timeline. You're still a freelancer here. You only just met her. You haven't even . . . it's just–"

"I can move to any timeline, any time, right?"

"Generally, most people pick the one with all the money."

"Yeah, but," Steve stares at his future wife. "Look at her."

Chapter 3

Dilbert takes Steve back to let finance and contracts do their thing. At the same time, Heller strolls into downtown Chicago grinning ear to ear. It's a huge sale. The final notch in Heller's belt. The final feather in his cap. It's the last link in the unbreakable chain leading from his very first sale so many years ago to earning the Platinum Vacation Package, his lifelong goal, which is the reward for closing his 100th sale, as stipulated in his contract.

You may be confused. In this current timeline, Steve is a gig economy warrior, a freelancer, a contract worker for various start-ups and IT companies–when they need him. When they don't need him, he sits at home writing bespoke code, hoping that one day he'll come up with an app that wipes out an aging service vertical and get picked up by Google. Until then, he's pretty much living paycheck to paycheck in a poorly decorated one-bedroom basement level apartment he shares with a bicycle, an outrageously overclocked gaming rig, his work station, and his cat, Ralph. In this present iteration, he could not afford a Platinum Vacation Package from Transluminal yadda yadda yadda. He couldn't even afford the paper mâché vacation package if there was one, which there is not. Transluminal Vacations, Inc. only sells the platinum vacation package. It's their sole product.

It's a very good product. It's an improbable product. It's unique. They don't advertise. They don't market. They don't make cold calls. What they do is send out teams of scouts into adjacent timelines, or nested translucent spheres of potentiality, or glow sticks, or however you wish to describe the simultaneous realties through which they flit like shades; they send out teams whose only job is to locate billionaires. Once they find a seven-figure figure, they backtrack into the timeline wherein this billionaire is broke and hungry. They give him a taste of the adjacent good life–for a couple billion a year. Which Steve freely gives to them for their service because of course he does. You would too.

This means Steve is in the finance office with Dilbert Sykes signing papers and contracts that give Transluminal Vacations, Inc. rights and points in Steve's adjacent timeline's billion-dollar cash machine which the finance team simply files then sits back and watches the money fill up their accounts like magic because Transluminal Vacations, Inc. also exists, like Steve, like Dilbert, like everyone living, everyone who has ever lived, and everyone who will ever live, in every timeline in this very office space doing this very thing. Their accounts are enormous and growing daily due to entirely illegal and unvirtuous investment fraud, which is, really, just a by-product of their work in adjoined simultaneity.

Heller ambles over to E. Juan Rieves, the oldest tobacco store in Chicago, checks into their members-only lounge to have a celebratory late afternoon cigar which he pulls out of his private locker along with a bottle of Kane Break 21-year-old Scotch. It'll take him an hour to kill this cigar, a period he spends shooting the shit with other accomplished men in worn leather chairs in a smoke-filled room lit dramatically by floor-to-ceiling windows looking west onto Wabash. He's thinking about what happens next.

"Lloyd Heller, you son of a bitch," it's an older man with hair the color of copy paper.

"Sparks, you ancient pervert. How are you?" Sparks is a retired salesman from Transluminal Vacations, Inc.

"Holding on tight. You?"

"Made my last sale today."

"Gonna retire?"

"Damn straight. Getting the Platinum."

Sparks whistles.

"Well, you earned it, Heller. You're a goddam machine."

"I been dreaming about it. Thinking about it. Rolling it over. I picked out a yacht—" Heller digs out his phone, calls up a GIF of a gorgeous fifty-four-foot luxury cruiser.

"I'm jealous, Heller." Sparks inspects his expensive cigar. "I came close. Racked up eighty-seven sales. The husband and I got a little place on the Cote d'Azur. It's nice." He takes a hit. Squints at heller through smoke. "But it ain't the Platinum."

"I was just lucky, Sparks." Heller lies. He wasn't lucky. He got up every day for twenty years with the firm intention of closing a sale.

"Lucky may ass," Sparks chuckles.

"I'm serious. Sykes had a screamer, so I dialed in and helped him out. Put the Heller touch on him. Closed like a box."

"You closed Sykes' sale?"

"Tech called me in."

"Well, I'm sure you followed protocol."

Heller looks past Sparks out the windows as the elevated train roars by. "Of course, I followed protocol."

***

Heller finishes his smoke. Walks around the corner to the office which looms over him, brown and sepia and white, sporting enormous silver Helvetica: Transluminal Vacations, Incorporated. In the very center of the facade, a deep, narrow door of ornate brass through which Heller swishes triumphantly.

The offices of Transluminal Vacations, Inc. are vast and vaguely mid-twentieth century analog. Security has the gate open for the elevator bank before Heller gets there.

"Wilbur," Heller nods, headed toward the executive lift.

"Mr. Clean," Wilbur says with a knowing smile. "Nice work."

The elevator doors open to a broad room with a frigate of high-end cubicles that are dead center and manned by a host of workers jabbering quietly into their headpieces. As Heller walks in, everyone stands and cheers.

He walks into the cubicles, into the center of the largest one, nearly an office itself, opens a metal wall-mounted cabinet door revealing a bank of switches labeled SOUND and OVERHEAD. Randall Jane, the office manager, sweeps into the cubicle on his heels.

"Don't do it, Heller. The Korean team is on a call–"

Heller turns to Randall Jane with a searing, regal disregard and looms them back out of the cubicle. He turns back to the box, punches a code into the keypad, brings up the overhead music program, and punches in another code. The opening drone of "Born on the Bayou" suddenly floats out into the office. Salespeople and clerks turn toward Heller, some of them stand up, one of them chair dances. Heller punches in another code, and the song blares through the entire suite as the drums kick in.

People come out of their offices; clerks rise to high five each other. Clients stare with confusion. Heller strikes a heroic pose, and strides out of the secretarial flotilla. Everyone joins in a crappy conga line[1] following Heller to The Board.

The Board is a white erasable wall stretching across the back of the office between Heller's cherished corner space and the matching corner suite, currently occupied by his Direct Report and the CEO of Transluminal Vacations, Inc., Rose Pilny, who hates him.

Heller snatches a forest-green dry erase marker and, with a flourish, with style, with panache, and while grinning at the staff crowding in around him, holds it like a baton.

"I stand before you on the tail end of twenty years closing landmark packages for Transluminal. Today I made my very last sale. Those of you who will now continue to remain gainfully employed on my magnificent coattails may kneel and adore me. Please, I'm not a shy man, I'm not a humble man, let's not pretend here. I'm a hardcore timeline hopping sartorial badass, and today I closed another whale. Peterson–"

Peterson drums on his desk dramatically. Heller turns to the Board to write CLOSED in the sales funnel bracket for Steve, but it's already there.

"The fuck?"

Rose Pilny grins as wide as her football-shaped head will allow and, stretched to her full four-feet-eleven inches, stabs a nubby miniature digit at the name aligned with the sale: Dilbert Sykes.

"I saved that deal!" Heller says.

"You dialed your reckless ass into his sales pipe without following protocol. It may be your work, but it's Dilbert's sale." Rose smiles warmly, pats him on the arm, waddles into her office, and shuts the door.

"Sorry, Heller." Dil doesn't know what to do with his hands. He knows how much this sale meant. Heller grits his teeth right through a matchstick. He looks over at his sales matrix, displaying the entirety of his career for the whole office to see. Ninety-nine boxes, all checked with precise, heavy exes–all except the last one. Long ago, Heller drew a green palm tree in that box because that box represents Heller's sole reason for continuing to push vacation packages for Transluminal Vacations, Inc.: his retirement bonus, the legendary and never delivered Transluminal Vacation Package of his dreams: The Platinum.

No regular salesman has been awarded The Platinum. But Heller is no regular salesman. He is the Jesus How You Doin' Christ of salesmen. He's a natural, a genius, a ghost. No one can outsell him.

"That cold coddled jigger of week-old cream. I will flay her." Heller barges into Rose's office. She's leaning against her desk (it's sharp edge digging into her shoulder blades) talking to someone.

"Heller, you can turn around and wait your turn."

"That was my sale, and you know it!"

"The hell it was, Heller. There are rules for a reason. You know that dialing yourself into an active pitch on the fly doesn't make the sale yours. You need written consent, department head authorization—you wrote the goddam protocol! Don't expect me to float you any slack because you can't remember your own regulatory statutes!"

"I saved the company a billion-dollar sale!"

"Thanks." She walks around behind her desk. Pulls out a leather folio. Tosses it to Heller. "Here's your next gig." Heller doesn't even try to catch it. The folio lands on the floor in front of some kid.

"That goddam platinum package is *mine,* Pilny!"

"I'm sure it is, Heller–if you close another sale. Read your contract. You get the platinum if you close one-hundred sales. Not ninety-nine sales. You're as far away from the platinum as Pluto. And you got one more day."

Heller growls. The kid hands him the folder. Heller snatches it out of his hand. He can't get it open, and his anger spills over and he pounds the folio on Rose's desk. She doesn't even look up. She's taking notes.

"FUCK STACK CITY!" He opens the portfolio. Scans it. Snaps the binder closed. "Rose Pilny, have you no shame? It's my last sale. Don't do this to me."

She doesn't look up. "Sales are randomly distributed, Heller. God did this to you, not me."

"He's a fucking priest!"

"I am aware."

"This is a challenge close!"

"You're making things up, Heller. There's no such thing as a challenge close. You have until," she tapped the phone on her desk which declared that it was currently 4:45 p.m. "Closing time tomorrow."

"He's a goddam," he holds the folio open toward Rose, pointing to a picture of his next lead, a thin Filipino man in an austere, humble black suit and army issue thick black plastic glasses. He's blessing an altar with incense. "He's Buddhist, Rose. They don't–how the fuck am I going to close a monk?!"

"He's not a monk. He runs a sandwich shop over on Lawrence. He's a lay priest. He dresses like Elvis Costello at a funeral. In one of his timelines, he owns a string of fast-food joints on both coasts and a private train. He's an eccentric nut job," She leans back. "Just like you."

"The fuck, Pilny. You just don't want to give me the package."

"If I ever give you a package Heller, you can rest assured it will be ticking. Please take Chris and leave."

"Who the fuck is Chris?"

"The new guy," she nods at the kid who waves weakly at Heller. "Your apprentice."

Heller stares at Chris. "This is bullshit." He walks out—storms across the office to the frigate. Creedence Clearwater Revival's still blasting. No one is dancing anymore. In fact, everyone is suddenly really, really busy. Two guys from Engineering are in the office with Randall Jane trying to get into the system. Heller leans over them and punches in his code. The music reverts to a shitty Muzak version of "Isn't It Ironic?". He storms off to the elevators. He storms out of the building. He storms down the sidewalk cursing. Finally, he stops, takes a deep breath. He pops a matchstick into his teeth, shoves his hands into his khakis, and stares up Jackson at nothing.

He whips around to glare at his employer, his face set into a fierce glower he reserves for moments requiring deep, risible hatred, but it goes nowhere because as he glowers at the brass doors, *She* glides out of the office for a smoke.

Suddenly the world moves like a waltz. Birds chirp. Small furry forest creatures pop their cartoon eyes over the edges of the architecture. The sun smiles down and doffs its fedora at Heller as a magical creature steps up beside him, steps close, looms into his personal space. He stares at her as if she's appeared like a sexy ghost rising up out of the ground: Octavia del Sol, the woman who carries Heller's heart around with her like a small, yapping, hairy, wildly annoying dog on a leash.

"What a shit show, Heller." She is unwrapping the cellophane from the end of a brick of Holliwell Lights and looking at the passing traffic as if every car is personally trying to destroy her *joie de vivre*. "Light me," she pops a cigarette between her lips and leans toward Heller. She glances up into his eyes and his heart races around her feet as if it needs very desperately to relieve itself, barking, whining, begging.

But Heller can't hear a thing she says. Her words have erupted into sutras spinning out into the sonic landscape. They burrow into his ears and into his mind like the swelling symphonic background track of a sappy love story. He only hears violins and the fragile voices of a children's choir and French horns as he falls through this movie into orbit around her face, falling closer and closer into the emerald sky-blue honey atmospheres of her eyes–

"The fuck's wrong with you?"

Heller snaps back into reality. He's leaning toward her in full pervert.

"Light. Me."

Heller stares at her helplessly. Octavia rolls her eyes hard enough to ruffle his tie and snatches matches out of his shirt pocket. She drags a stick furiously along the striker of the box. She holds it to the tip of her Halliwell as her brows furrow, and Heller measures them in long, slow millimeters. She hands it back. Heller accepts the box of matches like a dignified old actor getting an award. He drops the box into his pocket then folds his hands behind his back and gathers, as quickly and as discreetly as he can, his shit back, as they say, together.

"I hate that song," She snarls. "Who is it? Creedence Cracker Ass Revolver?"

Heller places the tips of his fingers on the bezel of his watch and turns carefully, cautiously counting the faint nodal bumps: one, two–

"I can't wait until you retire. You broken down old geriatric–"

–Seven, nine–

"–nineteen seventies eight-track tape on legs–"

–Eleven. He closes his eyes and lets go. Chicago flickers. Octavia del Sol gains a few pounds; her hair, which is normally strawberry blond and left to cascade in shimmering sheets down her back, has pulled itself up into a bun held together by a well-chewed pencil shoved right through it. She wears glasses. She stops talking. She touches Heller's arm.

"Rosie's difficult; but you'll close." She rubs his bicep then realizes what she's doing and finishes with a reassuring pat. She brings the cigarette up to her unlipsticked lips and draws smoke. She turns to stare into the traffic as if every car that passes is a problem only she can solve. "I know you will," she looks back at Heller. "You can close anytime you want to." She holds her hand up for a high five. Heller smiles warmly and presses his hand gently against hers.

"Platinum," Octavia whispers. She smiles at him, bathed in the magical light of a Renaissance painting.

He spins his dial and returns to his home line. Octavia's staring at nothing, her hip cocked out, eyebrows raised in all caps. She leans back with her brows knitted together like passionate folds in caramel-colored satin sheets. She flicks her cigarette into the street. Turns and slams her shoulder into Heller in a way that is most definitely not flirtatious but is, instead, a threat and a challenge and a dismissal and a bully move. "Oh, sorry. Didn't see you." She kicks the brass door open and strides into the deep shadow of Transluminal Vacations, Inc. leaving Heller alone on the sidewalk, staring up Jackson Avenue at nothing, his heart panting like an exhausted Pekinese.

Finally, Heller breathes.

Chapter 4

"Well, that explains the matches—although a lighter is cooler."

Fucklenuts. The kid. Heller shifts the match from one side of his grimace to the other side of his grimace slowly and deliberately dragging its fibrous edge across each tooth.

"I don't carry a lighter because I like to chew matches because matches are delicious. Particularly the Ohio Blue Tip which is the finest wooden match one can procure. Swans aren't bad for lighting a pipe, but they taste like shit."

"Not because you're in love with the J-Lo clone?" Chris reaches out for the matchbox. He's a quarter of an inch taller than Heller with a head of hair trying to fly away and teeth like bright white lights. His face is the picture of sincerity. Heller tosses the kid the box. Chris fishes a stick, rattling around with his fingertips maybe a teensy bit too long.

"I put those in my mouth." Heller stares.

"They're clean–" he wiggles his fingers in the air to demonstrate their fastidiousness, but Heller looks away.

"Keep it. I got more."

Chris puts a match into his mouth. He stares up Jackson with Heller.

"Cause she's into you."

What occurs next is a pivotal moment of pregnant silence, a phrase endlessly misused and constantly misunderstood since a moment has no gender and as far as this author knows has no sex life; yet, like you, gentle reader, the author has experienced moments drawn out to their most prolapsed and swaybacked intervals wherein something should be said but nobody knows exactly what it is so the potential of the moment gestates until the silence breaks and words, usually the wrong ones, burst forth into the world screaming and covered in grease. But that's really not a pregnancy as much as it is a festering boil or an explosive cyst, neither of which is poetic. Try saying 'it was a festering moment.' Or 'the moment festered' . . .

Actually, that's pretty good.

As Chris and Heller stared at passing cars the moment festered until Chris could no longer hold together the integrity of his pressurized curiosity and so like an enormous prom-cancelling zit squeezed into a spotty bathroom mirror, he sp–

"Here's how it works," Heller says. Heller is finely tuned to festering silences and knows the value of choosing the exact moment when the festerer is erupting so he may speak preemptively and therefore control the velocity and trajectory of the resulting gout of conversation (it's a sales thing).

"Here's. How. It. Works. See this?" He holds out his watch. "This magnificent chronograph transports us into an adjacent timeline."

Chris doesn't react. Then after another purulent moment, shifts his match amateurishly around a suspicious grin.

"Mr. Heller, I know you didn't want an apprentice. That's ok. That's fine. But can we not do the hazing thing? You don't have to make up a fal–"

Heller spins the bezel and Jackson Avenue shimmers through a blur of variations. Suddenly they're on a magnificently maintained boulevard.

The sidewalks have decorative cement moldings. The buildings are Franklloydwrightlike complex cement puzzles. Everywhere they look, every inch is ornamented. Festooned. Flamboyantly prairie-stylishly baroqued.

"WHAT IN THE LIVING HEL–" Chris swallows his matchstick and chokes.

"Oh, this is good. Look," Heller obliviously points to the building across the street. "I think Frank Lloyd Wright beat out Bau Haus for–" Heller notices the choking. He smacks Chris on the back and the moist match shoots into the gutter. Heller grabs the kid by the shoulders, yells into his face. "OH FUCK! OH SHIT! OH GOD! OH FUCK!"

"WHY ARE YOU FREAKING OUT?" The kid all caps back at Heller.

"I'M NOT FREAKING OUT! YOU'RE FREAKING OUT! I'M MAKING FUN OF YOU!"

Chris shrugs Heller off. He breathes deep. He bends over and puts his hands on his knees and dry heaves.

He looks around, flexing his fingers. He gets another match. Pops it into his mouth because he's not a quitter.

"That's a neat trick."

"Yeah," Heller admires the kid's recovery. "Yeah, it is. See here's what's happening. We're not in a different timeline, we're in a different model of our original timeline."

"Aren't they the same?"

"Yes, but also no. I'm a salesman, not a coder. I have no idea how this works. I just know how to make it happen."

"But how do we, I mean what if we, you know," Chris searches for the explanation. ". . . butterflies?"

"You mean the whole crush a butterfly and gain a letter in the alphabet thing? Yeah, that's real. But who cares? We're in a new pipe so it doesn't affect–look, this isn't time travel."

"So, we can't screw it up?"

Heller laughs. "Oh, we fuck it up all the time. I'm pretty sure every time I spin this dial, I wreck somebody's life."

"That's awful!"

"Eh. It's working out."

"Why do people do it?"

"Why do people do anything? For kicks. Check your wallet."

Chris's wallet is slim, made of beautifully tooled leather. His driver's license is staring back at him with a strange address.

"This isn't my wallet."

"We adapt."

"Yeah, hey, this isn't my address either."

"Really?" Heller pulls out his phone, a crenelated lozenge of jade plastic. It takes him half a second to get into it, find the current version of Uber and tap for a cab. One pulls up immediately, driverless and Jules Verned to the nth degree. A large round brass iris dials itself open and they climb through into the cabin. Forest green velvet with cream piping. Bright red ceiling. Brass. Bronze. A complex keyboard is directly before them with a tiled display. Heller grabs the kid's license and punches in the address. The tiles clack and rattle, showing a low rez affirmation. "So, we're in a Wright-Verne-Babbage kind of timeline. I'm digging it."

They disembark in front of a Chicago Greystone fronted by a wide walkway and beautifully designed geometric cement planters spilling flowers and sweet potato vines and brightly variegated coleus. There's a fingerprint keypad. Chris touches it and the door slides open revealing a tasteful, sunny foyer.

"We shouldn't do this. What if someone's home?" Chris says,

peering into the depths of the house.

"It's your house. You live here. You're home."

"Yeah, but the me that lives in this–"

"You're the you. You live in this timeline."

"No, I don't. I live in a studio on north Clark. I have roommates."

"Not in this timeline." Heller walks in, his boots clicking quietly on a gleaming marble floor. Chris joins him. The house opens up. The ground floor is beautifully composed, elegantly proportioned and keeps one's interest no matter where one points one's eyeballs. The second floor's been dissected for cathedral ceilings with a skylight carved into the roof. It's all mango and coral and jade.

Suddenly the warm and friendly tones of Marvin Pontiac float into the room from invisible speakers. Chris opens the massive stainless-steel fridge. It's full of fancy beers and cheeses and fresh fruit.

"I could get used to this," Chris says.

Heller grins out the windows into the garden. His expression collapses into resigned dread.

"Fuckwardian."

Chris follows Heller's deadpan gaze out through enormous windows into a garden patio where a handful of twenty-something men are drinking matche in a circle lined with handmade drums. One of them waves at Chris. He gets up then lopes through the French doors into the living room. He gives Chris a big hug.

"Hey brother. You ready to play?" The guy takes in Heller. "What's up, brother?"

The guy smiles, trots back into the garden. He's wearing turquoise crocs, orange socks with embroidered bright green windowpanes, a baggy white t-shirt with black Beethoven in shades and headphones. He's got a carefully coifed beard, ornate sideburns, and his hair is pulled back into a Samurai knob.

"Drummers." Heller grabs his watch. "We need to hurry–" but there is a thump from the garden and a group hoot. The guys launch into a poorly syncopated basic beat. "Kid, don't listen to 'em!"

But the kid is gone. He's out the door and before Heller can stop him, he's squatting on a stump hammering away on a goat-skin djembe.

"Chris, get back in here!" Heller glares through the glass, holding his hands over his ears. The guy with the t-shirt nods dramatically then says (not at all on the beat) "All. Right. Now we. Play. Our. Names . . ." Everyone simmers down, their hands barely brushing the skins. The leader spells his name, smacking the drum on each letter: C-U-T-H-B-E-R-T. The group repeats his name on the beat.

"I will slay them individually. I will throw them under this building. I will turn them into Mormons," Heller tears a paper towel into pieces. He balls the pieces into little cones which he plugs into his ears. He strides out onto the patio.

"Time to drag up, kid."

"H-E-L-L-E-and–R!"

"Stop it!"

"L-L-O-and-Y-and-D!"

T-shirt shoves a twosome of tiny, conjoined bongos at Heller. Heller holds his hands up like the bongos are on fire. He taps his watch at Chris.

"Go without me. I'm into it." Chris tilts his head back and plays a perfectly idiotic, fractured, nauseatingly arrhythmic tattoo. The other drummers nod and shout encouragement. A couple of guys come out of the apartment to join in.

"Hey, we heard you cats from the sidewalk. OK if we jam?"

Heller grabs Chris, peels his hands off the drums.

"Hey, pretty harsh, pops!" T-Shirt chortles. Heller drags Chris back through the living room and out the front door. Chris drums on every surface. Heller pushes him into a cab. They go back to Transluminal Vacations, Inc. Chris talks about drums, slapping surfaces and listening intently as if he's learning something from the tone, which he is not, except how to truly annoy Heller. He shoves Chris into the foyer of the office. Chris hasn't shut up since they left.

"I'm just saying there's a certain level at which we're all drumming, and every word is a beat, and it entrains–you know what entrainment is, right?–It entrains–"

Heller grabs the kid's hands and places them onto two gold handprints embedded in the wall with the words DRUM CIRCLE etched into the stone. There's a bezel set into the marble. He turns it.

"–your subconscious rhythm, your inner musician–you get this, right? It puts your tribal ID into the driver's seat and–"

There is a silent flash. Chris shuts up. He stands erect, opens his box of Blue Tips. Pops one into his mouth.

"Let's not do that again," Chris says.

Heller waves the kid outside.

"Drum circles suck."

"I know. I was terrible."

"I mean they suck like a vacuum. If you get near one, if you even hear it, you'll gravitate to it like water down a drain. It sucks you in and won't let you go until you have dreadlocks, or you've gone vegan. Stay away from drum circles."

"Does every timeline have drum circle resets?"

"Look kid, every thread has its pitfalls and traps. Drum circles are standard. Sometimes it's Vikram yoga. Every once in a winkydink you hit one where it's jazz record stores," Heller shudders.

"Jazz rec–"

"Can't get out. You go in, it's all innocent and you just want to pick up an old Blue Note 45 but someone asks you about Ornette Coleman and you tell them about Gato Barbieri and more people come in and pretty soon it's wall-to-wall jazz freaks and beards and pork pie hats and you can't stop talking about Milt Jackson and you can't find the door and you die like that."

"Come on," Chris takes the match out of his mouth in disbelief. Heller catches Dilbert walking out of the office doors.

"Dil—jazz record shops?"

"Jesus Herbie Hancock Christ, Heller. No." He turns right and heads east on Jackson. Heller pops a new pick into his teeth.

"What did I tell you?"

"Why were you so mad at Ms. Pilny?"

"She is a truncated goat-faced ladle of curdled buttermilk."

"I sense issues."

"She gave me a challenge mark."

Chris waits.

"This business is based on greed. We got people out there in every social striation; they're explorers; like spies. Like Vasco de Gama. They just stand around reading the paper and watching the news and hanging out in banks and bars keeping an eye out for billionaires."

"Don't we have enough of those here?"

"Oh, sure. But try taking a meeting with Bill Grates. Forget it. So, one of our Vasco de Gamas finds a billionaire she's never heard of. She comes back to the office and hands him over to the prospecting department who does their research and finds the guy in a timeline where he is penniless and desperate."

"Why? Why not just find them here?"

"Our timeline sucks, kid." Heller looks around at the world. "This particular 2020 is the kitchen junk drawer of the temporal universe. Every shitty thing that didn't fit in other timelines is here in spades. Listening to Phil Collins. On fire."

He chews stick for a second.

"Those same explorers find them, then we lure them in with promises of insane wealth that can only be enjoyed for brief intervals—"

"Why?"

"Why what?"

"Brief intervals. Why not just move there? Why not live in a better timeline?"

"I don't know. Nobody knows. We tried it, way back at the start. Put the first guy into his FYMT for six months before he ran the company into the ground and holed up in his apartment peeing into mason jars and growing a beard."

"Harsh."

"Took us a while to figure out." Heller looks seriously at Chris. "You belong where you belong, right? It's a clockwork universe and you are a gear that really only fits in this here machine," he waves around at the specific now. "The universe has designated this watery ass timeline for you so you'd damn well better stick around in it or the universe will fuck your shit, as they say, all the way up."

Chris digests this for a minute.

"That sounds suspiciously like a world view."

"It is what it is, kid. The universe is telling a grand and massive joke and you're the punchline. You can't be the punchline in another joke. It just doesn't work. So, we figured out that six weeks on, three weeks off is the optimal rhythm. Otherwise, you start trying to do the thing you're supposed to do in the wrong timeline and the universe will give you the hairy eyeball of stern rebuke."

"Six weeks in your better timel—"

Heller uses his matchstick to accentuate his words. "Ay kay ay *vacations*. We take them on a tour of their various timelines, making sure we–" Heller notices the kid is not buying it. "You don't believe me."

"I believe you, I mean, we just did it. But I just, I don't see how you convince someone. Actually, I don't see how you make money. I don't see how this works at all."

"Let your training begin." Heller spins the dial on his watch through successive Chicagos, keeping an eye on the Kid.

"So, here's one," Heller says. Chris reaches up and picks a cap off his head. GAGA emblazoned in frank white capitals. He reads the inside label: Get America Gooder A'ight?

"What's the first thing you see?"

"Hats?"

"Hats are norm."

"Yeah, but everyone?"

"What else?"

Chris turns in a slow circle. The people are white, blond, and unattractive. They're headed up Jackson.

"Maybe a baseball game?"

A passing pedestrian hears him. "Baseball? Son, it's a hangin'!"

"A...*what?!*"

The guy looks at Chris like he's from outer space. "Where're you from, boy?"

Heller steps in. "Sheeyut, Christian. He's my cousin's brother from Baltimore."

The guy hooks his thumbs under his suspenders. "Alright, well. I guess they don't hang too many indielecturals up there in Baltimalore."

"Indy–"

"Chris, we need to get moving."

Chris grins at the man. "It's intellectuals."

"Hey," another guy stops. "Wire you pronouncing?"

The first guy folds his arms and pinches his face into a sneer. A woman stops and looks at the second guy. "See pronouncing?"

An eddy of curious and slightly paranoid and definitely shifty hicks swells around Heller and the Kid.

"Say something!" someone shouts.

"What?" Chris says in a deeply fearful confuse. Heller grins. Chris tries to back away, but people are closing in on all sides.

"SAY SOMETHIN! SAY SOMETHIN!" hge points to his hat. "SAY GETA MERICA GOODER A'IGHT!"

"WHAT?!" Chris bellows back at them, teetering on the precipice of madness. Heller is grinning, buffeted by idiots who think they've bagged an indielectural. "HELLER!"

The man balls the kid's collar in his fist. He yells out at the passing crowd "WE GOTTA NUTHER ONE!" The crowd swerves toward them.

"Say, Christian, when's the hangin' start?" Heller shouts into the ruddy face of the nearest moron, looking at his watch.

"They's always near about seven. We just trine to git a gooder seat."

"DO IT!" Chris yells as people clutch his shirt, pulling him into the flow toward the hanging.

Heller spins the dial. The watch reaches out an invisible arm to snatch Christopher Aldous Abducted by Natives Montgomery out of danger. The ocean of maniacs yeets away. Chicagos shift.

"Always got to be ready," Heller says.

"HE'S GOT A WATCH!" Someone yells.

A skeletal man dressed in rags with a castaway beards grabs Heller's arm in a vicelike grip, tearing at his watch. Heller tries to fight him off. Chris is staring past them into the street at a horde of derelicts bearing down when the sky churns and he finds himself in his regular Chicago. Heller's straightening his clothes.

"Always ready."

A young girl, maybe fifteen, approaches Chris all shy and embarrassed.

"Are you Christopher Montgomery?"

"Uh, yeah."

"Oh My God, can I get a picture?"

"I guess–Heller?"

Heller just shifts his Blue Tip through half a grin.

The girl backs into Chris with her camera raised in video selfie mode.

"Ermagherd look who I ran into!" Chris waves meekly into the lens. Heller guides the girl back onto the sidewalk.

"Alright, ma'am. Thanks. Please tag us."

"Weird," Chris chuckles. Heller spins him around to look at a huge advertisement painted onto the side of a building. It's Chris' face. He's pointing at a phone. The copy at the bottom is just the one-word name of the app he apparently invented in this timeline: SMUGG.

People point, take pictures. A luxurious SUV pulls up. The doors gull wing open revealing a dark, cool interior from which a very professional woman waves them over. "Time's up, boss."

"Is this my rich timeline?"

"Definitely not an intern." Heller dials around through the nodal points and not much changes. Chris looks around for derelicts and unruly mobs but just finds himself in his original timeline.

"Anyway," Heller flicks a soggy match into a nearby trash can with astonishing accuracy. "That's the job."

"So what's wrong with our guy?"

"He's spiritual. Doesn't want anything. Heller inspects the deep-water blue tip of a fresh match. "How the fuck am I gonna close?"

Chapter 5

The Ravenswood Episcopal Church and Community Center was built in 1937 and has the plumbing to prove it. In the summer it just gets weird. The pipes rattle and the faucets drip and when it rains, seepage forms vast shallow puddles across the basement floor. They learned years ago to keep all storage raised six inches off the concrete and there's a protocol, but they've never had the kind of congregation that could pony up the fifty thousand or so dollars to seal the walls which is why Sydney Hearth Ough is on his stomach in the corner where they keep the donated grocery bags and plastic tubs, one hand gripping the shelves, the other hand poking the nozzle of a shop vac hose attachment he engineered from a PVC pipe and Gorilla tape to suck up a puddle of water way in the back underneath everything.

"Mother *forker!*" he stretches his body to reach his slim brown fingers as far into the dark under the shelves as he can. "Stupid…God dang…pipe—!"

Back flattened, arms and hands stretched as far as they will go, face in a rictal grimace Sydney–Sidd–finally hears a desperate slurping, closes his eyes, and breathes deeply, noting the hint of mold in the air, the fragrant tang of an onion that's rolled under the shelves and gone bad, the old book bouquet of thousands of brown paper bags, and listens as the vacuum swallows the last of the seepage.

When it's gone, Sidd slowly wiggles out from under the shelves. He is a thin, wiry man in a black long-sleeved Nehru shirt over stovepipe jeans, a shock of ink-black hair that never lies down, vintage black plastic Army-issue glasses, and a chain of pewter prayer beads looped around his neck. He unfolds himself and then stretches. He wraps the hose around the top of the shop vac and slides the PVC pipe onto a high shelf, then rolls the whole thing into a closet in the hall.

Most of the south side of the basement is a huge kitchen with a wide pass-through window and an impressive arsenal of pots and pans dangling from the ceiling.

Sidd picks a tiny tin pot to boil water. He pours a generous mound of Sanka instant coffee into a chipped cup, pours in too much sugar, then grabs a can of evaporated milk from the fridge, and pours some in. The water boils and he fills his cup, stirs the mixture until it's the color of a classical guitar, then he tosses the spoon over his shoulder without looking. It lands dead center in a bucket of soapy water.

Mooki floats up to the pass-through window. Sidd doesn't say a word, but he pours Sanka into a cup, pours hot water from the pot, and slides it over.

Mooki is fluid. They showed up eight months earlier to help with Tuesday night dinners and groceries and they haven't left. Sidd thinks of himself as a progressive, modern man of the cloth–a lay priest, not ordained, though that doesn't matter because this church hasn't had an actual Episcopal priest behind the pulpit in the eleven years Sidd's been working here–and he is careful with his pronouns, as he was trained in human resources video, and he likes to think he is not gender obsessive–rude–but every time he looks at Mooki he wonders about their form and gets lost in their floppy rag doll grace and then he gets mad at himself for not living fully in the spirit.

Although he's cursed luridly all morning while he was shoving himself under the shelves to vacuum up rainwater, it still counts as a sin so maybe a little distraction by Mooki's curvature is fine.

Mooki thinks Pastor Sidd is hot and can't wait to figure out how to tell him they're down, but they also love the whole waiting and chasing thing that's going on between themself and Sidd. They insist on They and Them for nametags and forms but in their mind, Mooki sometimes finds themself in a daydream involving Pastor Sidd, the coat closet, and a lot of grunting.

"Ambrosia," Mooki purrs over the rim of their mug. Sidd frowns and turns to studiously scour his coffee cup and the pot and the bottom of the sink and maybe his soul which has slipped again into an exegesis of Mooki's right shoulder, bare beneath whatever it is they're wearing for a 'shirt,' and sporting a tiny tattoo of a pontificating hamster. Sexiest thing Sid's ever seen, which is stupid, the man is in his forties, and he once went to a strip club to preach. But honestly, those women just don't compare to the sexy lava lamp ambiguity confronting him at the moment, so he scrubs the stainless-steel sink furiously to remind himself of his commitment to the Path of Righteousness while Mooki wanders around the basement singing old Sinatra songs in a voice that righteously curls his spiritual toes.

He's supposed to be reorganizing donations to weed out old food and out-of-date boxes and stuff that not even a desperate homeless veteran would eat (someone once donated a Thanksgiving dinner in a can, with stuffing, turkey, mashed potatoes, yams, cranberry jelly, and gravy stacked in a sheath of aspic. It was so old the label was fading out) but he can't because Mooki is out there smoothing down the paper bags, a completely unnecessary job, but a job that keeps their bare back toward Sidd who measures the sharp round dunes of their shoulder blades and is thinking about how he could just barely fit one of them gently between his teeth when someone knocks on the street side door upstairs.

"Thank God," Sidd whispers. He glides out of the kitchen and glides up the stairs, but Mooki says I got it as he takes the first step and they're young and they're fast so they scootch past him as they fly up the narrow stairwell smelling like warm blankets, and morning coffee, hip checking Sidd with a soft bump that draws Sidd up the stairs in their wake. Mooki opens the door.

"Hello, is this where we volunteer?" Sidd smiles at hearing this because it just fills his heart when his community comes to the side door to sign up. Also, he's pretty low on staff so–he looks past Mooki's delicious shoulder–two grown men to add to the roster.

The guy talking has his hand out, but Mook doesn't shake hands. Sidd reaches around Mooks. His long slim piano player fingers grapple with the man's short thick handball player digits and it takes a minute for them to come to grips but they do and the man in the straw hat and the Raybans filling the doorway moves aside to indicate his companion, a young man Mooki's age who is so handsome even Sidd can't take his eyes off of him and the guy sees Mooki and he pushes forward awkwardly all hands and hair and teeth and *Oh, hey, hi, how are you?* and he smiles and it's like the sun rising over a placid sea and he just takes Mooki's hand but it's weird so instead of a handshake it's more like he's holding it for a kiss and he looks at Mooki's knuckles and then into their eyes and he swallows hard and Mooki falls in love.

It's cool.

It's ok.

It's good, actually. Mooki's been alone for a long time and it's nice to see them suddenly, like explosively, like holy crapidly interested in someone their own age. Sidd welcomes Heller and Chris into the little side office and takes their names and tells Mooks to give them a tour. Then he goes back down into the basement kitchen and throws a two-quart saucepan against the wall.

Chapter 6

That night the Ravenswood Episcopal Church and Community Center serves onehundred and thirty one meals and loads nearly as many bags of free groceries. Even though Sidd knows the two men who arrived that afternoon and pitched in for the meals are named Lloyd Heller and Christopher Montgomery, he immediately renamed them Hat and Teeth and they worked their asses off and he can't be mad at them even though Hat could make a gargoyle laugh and Teeth is stealing his gir—his . . . his most preferred person.

Sidd takes a look at all the volunteers cleaning up. He finds Mooki in close orbit around Teeth's teeth.

"Great job tonight, Christopher." Sidd is bleached white by the sudden nuclear blast of Chris's lethal smile. He turns to Mooki, resisting the urge to cover his eyes and also resisting the urge to kiss them for the rest of his life. "Mooks, can you close up? I have an errand."

"Sure—but hugs," they flap their arms around Sid and hold so tight he can count their ribs through his shirt.[1] Then Mooki lets him go, looks

1. Mooki belongs to a class of people, homo hugsalottacus, who use their embrace to communicate and listen. Mooki is saying, through their hug, to Sidd, who belongs to the order homeo dumbassicus and cannot translate, *it's cool, I'm still super into you but you're an idiot and I haven't kissed anyone in a long time and my god, just look at this guy, I mean, scrumch, am I right?*

at him with a mere millisecond of an expression he absolutely cannot categorize[2] but feels a lot like pity, then turns back into the solar wind of the Teeth. Sidd disappears into the office. He checks the numbers. He talks to some of the staff about some of the office stuff. He grabs his coat because even though it's June, it's also Chicago so buyer beware.

Sidd walks around the corner with his coat collar up in a perfectly Kerouacian jaunt and one hand in his pocket and the other hand holding his lapels tightly closed like he's being photographed for the cover of a volume of existential poetry. He heads down Montrose into the restaurants and fitness clubs of the Ravenswood Business District. He slips into an alley between Whole Foods and Ten Killer Lake Brewery, holds his cracked and out-of-date smart phone to the door which opens with a soft click. Sidd steps into a lushly appointed Buddhist temple.

The floor is thick with Indian rugs. The opulent furniture is from a burlesque lounge that didn't make it because nobody wanted to pretend it was 1921 anymore. There is a cluster of crimson upholstered couches and chairs with gold-leaf baroque woodwork. A glass-topped table whose carved wooden surface seems to be giving birth to a bloom of *fleur de lis*. There is a bookcase set into the far wall. Another couch facing it. Soft indistinct music tinkles out of hidden speakers. Perfumed smoke from expensive Japanese incense fills the room like it's a fern bar from 1955. Slumped into a couch, an elderly monk is watching trash T.V. on the tiny flatscreen mounted high on the wall. It's *Amish Fight Club* and he doesn't even look up at Sidd. Sidd stands there fuming like a lightly-aged emo fanboy. Finally, he drops his featherweight carcass onto the luridly appointed settee facing the monk and says, "Master."

The Master says nothing. Sidd feels disregarded, though he's used to it. A finely attuned acolyte, however, would recognize the Master's esoteric message. The way his shoulders tensed, the way his lip curled

---

2. Also a means of communicating, to Sidd, the following: *honestly, you could kiss me right now and I'd forget this himbo's name. But you're not gonna do that are you? You moron.*

back a full millimeter. The deafening sound of his eyebrows furrowing. All these add up to *what is troubling you, favored dipshit?*

"I just," Sidd folds his arms and pouts. "Mooki's too young for me and anyway it's just another attachment to the material."

On the tiny screen, two Amish guys in Arthur, Illinois face off like furious Calumets armed with long razor-sharp fabric shears in front of a hardware store.

"Plus, there's this new volunteer who apparently crawled up out of the lost clone factories of Nazi Germany and Mooki's all over him."

The two Amish men, Aaron and Eli, are standing perfectly still, but energy radiates off their bodies and makes the hair of their long beards flare out like they're perched under a Tesla coil.

"I have no idea where I am. I think," Sidd unfolds his arms and leans forward toward his master. "I think it's time for me to take my vows and become a monk."

Eli pounces. He yanks the tip of Aaron's beard in one hand, swipes his scissors scythe-like just under Aaron's chin–

"Will you shut the fuck up?" The Master hisses. He never takes his eyes off Eli and the now mostly beardless Aaron as they flail around on the dirty small-town sidewalk while a bevy of teenaged Amish girls watch from a brace of coal-black exequial wagons. They are grim-faced and stern. The master points to a brand-new iPad on the table next to his seat. He never takes his eyes off the T.V. "The donations page is glitching."

His eyebrows are as loud as a jet engine, vibrating so clearly to Sidd, *no you are not ready for–are you serious? You can't even figure out how to get laid. You're not ready to be a monk, ya dork.*

Sidd sinks into the pillows. His master will probably not say another word. Sidd's lessons are infrequent and difficult and painful. His goal is to become a Buddhist monk. Maybe. He's not sure. Sidd doesn't know he's not sure because Sidd has an entire ground floor of encumbrances preventing him from stepping more fully onto the spiritual path offered by radical Buddhism. His master is painfully aware of every square inch of Sidd's spectral edifice and is patiently waiting for him to wake the fuck up and attend to the finely meshed gears of his interior, although the patient waiting of a Buddhist master is indistinguishable from the implacable fury of a nervous chihuahua.

Sidd changes into his temple smock. He gets out a white linen table cloth and snaps it open. He lays it flat on the temple's empty chess table. He gently removes the master's insanely expensive iPad, nestles it gingerly, precisely onto the cloth, and opens the online database. He cleans and prods and fiddles with the code and forgets all about Mooks. It's 11:45 p.m.. It's 2:30 a.m. when he hands the Master a working page. The master wrenches his iPad out of Sid's hands, flings it onto the couch and continues watching *Amish Fight Club*, Season 4, which is showing a recap of the bearding, with voice-overs and commentary by Eli and Aaron who are now beardless, dressed like Armenian DJs, and fast friends. They're starting a band. In the recap, Eli races away, disappearing down the small-town main street, waving Aaron's beard like he's captured a flag. The Master cackles.

Chapter 7

In order for Heller to properly train his apprentice, the ridonculously handsome Christopher Aldous Really? Seriously? Montgomery, he's been given a training booklet. It's pocket-sized, the contents divided into easily digestible paragraphs with enticing headlines like "When visiting a new timeline, always remember to check in with the office," and "Please do not transport unusual food items between timelines," and "Always Be Closing," which Heller finds infuriating.

They're standing in front of Transluminal's offices.

"Here's the thing, kid: we're not salesmen," Heller leans forward to see if the kid is paying attention. "We're vacation planners. And we're not even that—we're buds. We're their new best friend. And look, you get a lead and you close? You're gonna know that guy for the rest of your career."

"So you don't use the manual?"

"I use the manual to remind myself what not to do. Like checking in? Hell no. I don't want to see how good my office looks in other timelines. I don't want to know what Randall Jane looks like when they're hot. I don't check in. Unless I'm in trouble. And even then, it's got to be some fucknacularly horological fracas for me to call the desk."

"So what about the manual?"

Heller pulls it out of his shirt pocket. Hands it to the kid.

"Read it. Learn it. Memorize it."

"I thought you said–"

"Don't get distracted, kid. The manual will save your life. Internalize every remedial word. In the meantime," Heller rattles his box of matches. "Welcome to the advanced class."

Lesson Number One

Protect your shift device. Only take it off at the close of your day. Place your device in its secure container. Do not take it home.

—Manual of Best Practices for Field Agents of Transluminal Vacations, Inc.

"Never take this off," Heller holds up his watch. "It gets sweaty. It gets heavy. You're gonna be typing a report and it's gonna be banging against your laptop and you're gonna wanna take it off, but do not do that."

"Why?"

"Marsha Osner."

"Should I know–"

"Osner was given a lead in 1975–"

"1975!? How long have you–"

"Don't interrupt me, kid. So she's got this lead and it's an easy job except in this timeline, the lead's a kleptomaniac. They're at dinner when she gets annoyed and takes off her device. Lays it right on the table, right on the linen next to her salad fork."

"I mean, she can see it–"

"Then she goes to the bathroom."

"Oh. So he–"

"Guy ganks her device. He paid attention. Spins the dial."

"What happened?"

"Nobody knows."

"Then how did you find out–"

"Osner comes into the office right away. Got canned." Heller fiddles with his moist match. "I hear she's doing alright."

"What about the klepto?"

"What about him?"

Heller takes a slim jeweler's box out of his shirt pocket. It's one of those snap cases that is incredibly cheap but bears a resemblance to something expensive or at least suggests something expensive is nestled in the velour lining inside. It's a watch like Heller's.

"This one's yours," Heller holds it out. Throws the box away. Chris reaches out for the watch, but Heller snatches it back. "Negatory. You can have it after your training."

Lesson Number Two

"Here. Take this," Heller rips his watch off his wrist. Tosses it to Chris. "Let's throw you in the water and see if you swim."

Chris holds the watch out in front of him like a live grenade.

"No!"

"Put it on, kid."

Christopher slides the watch slowly onto his wrist.

"How are we gonna–" He doesn't finish this question because Heller reaches over and flicks the bezel. Chicagos boil. They land in a perfectly boring version where the hideously turquoise and nauseatingly pink design stigma of 1983 dominates. A guy walks by in parachute pants made from worsted wool under a matching Members Only single lapel jacket. His tie is surgically narrow. He's talking into a brick of a cell phone.

"Christ," Heller says. "This is terrible. You try."

The kid touches the watch.

"Come on, spin it."

"Which way?"

"Doesn't matter."

Chris grips the metal ring. He turns it with a jerk but stops halfway through the movement as the sky hesitates above him. He snaps it back. Everyone on the street seems to catch their balance. A stupid grin plops itself onto his face. He twists the bezel like it matters. Spins it almost all the way around. The city melts and hardens, dissolves and coagulates. They land in an open prairie. No city at all. A complicated covered wagon lurches toward them, no horses; it's rolls along under its own power. An Amish guy is lounged in a heap against the headboard. He glances up at the two men, stands in alarm.

"ENGLISH!" Another Amishman pokes his head out through the canvas. "Get the gun!" The first guy slides a long rifle out of a leather sling. He rams powder into the barrel and yells in Dutch.

"Oh, hey," Chris flings his hands out in front of himself. "Hey, Heller, I think we should go."

"You've got the watch, kid."

Chris looks at the watch. Heller lays his thick fingers across Chris's hand.

"Turn it slowly clockwise. You'll feel the nodal points. They're bumps that aren't really there. Hard to ex–"

"Oh, I feel it. Like a baby kicking."

"Excellent description. Do it three times and let go."

Chris follows instructions. Just as a hot chunk of lead blows the tops off the grasses beside them, they snap into existence in their home timeline.

Lesson Number Three

If you should lose your device, go
immediately to the office. If you
cannot get to the office, call for
a Manager's Special Device Global
reset.

*—Manual of Best Practices for Field
Agents of Transluminal Vacations,
Inc.*

"What's Manager's Special Device global reset?" Montgomery asks.

Heller takes the watch back. Puts it on. Looks at the kid.

"Don't. Ever. Use. One."

Chapter 8

They go back to work Heller's lead, taking an Uber from Jackson west toward Ravenswood. It's a slow trip so they have time to think.

Christopher Aldous Hollow Leg Montgomery is starving. His thoughts are firmly rooted in the material: *. . . And if I had one of those watches I could dial myself into the rich timeline every day for lunch at Alinea or Studd's and never actually have to pay. But why would I want to ruin Studd's? I mean, I'd get tired of it eventually. I never get tired of a decent chardog. When I get a watch, I'm going to check out every version of Clark Street Dog in every timeline until I find the one where they make the best chardog out there and then that's where I eat lunch because I'm–*

Heller thinks about his job.

. . . an apprentice. Might as well gimme a gold watch. They want me out and they're making it clear. Can't take the competition. No, wait, that's not it. I'm an idiot. This is literally my last job. I've made that pretty clear, but also, it's on the chart. I put it there. Then Octavia in the timeline where she likes me colored in the palm tree. Octavia. Octavia. Eights. She's a ten. She's an eleven. Another overture in a long line of overtures. Even today, the rub on the arm. "You always close," I mean. I can read. The kid has no

idea. Yeah, she's into me. But not in my home line. Not where it matters. I could just dial in. Any time I want. Take her home and–stop. No. No you can't. It's wrong. In the sweeter timeline, she wants me to get that platinum package as much as I do and she doesn't care that I'm ten years older–hell, she likes it. Last year. "You ever been to a beach, DelSol?" She looks at him in a way that a girl can look at someone they secretly openly love who is being a titanic jackass about it and says, "I'm saving it."

I'm getting that fucking vacation package and they know it and I know it and of course they assigned me an apprentice, they have to fill this gap and how the fuck do you advertise for job like mine? Where did they find this kid? Doesn't matter. This next job is gonna go all Alabama on me. A fucking Buddhist? How do you–ah, it doesn't matter. It's a challenge mark. I'm fucked nine ways to Sunday even if–

And on. Both men ride in silence, locked into the inflexibility of their inner monologue. Christopher Aldous Montgomery is always thinking about food and Lloyd Woods Heller is always thinking about his job. Both of them roiling in the near heavens of the immediate, worried about the tangible and the real, avoiding the thinner atmospheres of the upper psyche and not even imagining the finely wrought gauzy reality of the formative, of the divine. Never has Heller thought *I wonder what happens to the people we've abandon in unprofitable timelines? What is the me in an alt-line like? Is the God in this timeline the same God in another timeline? Does the discovery of massively multiple yet narrowly divergent present moments point to a determinate or an indeterminate universe? And did the guy who decided to call regularly fruiting tomatoes 'determinate' mean to make a cosmological joke?*

"Is this one yours?" The Kid rattles his box of Blue Tips at the entire world.

Heller stares out the window at the animated graffiti and holographic advertising that turns the Edens Expressway into a tunnel of light and color with the haunted image of low rise three flats and old automobile dealerships ghosting behind it all.

"Pretty sure."

"You're pret–"

"Look, kid; you do this enough you start to notice anomalies, weirdnesses; all kinds of alien shit you just didn't realize was there. You see people you've known in your baseline, known for your entire life as pitiful losers, you see them flourish. Or fuck up. How did nearly getting shot by an Amish tech distributor change your philosophy?"

"I suppose I–"

"Exactly. You get cynical. Makes it hard to believe in things. Makes it hard to hope. You just plow on toward the Platinum Package."

"Your reward."

"My reward," Heller relaxes back into his seat. He smiles out the window.

"What's that like?"

"Are you asking me, kid," Heller points his toothpick at the kid. "Are you asking me about product?"

"Yes? You seem pretty excited about–"

"Here's the thing. It's different for everybody. Statistics runs a trace through all your timelines to measure your happiness quotient in each one. It's expensive, that's why it's an upgrade. You got to already be paying in. But they run a trace and they look at a densely woven thread of potentialities, of measurables, of subtle realities that persist through your verticals until they get this portrait of you that tells them where you'd be happiest."

"Is it–"

"And it's not always what you think it is. It's not always the fuck you money line. Sometimes it's just . . . no big deal. Those are the ones I don't understand. I haven't been scanned. This–” Heller stares at nothing over the kid's shoulder. “This is about as happy as I get. But somewhere on my timeline is a version of me where I'm making crazy money and I'm on a private yacht and I'm hip deep in pussy and cocaine. So, you know, I have that to look forward to.”

“And that's your pl–”

“But that's just the accounting line. That's just the money. I don't know if it'll make me happy.”

“Jesus.”

“Yeah, well, I get the upgrade.”

“If you close thi–”

“Unless I blow it.” Heller grimaces out of the advertising images projected onto his face. “That's the thing about a challenge mark. And let me tell you, this guy,” Heller waves his match around at nothing in particular to indicate the Buddhist. “This guy is a challenge.”

“Wait, how is there an upgrade if we only sell the plati—”

“That's why we have staggered packages—or why we tell them that. We tell them there's a silver, a gold, and a platinum package. But the silver and the gold are just part of the sales pipeline. We take them to their PGMT, their pretty-good-money-timeline to whet their whistle and get the greed dialed up. Then we kind of let it slip that there's still another level. The Platinum's the only product we sell. If we sell.”

“What happens if—“

“Rose pulled a ticket on this sale. I'm sure of it. That truncated oscillating nozzle of yak pus. One day I will open a timeline where she is a clerk and I'll have her fired. A ticket–so she's ticking off the seconds to the end of this close as a kind of Human Resources thing. Checking on my work. Seeing how long it takes me to close–if I close–because if I don't, if I don't,” Heller looks down at his shoes. Smooths the fabric over his knees. "If I can't . . . then I lose the bonus."

"How many years do I–"

"Been on the job for twenty odd years, sweetheart. "Heller's face folds into a fierce visage. "I earned it."

Chapter 9

It was worse than he thought. It was worse than he could imagine. It was earth-shattering. That phrase is rarely used for anything but recreational hyperbole, but rest assured that in this moment, as Ovale Calvarium had backed himself up against the wooden doors of his lab table; as his eyes, already magnified by vintage multi-lensed watch repair goggles inflated themselves in horror against the limits of his orbital sockets; as his lips peeled back like pale strips of anchovy under his nose while his jaw opened wide enough to detach itself from his skull; as a scream built momentum racing up his windpipe to blow itself out through his quivering teeth; as all this was occurring, Ovale was realizing he may have just broken not only the celestial body he shared with so many other not-quite-so-horrified-(yet)-people, but the universe in which it wobbled; therefore his brief mental deployment of the word earth-shattering was a thing of gleaming syntactical precision.

On the floor between his knees, in the delta formed by his legs which had shot out into a frail V, glistened a glistening puddle of pond water and broken glass that, if a couple of hundred ancient elven craftsmen labored over it for decades, may have been put back together in the form of an oversized vacuum hydrolysis tube which had, until moments before, contained the pond water which, still glistening on the glistening floor, contained a complex micro-eco-system which Ovale was paid handsomely to maintain.

In that ecosystem, in fact, were the microscopic kings of a soggy aquarian jungle: a tiny handful of rare tardigrades. It should be noted that of the thirty families, one hundred forty-two genera, thirteen hundred species, and thirty-six subspecies of Tardigrada, only two were classified as SECRET LAB ONLY and PROPERTY OF TRANSLUMINAL VACATIONS, INC. RESEARCH FACILITY, UNIVERSITY OF CHICAGO not found anywhere on the planet except in an oversized vacuum hydrolysis tube, now shattered on the glistening floor of this lab; they were: tanarctus chronochalarapoutinka (translation: a tardigrade that treats time as if it were a loose pudding; TC-1) and tanarctus chronosfichtosvarelli (a tardigrade that reacts to liberated custardy time by sighing then laboriously gathering all the time back together, as it should be; TC-2) both of whom exist in microecologies so precise that a temperature change of a half of a half of 100th of a degree would cause them to explode. However, maintaining such a weirdly consistent temperature was not nearly as vital (nor difficult, it's a lab after all) as maintaining perfect stillness because tanarctus chronochalarapoutinka and tanarctus chronosfichtosvarelli are cantankerous little bastards who don't like their pond water all swirly.

A curious fact of TC1 and TC2 is they are essentially the same subspecies of tardigrae, just with different reactions to having their comfortably motionless environment turn turbulent, as noted by the eminent nano biologist, Jimotheen "Tits" Barnardi, from the Zoology Department of the University of East Ocoee, subsequently redacted from the records by very determined and totally secret field agents of the Transluminal Vacations, Inc.

TC-1, who like all tardigrae spends most of its time sleeping, will ignore the swirling of water which washes over its skin in an equatorial fashion. TC-2, also mostly asleep, will ignore any swirling water washing over its skin in an uppy-downy way (which is perpendicular to equatorial swishing, but I can't remember what that's called).

However, when water is swished against their grain, they blink into an adjacent timeline where such movement is not happening–TC-1 moves right, TC-2 moves left–carrying with them all their microbiological neighbors and the local supply of algae and rotifers on which they regularly dine.

Ovale's job is–was–to keep a tube of these particularly scarce tardigrades in the lab in perfect stillness at the perfect temperature until such a time as Transluminal Vacations, Inc. might need them, whereupon Ovale would use a tiny siphon to carefully remove a single TC-1 and a single TC-2 along with some of their adjacent rotifers and algae then deposit them into the cavity of a Transluminal salesman's Quartz Action Timepiece which, instead of watch parts and gears, contains a carefully curated dollop of pond water.

When Heller turns the bezel on his watch, tiny magnetic paddles stir the liquid inside over one of the tardigrades which irritates them enough to flick themselves and their ecosystem–which contains the salesman and anyone he's with–into an adjacent timeline. They also eat harmful bacteria and dream mostly about impeccable stasis.

Now, between Ovale's knobbly knees those tardigrades are whooshing through the imperceptible and violent vortex of a nanotsunami because Ovale was practicing speed yoga and sprang thoughtlessly from the classic "unflappable peering ostrich" pose into the little-known "formidable metropolitan bus bench" pose with a little too much gusto and lost his balance so he involuntarily flung his arms out and knocked the vacuum hydrolysis tube off his lab table as he crashed to the floor where it smashed into a bajillion shards between his trembling patellas.

Ovale and the rotifers and the algae and the small family of tardigrades are now flickering through successive timelines. Many of these flickerings are from TC-1s and many are from TC-2s and all of them are happening simultaneously which is causing some temporal friction and putting a lot of pressure on the seams of the universe and Ovale, who studied hard in school, knows that if he doesn't figure something out the whole cosmic casserole is going to disintegrate into a fractalicious Alabama-hotpocket of steaming gray gloop, and the earth, within this infinite splintering, will shatter.

So, yeah, Ovale is accurate on that count.

Chapter 10

(Flicker.)

Chapter 11

They arrive at the Ravenswood Episcopal Church just in time, all hat and teeth and handshakes and home spun charm. They literally roll up their sleeves and leap into the work like they've been doing it for years. Teeth's never more than a smile away from Mooki. Hat somehow ends up working with Sidd no matter where Sidd sends him. They work hard, throwing themselves into every task, working with volunteers so seamlessly and with such deference that everyone on the crew falls in love with them again and Sidd just can't be mad at all.

Transluminal donates a massive check to the church which Hat gives to Sidd in semi-privacy while they walk down the stairs to the basement for supplies. He just whips it out of his shirt pocket and hands it over. Says, "From the company outreach program," and Sidd's looking at an extra ten grand. Hat gives him one of those nods that means *This is just between us. No grandstanding. No need to say anything, this is serious business between serious people* then he disappears into the volunteers in a flurry of activity and jokes and charm.

Sidd can't help himself. He likes Heller. He even likes Teeth. He's a sucker for enterprise and these cats work hard. At the end of the night, when just a handful of volunteers are cleaning and the dirty blues moans along to the percussion of banging pots rising up from the kitchen in the basement, Sidd sneaks out into his favorite space behind the parsonage for a smoke. Heller's there.

"Don't tell anybody," Sidd says.

Heller holds out a match.

"Tell who what?"

Sidd grins. They sit in silence in the warm June night. Sidd leaning his beanpole frame against a light post. Heller parked on the edge of a picnic table fiddling with his watch.

"You don't smoke," Sidd observes.

"Naw. I chew on 'em." Heller rattles his box of Ohio Blue Tips. "Nervous habit."

"Nice watch." Sidd blows a cloud across the small courtyard.

"Comes with the job."

"I've heard of company phones," Sidd stares at the watch. "Which all tell time. But a watch? Is it an image thing?"

"That was a good supper. What'd you do, 80 people?"

"75. Slow night. Why change the subject, Mr. Heller?"

"It's just Heller and I didn't change the subject."

"What kind of company drops ten thousand dollars to a local church without even filling out a form?"

"We're committed to the community."

"And requires you to wear a clearly expensive watch when you can just look at the time on your phone?"

Heller puts the watch back onto his wrist.

"A broken watch," Sidd observes.

The little hand is on the seven and the big hand is between four and five but it's almost midnight. Heller resets the hands. "Damn thing's never right."

"Who are you, Mr., Heller?"

Sidd's cigarette is pinched between his index finger and thumb, like he's signaling everything is ok. Like he's going to throw the cigarette away after one last drag. When he inhales, his eyes narrow. He smokes like a suspicious cowboy. Heller watches him then looks off into the dark past the roof of the rectory. His pose suggests he's thinking about telling Sidd an important secret and despite all Sidd's training and education he imagines Heller's a spy and he's been sucked into some kind of political power play. But what Heller's actually doing is waiting because Sidd is closing in on Step Six in the Eight-step Transluminal Vacation, Inc. Pipeline to Conversion from the Manual.

1. **Find a gajillionaire in *any* timeline**

2. **Find the poorest version of them in any *other* timeline**

3. **Gain their trust**

4. **Get them to notice your watch**

5. **Change the subject**

6. **Wait for them to come back to it then pause dramatically until they insist you tell them "the truth"**

Sidd slips the check out of his wallet and hands it to Heller.

"I think maybe you should go, Mr. Heller."

"It's nothing bad."

"I raise funds for a living, Mr. Heller, and nobody hands out ten grand without a meeting. We don't need the money that badly. Please take Christopher with you."

7. Tell them the truth.

"I sell vacations."

"And I'm a parachute repairman."

"It's just, our vacations are . . . special."

"You will not be using our church for passing anything illicit from—"

"What do you want?"

"—huh?"

"What, Sidd? What do you desire more than anything in the world? Not what you're supposed to want, not what you tell people in polite company, but—man to man—what is it you want the most?"

"I want people to be happier."

"Are you happy?"

"What is this, Heller?"

"Sidd, my job is to make people happy. Not just happy yer, but as happy as they possibly can be. The most happiest. Like, sitting on a beach in the Maldives drinking fancy umbrella drinks with nothing to do happy. My job is to sell them the platinum-level vacation package of their dreams."

"I have work to do, Mr. Heller."

"I'm sure you do."

Heller waits. Sidd smokes. They look at each other. Sidd is weighing the sincerity he hears in Heller's gravelly voice while Heller is counting the seconds until Sidd says, ok, fine, show me your brochure.

"Ok, fine." Sidd stubs his cigarette out in a coffee can half hidden behind a drain pipe. "Show me your brochure."

8. Jump

Chapter 12

Heller grins.

"How you feeling?"

"Suspicious."

"Natch. Do me a favor, just, flex your knees a little. Yeah, like that. Roll your neck. Here," Heller steps up to Sidd and pats his shoulders and brushes imaginary crumbs off his shirt which is all a pretense to make sure Sidd is within the sphere of temporal protection offered by the watch. Heller looks into Sidd's eyes, then very studiously, he turns the bezel.

Reality churns.

Sidd and Heller are still facing each other. Sidd blinks. Looks around. The courtyard is lit up by string lights. It's bigger. A lot bigger. And nice. People in clumps, hands full of tiny plates with tiny bites of tiny foods. Everyone dressed nicely. Sidd looks down. He's dressed nicely. Heller's in a bespoke suit. Sidd breathes short powerful breaths. Mooki shows up in a flowing peach tuxedo with a cream-colored sash, holding out a clipboard with names and dollar figures. They're grinning ear to ear.

"We shot past our goal in the first ten minutes. We're thirty thousand up, Sidd. Thirty thou—"

Sidd's eyes widen. He turns away and pukes all over the drain pipe. Heller sighs, dials them back into the duller timeline. Sidd yelps. Backs up against the wall.

"The fuck?"

"Something, ain't it?"

"People were mingling!"

"Are."

"What'd you do to me?"

"Nothing. Nothing at all," Heller pops a hose off the back of the parsonage and washes gunk off the drain pipe. He hoses off the toes of Sidd's boots. "I just used my company issued watch to pop you and I into an adjoining timeline—"

"Don't fuck around! What kind of—how did you do that with all the people and Mooks and—"

"Into an adjoining timeline where your situation is different."

"I was in a suit."

"Looked good, too."

"Mooks."

"Also good."

"It smelled . . ."

"Different timeline, different air. Contamination's not a concern, since you're you in that timeline so you're conditioned, but you're right. It's noticeable."

"The church!"

"Sidd, here's the thing. Transluminal Vacations, Inc. makes me wear this watch cause it's not actually a watch. It's a highly technical device that I use to transport myself—and others—into adjacent realities."

"Time travel is—"

"Not a thing. Correct," Heller says. "But as it turns out, the multiverse *is* a thing, and we can jump around in it. We can't go forward or backward, but we can go sideways. You might say we travel more room-to-room than day-to-day."

Sidd drags a cigarette out of his slightly crumpled pack. Heller has a flame under it before he even gets it to his lips. They sit there for a minute while Heller chews a match and Sidd smokes slowly, thoughtfully, staring out at nothing trying to decide if what just happened was real or not.

"So that just happened?"

"Yes, it did."

Sidd smokes more. He looks up at Heller. Heller grins a wide alabaster grin as welcoming as a low picket fence, as comforting as your mom's coffee cups, as soothing as a white cat stretching in your lap. He holds up the watch.

"Wanna do it again?"

Sidd flicks his cigarette butt into the coffee can without even looking.

"Fuck yes."

Heller grins. He spins the dial. Reality churns. Nothing changes.

"Didn't work," Sidd says. There is a plaintive scream in the sky as a pale, manta-ray-like creature drifts low across the courtyard's postage stamp square of stars. Two more follow. Sidd reaches into his pocket for smokes and comes back with a short pipe and a satchel of tobacco. He laughs. "What?"

Heller spins again.

It's the party. Mooks is in the peach suit. Sidd is holding a Halliwell Wide filterless in his hand. Mooki snatches the cigarette and gives Sidd an intimate look which he has never seen before but which, apparently, contextually, in this timeline, he has. They shove it back into his pocket then turn to the minglers.

"Can I have your attention, puh lea yuz. Our patron has a few words." They step aside, turning to Sidd, clapping along with the group. Sidd panics.

"Heller, do the thing."

"And miss your speech? Come on, Sidd. You got this."

"I'm serious. Spin the—USE THE WATCH!"

"Nope."

Sidd grabs Heller's collar and leans in. "I don't public speak. Get me out of here."

Heller flips them back into Sidd's baseline.

"Ok, let's pick a new place. The visuals here are pretty plain and I'd really like you to see some dramatic change."

"That was dramatic."

"Yeah, but just–" he leads Sidd out front, they plop down on a bench at the corner of Lawrence and Mango. Sidd lights a smoke and takes a vicious drag as a local walks out of Moynihan's across the street on the corner. He loses the guy as he passes behind the Church sign, a wide low horizontal brick thing from 1954. Then the guy appears from behind the trunk of the white oak at the corner, its roots decorated with black cohosh and joe-pye weed. He crosses Lawrence under amber lights as Sidd draws a deep drag. Looks up at the full moon. Heller explains, "It's better with a view."

Heller dials. Chicago boils. Sidd marvels.

When the sales department puts together a lead package, it's been thoroughly researched. The field teams have determined at least three of the client's Fuck You Money Timelines and three of the less filthy rich versions. The idea is to whet their appetite, work them up to one of the really good timelines where they're raking in 500 thousand a year then say, *hey, want to see something really cool?* And drop them into an FMYT. Then you close.

But before that, there's a thing Heller does. It's part of his schtick. Every salesman has a schtick. Doesn't matter if you sell used cars or United Oil, you've got your personal theater, your patter, and it works, and you won't deviate an inch. Heller's goes like this:

He spins them into a timeline: Moynihan's sign changes to a wooden slab with a bas-relief of a red buck and block capitals spelling Cerf Rouge. The guy who walked out of the bar and is stepping up onto the sidewalk on the other side of Lawrence is now wearing a wildly epauletted deep green velvet jacket with gold piping and buttons so highly polished Sidd can see them glimmer all the way from his bench. The man has a sword and a ridiculous wig. The doors to the bar fly open and a guy just like him but in blue holds up a tankard and yells "putain d'enfant, reviens boire un verre!" before a couple of other wigs drag him back inside. The sign for the church is small and squat. The white oak is a stand of fir, and the cars are all carriages. No horses. Just the carriages.

"Nah," Heller says to himself. Dial. Churn. Every building is precisely chiseled from granite slabs. The sign is a moss-green stone tablet. The white oak is rectangular statuary. The door to Moynihan's slides open. A man steps out in clothes that look like they could slice cheese. He opens his mouth and says "asflkafpsdfpihpiufg!" Sidd grins.

"Sucks," Heller says, looking at the corners. Spin. Roil. Sidd breathes a cloud of smoke. The sign is floating in midair. So is their bench. Sidd turns to look at the church. It's hovering six inches off the ground.

"Why aren't I scared anymore?"

"You weren't really scared the first time. It was just jump anxiety. Thing is, this timeline is normal for you."

Sidd watches as reality blurs again.

"Weird." Heller mumbles. Turn. Churn. Sidd stands up and takes in the Church. It's the same, only now it's fantastically detailed, with each aspect of its construction somehow overwrought, almost cartoonish. It's gingerbread baroque with colors that are, well, he'd never have painted the place salmon with a dull blue trim but, hell, it works. The bushes are trimmed into abstract ornamental shapes. The lighting is amazing. Yet, he hates all of it. He is strangely alarmed. He glances up at the moon and it bears a familiar silhouette: an enormous tattoo of Mickey Mouse.

"Fucktrifyingly nope," Heller growls. Twists. Flicker. Moynihan's is Monaghan's and it's fixed up nice. Brick facade, beautifully painted doorway, gold leaf details. A girl steps outside for a quiet call. She's dressed in a tweed hunting suit, high boots, and a cap. The moon hangs unbranded in the dark.

Sidd turns to the Church. It is in fine shape, really well-maintained. He walks around to the front and it's illuminated by lights embedded in the sidewalk. The facade is refurbished, the mid-century central verticals have been turned into living walls. The slabs of rock cleaned and fresh and bright. Sidd is wearing a nice suit. Nothing special. Just nice. It fits. There's a bus parked out front with a crew in matching t-shirts loading music equipment into the luggage compartment. A small delivery truck pulling away. As it drives past Sidd, the letters on the side read "Ravenswood Episcopal Mobile Food Pantry." One of the band members waves at Sidd. "It was a good night. Pretty nice." Sidd nods to him.

"Is this real?" Sidd watches the bus crew board.

"It's real. It's now. It's permanent."

"How can I afford this?"

"Funny you should ask," Heller spins the bezel to one of the predetermined FYMTs. The church blurs and is now the center piece of a much larger complex. There's adjoined housing with a graceful plaque on the brick exterior reading "Ravenswood Episcopal Apartments". Sidd opens the door. They walk into a nice foyer with a reception desk, mailboxes, coat closets.

"Apartments."

"Pastor Sidd?" it's the receptionist. "Hey, how you doing?" Sidd checks himself. He's in a clerical outfit.

"How's business?" Heller asks.

"We have two units to fill." Elevator doors open and a family hurries through the foyer. They say a warm hello to Sidd.

"It's for the homeless?" Sidd asks.

The girl looks at him weirdly. "You told us not to use that word. You said they's residents."

"Residents. Yes." Sidd turns to Heller. "This is my dream. To put all the people we feed into residential apartments. This is it."

"Pretty good idea, Sidd."

"I don't understand how this works. I don't know what's going on." Sidd says quietly.

"Excuse me," Heller says. "but just to humor us, how does the church pay for all of this?"

"You must be new. The Church doesn't pay for it. Pastor Ough pays for it from his sandwich shops. He's one of the good ones, like Will Bates. Puts his money to work for the people, right Pastor?"

Sidd notices a stack of menus on the counter. They're for his sandwich shop and they look expensive.

"There aren't any prices," Sidd flips through them.

"That's how they's supposed to be? Did I get the wrong ones? Oh, shoot. You said you didn't want the people to think about how much this stuff costs, so you printed—"

"Priceless menus."

"Catchy," Heller says.

They walk out front and dig the quiet face of the church.

"What's your take?" Sidd asks Heller.

"From here? Nothing."

"What do you mean?"

"Every thread has a designation. This one is an exemplary thread. We haven't been to the account thread."

"How's it different?"

"Makes this look like small potatoes."

"But the apartments, this," Sidd points at the building. "This is what—" he turns to Heller. "This is what I want."

"Sidd, in the accounting thread, you can do more."

"Yeah, but . . ." Sidd reaches out to run his finger along a brass accent on the edge of the doorframe. "Just look at her."

Chapter 13

A Tanarctus chronochalarapoutinka was strolling down the avenue on a Tuesday evening.[3] He didn't know he was a Tanarctus chronochalarapoutinka, he only knew that it was a beautiful night. The lights of Rotifer Lane pulsed gently, illuminating the fronts of shops[4] and businesses in a softly verdant glow. His name was George[5] and he was on his way to a meeting.

George drew up alongside a pale authoritative building, trotted happily up the steps and through the door. He hung his hat on a hat rack, chose a clean white sash from the wooden box of white sashes by a set of double doors that opened onto a broad, dimly lit, well-appointed room with a parquet floor and theater seating along both sides. On the far end of the room a raised dais sported a large ornate chair in which a bearded, ancient Tardigrade in a fez was going over the agenda.

---

3. Of course it wasn't an actual street. I could have been pedantic and literal and written 'trod infinitesimally slowly along an established scent corridor' but who wants to be pedantic? Look, translating Tardigradian into English is almost impossible as their language is mostly smells and response where ours is mostly forcing air through a hole and yeah, there are obvious similarities and sometimes scents but let's just be serious for a moment. I think I got close.
4. No, of course they aren't actual shops, but probably more like nodes of communal gathering for various nutrient-dense patches. Just . . . just stay with me here.
5. Literal Translation

"Good, I was worried I was late," George said to the old, elderly, decrepit, antediluvian, and nearly extinct Tanarctus chronochalarapoutinka who eyed him suspiciously through a brace of eyebrows that would have made an impressive hedge as George tried to walk through the doorway.

"Password," the prehistoric patriarch purred.

"Frank, old pal, have you finally slipped into dementia? It's George. You obligated me into the order twenty years ago."

"Password," Frank muttered.

George sighed. Reared erect. He took a fez from the box by the door, its face imprinted with three wavy horizontal lines, put it onto his head, then delivered the required shibboleth, "latitudinal," and swished his pudgy eight-legged corpus through the open doors to take a seat for the argument.

The ancient tardigrade in the big chair rapped a gavel two and a half times. Everyone stood up.

"You will come to order as assembled Champions of the Alabaster Sash!"

The tardigrades standing along both sides of the room arranged their lower feet in a complicated stance and tucked their upper thumbs beneath the hems of their mostly white sashes. All eyes were on the Tardigrade at the front. Suddenly, he pinched the edges of his sash and with a flourish, spun it rapidly until it whirled around him from shoulder to hip.

A susurrus whispered through the hall as the Assembled Champions of the Alabaster Sash swished their sashes. As the circlets slid around them for the sixth whorl the group shouted "DAMN STRAIGHT" rather sternly then blushed for using an expletive and for making so much noise. It all ended abruptly when the Tardigrade on the dais, The

Guy Who Sits at the Front in the Big Chair, rapped the gavel twice and fell back into his chair on his ample, dimpled terminal plate. He looked around the room, puckered his stylets, and considered his next words carefully.

"Champions," his voice was stentorian, a gravelly grandpa's voice that was calm and reassuring while simultaneously informing you, from its tone, that you would probably never amount to much, but he loves you anyway and also, these next couple of words are going to set you off. "It is time we recognize the uppy-downies."

It was as if he had taken their universe and shaken it violently, swirling the placid water they breathed then shit in their beer. The Assembled Champions of the Alabaster Sash leapt out of their seats. Some of them shouted at The Guy Who Sits at the Front in the Big Chair, some of them shouted at the shouters, some of them grumbled and gathered their belongings as if they were leaving, which was pure theater because they wouldn't miss this argument for all the rotifer cheese in the world; some of them rattled their sashes and glared. Five of the A.C.O.T.A.S. stood silently, their top four legs posed in a pretzelish loop to indicate their formal displeasure to the Guy Who Sits in the Front in the Big Chair and to make certain it was recorded in the minutes.

The Guy Who Sits at the Front in the Big Chair sighed. Disorder was not his strong suit. For five years, and indeed for the previous twenty decades or so, the various Guys in the Front Who Sat in the Big Chair had maintained a nearly motionless state of bliss and harmony among the A.C.O.T.A.S. during lodge meetings (first and third Thursdays (excepting those weeks wherein they hosted a rotifer fry or a protozoa-cake breakfast (or holidays))) which were comfortably torpid and blissfully silent.

The uppy-downies were Tanarctus chronosfichtosvarelli, a vapid cartel of riotous Neanderthals who wallowed in longitudinal lethargy openly satisfied by the swishing of pond water flowing from the bottom to the top or vice versa—which was sickening.

If you were a Tanarctus chronochalarapoutinka.

To the uppy-downies, it was just a Tuesday. The uppy-downies paddled the parts of the land where the water rose from the bottom of the known universe to the infinite upper end, where scripture dictates the water terminates at a surface (a parable for children) wherefrom light flows in an unending pearlescent cascade.

The A.C.O.T.A.S. and their friends and families lived in the part of the land where the water swirled in a nearly static vortex shaped like a flattened cantaloupe. The two societies almost never met, and when they did, as in for instance, business meetings or when an uppy-downie needed to traverse the Great Wide Whirl to trap protozoa for their farms, both parties had to endure insane levels of itchy discomfort and vile, secret loathing.

However, there'd been rumblings since the time of the Sudden Sploosh. Dangerously liberal ideas drifted through the Great Wide Whirl, things like "Uppy-Downies Should be Townies" and "Aren't We All a Little Uppy Downy?" and the worst of them, *Is Flat All That?* with its saucy italics. These grumblings were a symptom of better education and greater everyday freedoms and a long, long period of perfect stasis with a seemingly endless supply of protozoa, ciliophora, diatoms, and even an instance of the (previously) mythic brefeldia maxima which had engulfed an entire lobe of their static environment and on which herds of eukaryotes grazed placidly.

His own grandlarva had lived their lives without once having to venture into the wilderness to hunt, without braving the irritating sluice of the vertical vent wash, without climbing in silent terror over ravenous xenophyophores with their horrifyingly crenelated crevasses and their hideous enormity. They didn't know how good they had it, these kids.

And now here they are saying the uppy-downies ought to be allowed to visit his town, to walk down his streets, to shoppe in (shudder) his shoppe? Blasphemy!

Yet, here was his own Guy Who Sits in the Front in the Big Chair telling this revered organization, this ancient and honorable institution, these defenders of equatorial rapture, ought to sit in lodge with . . . virts.

Chapter 14

Heller's other trick is part of Transluminal Vacations, Inc. sales canon, which he explained to Christopher Aldous I Know it looks Like I'm not Listening, but I am Listening, I Swear Montgomery way back two days ago in training.

"Alright, boss, but—" Christopher shifts his soggy toothpick around his Aaryan smile. Heller makes a face, like the kind of face you make when someone accidentally drops their pants and they have really weird, pale legs with sparse but exceedingly thick hairs, more like wires, really, like they have a hilltop copse of starving trees poking out of their kneecaps. "But what I don't understand is how you get someone to close. I mean, this is all terrifying."

"Reverse Psychology," Heller says, very pointedly taking a brand new entirely crispy and dry match from his box slowly enough that Christopher gets it and tosses his own limp stick into the gutter. "Here, I'll show you."

Heller dials them through a knuckle biting carousel of realities, landing suddenly, rocking slightly like he just stepped off a boat. He looks up at the giant advertisement on the side of the brick wall of the building right next to Transluminal Vacations, Inc. It's Christopher pointing to a phone with the word SMUGG, alone, in the copy space.

"Lesson one, kiddo: Show 'em the money." Heller slips Christopher's phone out of his pocket, waves it in front of his Aaryan eyeballs to unlock, then taps open SMUGG from the home screen. A social media profile pops open. It's a thumbnail of Christopher looking smug, his name and details (Christopher Aldous Montgomery, CEO, SMUGG, smugg@smugg.smugg, net-worth: $321,943,211.03). He hands it to Christopher who quietly holy shits all over himself.

"Maybe I should stick around," Chris says.

"Should you?" Heller whips them through another wheel of Chicago's, the advertisement melting through successive iterations of Christopher (a wanted poster, a before image for an erectile dysfunction drug, a stock picture for a shoe ad, three versions of Smugg) finally landing in a thread where the painting on the side of the building moves. Christopher stares in awe at himself as his giant head, bulging out of the wall, turns to waggle its eyes suggestively at the phone in his hand where his net-worth is rising by the second and has a new digit up front.

"Billions. . ." Chris is mesmerized. A very sharp, somewhat familiar looking woman leans into his field of view.

"Chris?"

He snaps out of it. Looks at her. Looks at Heller. Looks back at her.

"Is it on point?"

"Is it . . ." He confuses.

Heller dives in. "Sorry, Cassandra—"

"Again, it's Marcus, Mr. Heller."

"—Chris and I were talking serious bizwax and he's a bit kerfuffled."

"Chris, you said 'I want to stand in front of it. I want to see if it hits.' I think you were wondering how it affects the average viewer."

"Heller?"

"See, this is just like the other one, but better," Heller says.

"Other what?" Marcus asks.

"What . . . How do you get them to . . ." Chris remains fuffled.

"Mr. Heller, would you give us a moment?" Marcus unpleases.

"Sure, let me just check the time."

Reality roils. They skid into their baseline.

"Why did I feel so . . . I don't even know how to explain it." Christopher's usual sheen of arrogance and privilege has evaporated.

"See," Heller says warmly, quietly. "This is the kicker. In that timeline you were one of the richest men on earth."

"Shouldn't that feel good?"

"You'd think. But what I've found is as you take people into the higher tax brackets of their FYMTs they get nervous. Paranoid. The whole planet's got it in for you, yet you depend on the whole planet, on billions of people, to keep you on top." Heller lets it sink in. "So everyone hates you."

"How the fuck do you get them to close?"

Heller dials them out then dials them back in somewhere else.

"You already closed. This part of the pipeline isn't about conversion anymore. You may not have signed—and I'm saying not you you but . . . you know I mean the client—"

Christopher's eyebrows do a thing that means this caterpillary copulation dance is what happens when I think hard about something, it's my frontal sinus muscles twitching and stretching as if I can pull the meaning out of the numinous with my forehead muscles alone. "Yes."

"—Now we're negotiating. We need to compare products."

"Hey, is that Montgomery? Hey! You rich dick!" A guy barrels off the sidewalk. Suddenly, an android of spiderish contours races past Heller and Chris to tase the shit out of the guy. Chris looks up at the ad on the side of the building. Someone's gratified over it, blacked out a tooth, painted 667 on his forehead and in large red capitals: TRAITOR TO EARTH!

The android dog drags the unconscious man away. Someone very much like Marcus whistles and the robot dog trots back to them. It doesn't even turn around. Just reverses course. Chris looks at Marcusish, Marcusish says:

"Like you always say, Boss. Fuck 'em—we got their money."

"Heller?"

"Billions, kiddo." But he dials and they're back to baseline and Christopher Aldous Perhaps He Has a Soul After All Montgomery is crying just a little bit.

"It was awful. It was awful. The way I felt. The hatred. It was like a hunger."

"I can imagine."

"And that makes them close?"

"No. They always—and I mean always—back out. Hard pass. Then I say, yeah, of course, sure, let me just take you back to square one. But on the way, we stop in their TOOC, their Timeline of Optimal Contentment—"

"Take me there now, please"

"Kid," Heller feels terrible. But the lesson is important. If Chris ever wants to sell a vacation, he's got to know how this works. Plus, Heller has a legacy to hand off. Might as well be Teeth. "If I could, I would."

"What happens in their Optimal—"

"Guaranteed ninety-percent contentment quotient. It ain't necessarily king of the world stuff. For some people it's more like an enduring childhood memory. One client, this lady from Sauganash, hers was owning a library. I mean, it was in a smoking apocalypse of terror, but she'd somehow ganked this beautiful fortress of a library. No money to speak of, but she was perfectly happy. Never seen anything like it.

"How can I get—"

"Every employee gets scanned. You don't get the results until you're vested, which for Transluminal Vacations, Inc. is ten years, kid. You have to make partner. But then, well, they give you a taste."

"But wait, the timelines you took me to—"

"Convenient. I have no idea if they're your FYMT. But if they're not, they're close."

Heller fishes the matchbox out of his pocket. Offers one to Chris.

"That's enough for one day. Shit will wear you out. Let's drop brass and head home. You need a ride?"

"I need a ride."

Heller dials up an Uber and thinks about firing up the grill.

Chapter 15

Ovale Calvarium gathered himself back into the form and shape of a qualified scientist and lab technician curating the motionless life of timeline hopping Tardigrades in a normally unbroken vacuum hydrolysis tube.

The watch around his wrist, assigned to him by Transluminal Vacations, Inc. at least a decade ago, was vibrating urgently. Calvarium waggled the knob which silenced the notifications. He didn't need to hear the terrified tones of whomever in the company had called in a loop breach. It would just make him feel worse, which might be impossible since he'd just broken the world.

Calvarium wondered if they knew it was him. Rose would get there eventually. Octavia would tell her. None of the agents would figure it out. *Could* figure it out.

Idiots. They were mere users. It was *his* work with the watches, his careful and endless curation of Tanarctus chronochalarapoutinka and Tanarctus chronosfichtosvarelli that ran their stupid devices. He'd made up the hermetically sealed torus watches based on magnetic confinement fusion reactors that balanced perfectly so the encapsulated pond water never swished nor swashed and the encapsulated beings never realized they were in a miniature Tokamaks nuclear reactor (sort of). You could duct tape one of them to a propellor and fly it to France and the tards would never know.

Unless you moved the dial. Then strong magnets clustered tightly around the tube caused the water to flow through the tube lengthwise, or to whirl around the tube sideways. He'd invented the entirely useless device, the 'recharger', a stupid name for a brick. Those mongrels in sales could never quite grasp the concept that a powerful scientific device can be fully analog. The sheer volume of cretinous emails he received asking for batteries. *Morons.* The recharging station doesn't do a damn thing— except bring a Grinchian smile to Ovale's lips every time he thinks of those truncated apes going through their pointless ritual every night. He'd told management the charging station was really to lock down the magnetic field for a few hours so the pond water would definitely be still which was bullshit. He'd designed it to be still, so it was fucking still.

Or it had been.

Calvarium stared down at the puddle on the lab floor. He lowered a couple of the lenses on his modified Qolteck goggles, nodded to open a window, subvocalized for a pop-up security monitor which irised open in his upper right, seeming to hover over the spot where the vacuum hydrolysis tube once stood unshatteredly. He was looking down out of security camera TVI-12 at a potted plant just outside the TVI building. It looked perfectly normal for a glass-stemmed dwarf spruce fir pulsing with an intense scarlet radiance.

(Flicker.)

The fir became a barrel cactus.

Flicker: a massive corpuscularia.

Flicker: a colony of sentient plover's egg succulents.

Flicker: screaming monkey orchid bush.

Flicker: vibrating bat plant.

Flicker: giant purple Dutchman's pipe.

Calvarium swallowed and very briefly shed the impenetrable cloak of atheism he always wore so he could give thanks to the entire spectrum of listening deities because he was inside his lab where the ground hogging wouldn't affect him. Also, because he knew how to fix it.

Ovale opened a closet door, peered into the bracken of Pyrex tubes, grabbed a No. 7 thermionic cylinder and a No. 12 vacuum hydrolysis tube and a roll of paper towels. He used the No. 7 thermionic cylinder to slurp the violently rebelling tardigrades and their known world into the new No. 12 vacuum hydrolysis tube which he then placed into a cradle on the counter.

It was just a matter of magnetic submersion. Just move the No. 12 vacuum hydrolysis tube into the magnetic field micro chamber which was affixed to the opposite wall of the lab looking like a complicated sci-fi mood lighting sconce. Then, shut the door, dial up the field, kick back for an hour, maybe watch T.V., maybe read a book. Definitely not speed yoga. That was a mistake he'd never make again.

The whole thing was protocol he'd written ten years ago with the arrogant assurance they'd never have to use it. Which is why you write emergency protocol in the first place. Follow protocol. That's all he had to do.

Ovale carefully lifted the No. 12 vacuum hydrolysis tube, carried it carefully across the lab (not that it mattered, they were already agitated), placed it into the spider-like claws of the magnetic micro chamber, slid the curved glass door closed till it clicked, then slipped in a slick of pond water he'd missed with the paper towels and fell. Again.

As Ovale windmilled, he grabbed the frequency knob for the

magnavibratron with both hands, slammed his forehead into the time lock, knocked himself out, and crashed to the floor, inadvertently turning the magnavibratron to its highest setting, featured on the calibration graphic in the international bright crimson indicating that this here section of range was pure madness. In his heads-up display, the window featuring the plant outside the TVI building showed a rising shimmer of new species in the pot, the silent whoomph of each flutter hitting like the beats of a popular song.

Chapter 16

Lloyd Heller was smoking a pork shoulder in his backyard on the north side after coming home from serving dinner at Sidd's church. He'd dropped Christopher Whitfield Aryan Nation Montgomery at the blue line. There's only so much you can teach a new guy and besides, all the kid talked about was his new floppy friend of indeterminate pronouns.

The pork shoulders were enormous. They looked like miniature western buttes and Lloyd, having employed a tall can of British War Widow (or three) grinned to himself as he imagined a small native American village of the 1970s late-night television black and white racist rerun variety which looked perfect perched on the edge of his pork shoulder with their little tee pee and their cooking fire with its needle thin tendril of woodsmoke–

"Fuckitudinal." Lloyd hung his tongs on the grill, put the lid back on, slid the vents closed, then walked toward his bungalow which shimmered through a series of improbable architectural styles as he got closer.

"Nope. No. Negative. Nuh uh."

He grabbed his cell off the kitchen counter and pecked in a number that dialed all agents, engineers, Rose and Randall Jane. He didn't wait for them to pick up. He recorded this message:

"We're ground hogging."

He slipped the phone into the pocket of his jeans and hoped he could catch a train back to the office that didn't have eyeballs and scales.

Ground hogging is worse than losing a Watch. Ground hogging is a time loop–like in the movie starring Will MacMurray where he's a postman who accidentally opens a package addressed to the old creepy house in the town and he has to live the same day over and over until he finally delivers the package–you know the movie. Ground hogging meant someone screwed up in an exquisitely fucknomenal manner resulting in a glitch wherein reality blinks through adjoined timelines like a train on greased rails; worse, not everyone would know. Only the agents who picked up when they heard Heller's terrifying intonation of "We're ground hogging" would have time to grab their device and spin the bezel to the special emergency-only node labeled in heavy crimson all-caps DON'T STOP HERE. The ones who didn't wouldn't know anything was wrong, unless they were finely attuned to the liminal hem of reality's favorite bowling shirt, as was Lloyd Heller, now Ubering toward H.Q. in a dreadfully dreadful dread.

Rose nearly bowled him over as Lloyd stomped through the front door of Transluminal Vacations, Inc.

"Hurry up, Heller!"

"What happened?"

"You called it in, don't you know?"

"We're ground hogging. I know that. I don't know where it started." They marched side by side through a corridor of freaked out agents and office staff acting like they were doing something when they were really just trying to calm their own terror by pretending to work. Rose and Heller walked into the flotilla of cubicles to where Octavia del Sol and

Randall Jane were rapidly auditing adjoined whiteboard schedules of the TVI field agents.

"Miller?" Octavia says, perfectly calm, perfectly in control, following her protocol like a pro. She doesn't look up as Heller and Rose lean into the cubicle, but she turns very, very slightly toward Heller. Randall Jane runs her finger down her own whiteboard, stopping at a row with the name Miller in small caps.

"Six lines east."

Octavia marks Miller off her board. She glances at Heller. "The fuck, Old School?"

Heller deers-in-the-headlights for a half a second too long before he speaks, "I just–"

"Sadler!?"

"Sixteen east."

"–I saw a tiny Indian camp on my pork shoulder–"

"Ashton!"

"41 West."

"–was thinking maybe it was the beer, but then I realized it was real and I realized we were glitching–"

"Morlay?!"

"Off line."

Heller watched Octavia steadfastly ignoring him and shut the hell up. His gaze slithered down past her ribs to her hips, and he saw they were cocked somewhat himward.

"Archie?"

"Can't find him."

His training included constant non-verbal classes that taught all the secret body language indicating someone is immune to the pitch (feet together, shoulders facing away), or into it (hips cocked toward salesman) long before they knew they were going to say yes. It was a promising tell. Rose kicked him squarely in his instep. He looked up at Rose, Octavia, and Randall Jane all glaring.

"You think maybe you can keep your head in the game, Old School?"

Octavia's glare was frigid as the center of Pluto. Her hips had turned to the board and lost all interest in him.

"Heller, I'm routing all the unassigned agents to rope in anyone working a mark."

"Just point me where you want me."

Octavia explodes. "We want you to go wherever it is you have to go to fix the goddam loop breach and maybe SAVE THE GODDAM WORLD!" She walks over and pointedly and robotishly ratchets her entire body a half an inch away from Heller's hips with a face as hot as the heart of a volcano. "Now's your chance, Old School. Impress me."

"I have some ideas," Heller said, devoid of a single idea, not even a conceptual inkling of a hunch.

"Look at Old School trying." Octavia turns away like Heller was never even there. Her words shoot through his heart like a frozen bolt of pure fire.

"Manson!"

"Retired."

Heller stops by the kid's place. Chris opens the door wearing a fluffy housecoat, gray sweats, big fluffy assed slippers, holding a bowl of cereal. Behind him a giant TV is stuttering through a cut scene in a video game and the tousled head of a roommate can be seen.

"Kid, we got problems."

Chris disappears into the dark apartment, comes back in jeans and a t-shirt with a blue tip in his teeth. Heller shakes his hand to bring him into the breach.

"Let's hit it, boss."

On the street, Heller tabs for an Uber.

"We're ground hogging."

"Like that Will MacMurray flick?"

"Fuckzactimundo. Except this is real and we're in the weeds. Someone's opened a breach, and nobody knows where it is."

"Shouldn't they send some kind of crew?"

Heller stares.

"Oh. Ok. We're them."

"I have some ideas, but I don't know. It could be anywhere. It could take us days to find it."

"Sorry."

"What? For what?"

"You're not gonna close."

Heller looks at Christopher Aldous Oh, Shit, the Bastard's Right Montgomery as he feels the impossible sale become even more impossible. A flock of airborne jellyfish explode from the building above them then float quickly out into the sky and Heller feels his Platinum Vacation Package following them.

"Yeah, well," Heller rattled a match around his frown. Tears his eyes away from his disappearing future and looks for clues in the gutter. "It's off in the wild blue yonder, kid. Off in the wild blue yonder."

"No, wait—no." Chris gets excited. "Let's just take them with us."

"I love your passion, son, but we're headed into hazardous territory. I can't be responsible—"

"What's the worst that could happen?"

"Do you have any idea how often those are somebody's last words?"

"What happens if we don't shut down the—"

"It's all over, bucko. The world'll blow into a million pieces."

"How much more hazardous can their life get then?"

Heller looks away, up the street, into the sky, back at Chris.

"Fucking smartass."

They get to the church. Mooki is in fatigues.

"Hat. Teeth." Sidd doesn't smile.

"Who is–?" Montgomery tries to smile but he's wondering which one–oh, right. Teeth.

"We need to talk." Heller says this with a tone which brooks no argument.

"Would you consider brooking an argument?"

Heller's face reiterates.

"My office," Sidd says curtly.

"I was thinking a bar is in order."

"Is it?" Sidd looks at Heller with a smidgen of disdain.

(Flicker).

A flicker rumbled through the low hanging clouds. Mooki was suddenly decked out in a roaring twenties fringe trim dress with a cabbage leaf hat. Heller grabbed both of them and drew them closer.

"Don't freak out."

He raised his watch and dialed them into the loop just as a herd of crab giraffes hustled past the church. Sidd watched with mild suspicion. Mooki almost ran after them, but Teeth grabbed their skirt.

"We're not volunteers." Heller ran his fingers through his hair, a gesture not covered in his training because he was working off script and despite his admonition to them, he'd never been through a Groundhog breech and he was freaking out the tiniest little smidge of a bit.

Sidd looked down Ravenswood at the crab giraffes skittering around the corner throwing up a cloud of dust. He smoothed down the front of his plain shirt. Despite Mooki, Heller, and Teeth being in full Gatsby drag, Sidd was wearing the same exact black shirt, Roy Orbisons, and pewter prayer beads he always wore.

"Maybe I could use a drink."

Chapter 17

"I suspect our priorities are askew." Teeth tried to keep up with Heller as they followed the sidewalk toward a tavern luridly festooned with neon signs.

Heller pushed the door open into The Narrows, his second favorite bar (his first being The Oxford English Dictionary, but it was across town) and held it for Mooks, Teeth, and Sidd. They filed past him into the dark interior, their gaze held briefly by A Standard Local Band, who were noodling their way through a collection of 70s soft rock super hits.

Tripping your balls off on Bakers treats

Buzzing and laughing, feeling the heat

Hey it's another lazy day

Let's get us a cupcake

And put on some Dan and sing...

The four of them took stools at the bar. The barkeep nodded at Heller. They were pals.

"Lazlo. A round of Poor Life Choices."

Lazlo went to work. In a flash, he distributed five pints of British War Widow accompanied by five shots of Malört with a dash of creme de menthe. He and Heller dropped the urine colored (flavored) shots into their beer, raised their pints, then drained them dry. (Flicker). They turned to the rest of the group with expectant faces. Lazlo raised his giant lobster claw to his antennae and saluted.

Mooki and Sidd stared at Lazlo. Mook glanced at the band who were bobbing gently on their decapodal legs, their exoskeletons resonating the beat. The lead singer skittered up to the mike, opened his mandibles, and sang.

This cromuffin top is just so bold

It's got, pecans and walnuts, but it's got no soul

And it's taking me so long

To find out I am wrong:

I can eat it in just two bites.

Mooki turned back to their drink, a bamboo tankard with steam rolling down the sides. Lazlo waggled one of his furry eyebrows at them. Mooks recoiled. Bandoleros of airline-sized Malört bottles criss-crossed his hairy chest. He wore a weird mountaineering hat and spoke to them in German-accented Esperanto.

"La sepdekaj jaroj sciis luli, pravas?"

"Lazlo, Mooks is people," Heller said. Lazlo shrugged an apology.

Sidd, Mooki, and Teeth followed Heller and Lazlo's example and drained their Poor Life Choices (flicker). Lazlo's tentacles blurred behind him then snapped another round on the bar, shooting a cloud of blue fog through his siphons while flashing a series of blobbish colorations across the knobby surface of his carapace that looked like old school New York subway graffiti in a poorly focused polaroid. Heller laughed at Lazlo's projected joke.

"You're an incorrigible raconteur, Lazlo." He glanced down the line. Sidd. Mooks. Teeth. The band flashed bright blobs across their mantles. Their sucker cups shivered as their tentacles wanged out the song.

> *You used to make your pastries, so easy*
> *You used to claim they tasted so greasy*
> *But you're frying, you're frying now.*

"Here's the deal, Preacher." Heller turned to Sidd, (flicker), ignoring Lazlo who'd warped into a luminous translucent bubble with a rainbow sheen of oils roiling over his surface. The bubble extruded another round of glowing orbs.

"Lay minister," Sidd corrected.

"I'm sure someone will eventually," Heller quipped. Mooki stared at the bottles behind the bar and grinned to themself as they sipped their drink through a straw. "I didn't come to your church to volunteer. I came to sell you a vacation package." Again, Sidd reacted with the fluid alacrity of granite. However, Mooks (flicker) slammed their illuminated globule on the counter (where it burst into a starlit puddle, which Lazlo cleaned up by extruding a long podlike extension that absorbed it with a quiet slurp).

"He's never even *been* on vacation," they said. "He works all day at the church then all night at the grille then stops by to clean the temple on his way home!"

"My devotions are rigorous," Sidd mumbled curtly (flicker). "Besides, we've been through this, Mr. Heller. You showed me how it works."

"Doesn't matter," Heller winked at Lazlo, who was giving him the eye and twirling her bright red hair. Her slim tail flopped across the bar and wound itself around his left wrist. He felt a telling pulse beneath the soft crimson velvet, throbbing to the beat.

"It's not a vacation. It's this," Heller waved his hand insolently at everything and nothing to indicate the runny reality in which they were currently drinking. "I wasn't just sent to find your fuck you money timeline. I was sent to persuade you to take a tour of your best possible life."

"Am I not already living my best possible life?" Sidd asked. (Flicker.) Mooki snorted. Teeth smirked at them, then noticed Lazlo's naked gleaming skull and stopped.

"I think you're trying, but look," Heller spun his barstool to face Sidd. He leaned in. "I'm not talking philosophy. I'm talking architecture."

"I'm not following you."

"I'm sure your efforts at finding nirvana are on point–"

"It's not," Sidd huffed. "Everyone gets that wrong. We're not looking for nirvana; we're trying to achieve *samadhi,* which will make us worthy vessels for Buddha. *Then* we find nirvana."

"Cool. Look, what I mean is, that's a part of you that doesn't change. That's residence. This," waving the arm again (flicker.) "This is the architecture in which you reside. Even though right now, it's gone batshit ape knuckle–"

"Meeep?" Lazlo parked a massively knuckled paw onto the counter, its silver fringe of fur spilling into Heller's coconut of beer.

"Sorry, Lazlo."

Lazlo signed it's cool, unclothed monkey and turned back to his typewriter.

"My company has technology that allows us–and anyone with us–to jump into adjacent timelines in the multi-threaded quilt of reality."

Sidd stared.

"You know about the multiverse?"

"He's a Buddhist monk," Mooki said. "They invented the multiverse."

Sidd uncrossed his arms to quote scripture: "'Disciples,' the Buddha said, 'nowhere between the lowest of hells below and the highest heaven above, nowhere in all the infinite worlds that stretch right and left, is there the equal, much less the superior, of a Buddha.'"

Heller shifted his Ohio Blue Tip from the infinite reality of the left side of his mouth to the infinite reality of the right. "So we're on the same page. Thing is, Transluminal Vacations, Inc. discovered technology that takes you there. My assignment was to ease you into the actuality of that concept (flicker) then escort you through a series of increasingly delectable timelines to whet your appetite then finish with the big kahuna, your fuck you money timeline."

"Sign me up," Mooki said. Teeth laughed then caught a glimpse of Lazlo floating in endless cthulian dread mere inches above the bar, his spectral incandescent absinthe colored face pulled tight against his skull as he screamed in mute terror and wordless pain. The band, verdant and luminous, transparent as smoke, played soundlessly from the grave dark stage. Somehow, they all heard the words, seeming to echo from the Stygian depths of a cold crypt.

> *You down the treats and there's a light hazy daze*
>
> *It opens the doors and gives you trippin' balls face*
>
> *You wonder where you've been*
>
> *You wonder what you've seen*
>
> *And you talk about groundhog ging (flicker)*

"I'm fine," Sidd said. He took a tentative sip from a thick-walled specimen jar containing a light gold liquid and what looked like a spectacularly detailed example of an interdimensional demon larva. He reluctantly looked up at Lazlo, who was a gargantuan solid black snail wearing steampunk goggles and a leather pilot's cap. Mooki dipped their finger uncertainly into a puddle of slime on the bar.

"Ew."

"I suppose after the last couple of minutes, you kind of get that what I'm talking about really works (flicker)."

"Does it?" Sidd nodded toward the stage. Four trees stood perfectly silent. One had a guitar.

"Usually. That's why I'm here now. It's why I'm giving you the speed reader version. In one of the million trillion adjacent timelines there is a version of your current life in which you are magnificently wealthy. Your restaurants became a national chain. You have a yacht, a beautiful wife–" At this, Mooki unconsciously glanced at Sidd, who unconsciously glanced at Mooki, his glance landing square in the middle of theirs then glancing in pure embarrassment off their eyeballs into the room where it got stuck in the ceiling fan. "–and pretty much all the money you could ever hope for. You can have anything."

You have this dream about frying some spam

You're gonna, give up the fruits and the nuts for ham

And then you'll chill on down

On some chilly little couch

And forget about cromuffins...

(Flicker).

Sidd's steady gaze slipped slowly off Heller's grin to take in the rest of the room. He looked at the bottles behind the bar (mostly filled with liquified wasp elbows), the neon beer signs buzzing on the wall (Derp's Herp, BWW, Pooli's Revenge), at the band in their glittering glassine hulls. His gaze swung slowly, searching for a perch, a place to pore over this idea, to take a breath and maybe not be surrounded by an acid trip, then it landed on Mooks, who was looking at him with an inscrutable expression.

If Sidd had been a player, if he had any real experience with floppy beautiful fluid people, or anyone in love, ever, he would have recognized this look. It was the look countless humans had leveled at someone else at some time in their life when there was a moment of significance, a hinge of certainty, where the one they were desperately aswoon over might recognize a crack in the doorway to their heart from which a languid, golden light shone lovingly toward them.

Mooki grew up poor as dirt, mostly homeless, mostly kicked out from one grandma, aunt, or well intentioned-but-utterly-clueless-doting-neighbor-lady to another exactly when they pressed them about finding a nice boy and then couldn't deal with the ambiguity. *Are you gay? Jesus Heteroflexible Christ,* they'd think. Then they would pack. Then they would leave. Everything Mooki owned fit in a backpack and one tiny drawer in a scratched and dented side table by their bed. They'd begged, borrowed, and stolen to get by for the last several years. They'd slept in bus stations, under overpasses, in the backseat of friends' mom's minivans, and for a few days, until Sidd had noticed them, in the side door archway of an Episcopalian Church. Mooki knew what money was. Mooki knew it could and did buy all the happiness you could stuff into a suitcase, and they knew what it would mean for Sidd if he had some.

Cause Sidd wasn't a money guy. He was an organizer. He ran his little storefront cafe on a spreadsheet and by hiring competent people who didn't need his help and didn't steal very much and knew how to cook lumpia and sticky rice like they were 90-year-old Filipino grandmas. He stopped in sometimes. He took a meager salary.

Sidd lived in a one-room apartment at the back of the church garage, slept on a twin bed, kept three identical shirts folded neatly in a small dresser, three identical pairs of pants hung in a narrow closet; he listened to one slab of vinyl on a vintage record player; he kept a wall of books.

Money would be just fine, Mooki thought.

But the sliver of honey-colored light spilling over the threshold of their heart wasn't their desire for Sidd–strong as that was. It wasn't desire. Of course they wanted him. That was obvious. But this time, at this moment, in this stupid Salvador Dali tavern painting, the tiny shimmer wasn't the delicate and growling grope they so often fantasized over in embarrassing detail. It was love. Pure as a diamond. Mooki loved Sidd all the way to their toenails, and if he never took them in his arms, that was ok–although they were very, *very* ok with it if he did–they just wanted him–swear to God–they just wanted him to have everything he ever wanted. They just wanted him to get some *rest.* They just wanted, with all their heart, for just the span of a breath, for just the infinity of a heartbeat, to see Sidd *happy.*

> *But you know you'll always eat muffins*
> *Doesn't matter bout the damn stuffin'*
> *Cause these muffins, they're for trippin balls*

But Sidd was a fucking idiot who only had eyes for the path of the spirit. Mook knew that path wound deliciously up their spine and along the dappled moonlight on their skin. They had no idea how to show it. Every time they got close, Sidd let them down. Even now, even as his glance peeled itself off the ceiling fan to slide down the high vertical ladder of the light of love leaking out of their heart to land on their face, which was the dictionary entry for absolute ride-or-die, forged in fire, eternal love, he blinked slowly, turned to Heller, (flicker) and said:

"Thanks, Mr. Heller, thanks for this. I appreciate you throwing us a lifeline," Sidd didn't exactly look at Mooki. "But it's Tuesday, and we have to do inventory for the food bank. So, again, thanks for," Sidd glanced at the barkeep who flittered across his web to snare a bottle of Kane Break with a silk thread, "this . . . But we have to go. Better luck with your next prospect."

There was the incredibly loud imaginary sound of a heavy door slamming shut. Sidd Flinched. Mooki grabbed Teeth and dragged him onto the dance floor. Mooks flowed through a series of liquid poses like a national geographic video about wave structure. Teeth was trying to be graceful but looked for all the world like a series of mid-century academic illustrations of involuntary seizures.

Heller watched Mooki dance and realized they were not merely floppy. They were exquisitely lithe, fascinatingly supple, a mercilessly hypnotic expression of unrelenting craving. Teeth experienced a collection of alarming convulsions next to Mooki, who ignored him entirely. They writhed a blunt invitation, their eyes filled with primitive fire, staring at Sidd in a way that made Heller want to move out of the way.

(Flicker).

Sidd stared back, his face ablaze from Mooki's flames. The band morphed and melted through a disturbing zoology as Sidd broke his gaze, took an interest in the floor tile (currently mostly eyeballs), slid off his stool, then staggered out the door of the bar.

He stopped on the sidewalk and bent over. He put his hands on his knees. He took deep gulps of the frigid air. He sobbed violently.

After a minute, Sidd pulled himself together like a puppet unfolding from a suitcase. He tweaked his collar and shot his cuffs. He wiped his eyes. He walked away, toward the church, the last lines of the song leaking out of the door and fading away behind him.

And when you wake up, it's a new morning

Mooki loves you—here's your last warning
If you're stupid, you will die alone

Chapter 18

George was furious. His family built this lodge. His Tardigradian foremales had served as the Guy in the Big Chair in the Front at least eleven times. It was his legacy. In all eleven sessions, decades of service since the Great Sploosh, they had never–*ever*–tolerated a visitation by the Uppy Downies.

This was his moment. His wife had been wagging her papilla at him over coffee and just, you know, out of the blue bringing up Lauren's husband Steve's recent expansion of his paramecium farm and then just, you know, dropping in that Steve also got promoted in the A.C.O.T.A.S. Grand Lodge to Most Exalted Chancellor of Aquaferic Fauna Relations which George already knew but had shelved for being angry about sometime later when he had the time to go over how he'd missed that opportunity to serve his esteemed brethren, like that son of a bitch Lauren's husband, Steve.

George sprang up. He snapped his upper legs into the ceremonial genuflection indicating his desire to be recognized. The Guy in the Big Chair in the Front glanced at George, rapped his gavel one and a half times, then almost said:

"The Big Chair recognizes George," but only got to "The Big Chair Recognizes–" when Frank yelped, and the double doors flew open revealing a tanarctus chronosfichtosvarelli wearing an ornate purple lanyard that hung in a perfectly vertical droop from his shoulders to his second waist. Three wavy vertical lines adorned his fez.

"The Most Esteemed Lord of the Ennobled Chaise Located in the Fore," he propounded. "Exalted Among All Tardigrae, 22nd Servant of the Grand Protectorates of the Upright Drafts–"

–behind him his cadre of fellow chronosfichtosvarelli shouted *properly perpendicular, pal!–*

"–desires admittance!"

George growled. He was too vexed to take note of the historical importance of this disruption nor note the hysterical indignant posturing of his fellow sashers, leaping to their feet and harrumphing.

The Guy in the Big Chair in Front rose slowly. He'd prepared for this. He'd discussed it with his peers and Most Revered Former Guys in the Big Chairs up Fronts. He'd spent hours with the Grand Librarian finding the exact words, the correct ceremony, and the perfect protocols to make everyone feel at ease.

"Most Esteemed Lord of the Ennobled–"

He never finished the sentence. George unfurled a savage cry. He leapt onto the Most Esteemed Lord of the Ennobled Chaise who quickly became the Not So Damned Esteemed Lord with a Very Bruised Face.

From the foyer, the Grand Protectorates of the Upright Drafts swarmed into the hall whirling heavy shell-cracking plumbs and wielding sharpened L-squares. The Champions matched their savagery. They flew across the floor slamming heavy levels as long as their middle arms into the upper thoraxes of the advancing tardigrae.

In his big chair in the front, the Guy in the Big Chair in the Front gaped in horror. This was supposed to be a peaceful visitation, a testing of the waters but it had devolved into combat. Looking past Frank, who stood in the doorway tightening his sash around the fat neck of a Grand Protectorate who had his upper hands gripped around George's throat, he saw the front doors fly open. A new stream of well-armed Protectorates surged into the hall. He had no choice. He carefully removed his fez, pried open a secret compartment in the arm of the big chair, which revealed a giant upright needle labeled "Seriously, NO!" then swung his closed fist down onto it.

There was a sudden silence, a shivering, spectral no-sound that drew the attention of every Grand Protectorate and Assembled Champion who stopped inflicting carnage for a moment to stare at nothing in particular as they listened with a part of their tiny tardigrade minds to a turbulent lithic calm gathering toward them.

George turned his purpling face to the Big Chair in horror. Beneath him, the nearly unconscious Esteemed Lord Mostly Bruises growled as loudly as he could, "They've launched the Swirl!" He reached under his vertical sash for a small device like a car alarm remote, poised his thumb over a short needle surrounded by exclamation points and whispered, "May God have mercy on my soul," then passed out.

Beneath the growing stillness, another virulent hissing could be heard, like a steam engine pierced by a native spear. It grew louder and louder as the silence grew bigger and bigger until the two monstrous events met like crashing tsunamis and the great hall was flooded first with enormous cliffs of horizontal flows that gathered most of the tardigrae in their bosom and used them to break through the walls and flood out into the city, only to be stomped mercilessly by ponderous pile drivers of vertical downpours and upflows which grappled with the horizontal swirlings like Poseidon learning how to do the robot.

George, violently adrift somewhere in the eaves, felt his stylets sag and his papilla retract. This was the end. This is how it all broke apart. With great sadness, thinking of his family, he withdrew his consciousness into the depths of his mind. He fumbled around down there for the switch and, taking a short courageous breath, flicked it.

***

George sat in his favorite armchair in his den smoking a pipe and reading the morning paper, his lower legs crossed, his middle ones turning pages, and his upper arms behind his head. The paper didn't say a thing about the fracas at the lodge because George had flipped the switch.

Every Tanarctus chronochalarapoutinka and every Tanarctus chronosfichtosvarelli shared a curious feature other than their preference for being undisturbed. It was a toggle, deep in the folded blanket forts of their minds, which, when togged, bumped the tardigrade and all that it held dear into an adjacent timeline.

It was an evolutionary stub left over from the Presplooshian period, a spurious nubbin bulging off the brain stem designed to assist in fleeing predators or when one was in excruciating pain. It was a fleshy panic button, a neoplastic toggle which, when pressed or toggled, sent the tardigrade and its adjacent tardigrae, in this case George's immediate family, into a neighboring timeline. Ordinarily, this would move the tardigrae out of danger, replacing them into the exact same place they had been before with only minor differences. A fin here. An extra arm there. Small price to pay for safety. Most of them barely even noticed.

George had flicked that switch with grave reservation as he wasn't sure if it would work. But it had. As evidence: his perfectly happy family, his perfectly tamped pipe, and his perfectly boring morning news all pointed to the success of the jump. Now he'd get some rest and who knows, maybe go take a look at that Exalted Chancellor position Lauren's husband Steve kept talking about. He should give Steve a ring, talk about old times. They didn't see each other enough anymore.

He turned to his wife who was bringing him a mug of hot cocoa and stared in mute disbelief at the massively muscled Tanarctus chronosfichtosvarelli who's bulging arms were locked around Marge's capacious neck. Marge's pigment cups were as wide as they could widen. Her papilla trembled toward George, pleading. The Tanarctus chronosfichtosvarelli had a sharpened L-Square in its hand. The blade bounced maliciously on Marge's pulsing jugular.

It hadn't worked.

George fell backward into his mind space. He flew through the corridors to his Nubbin. He didn't even reach for it. He kicked out like a ninja and swept the switch up with his foot.

Something flickered. George ran back to his den. Two Tanarctus chronosfichtosvarelli were having coffee and flirting with Marge who looked at him with disdain.

Merde.

He ran back, kicked the switch.

Ran back . . . Three of them now.

Back . . .

This went on for a long time.

Chapter 19

Octavia del Sol kicked a trashcan across her cubicle. It bounced off the grey felt-covered wall, which shuddered from the blow. On the other side an accountant flinched and whispered, *Octavia, Goddam–Tranquilo, Tranquilo* under his breath but continued crunching numbers on the emergency stats review.

The entire accounting department had shifted onto stats analysis. They were using mathematical triangulation to locate anomalous bulges of potentiality in the local field. Octavia had given this particular accountant the North Loop sector, and he was combing through it like it had lice.

Working next to Octavia has its pitfalls. She went through trashcans. The current victim rolled around the low flimsy wall of their shared space and bumped against his chair. It left a trail of wadded paper and crushed diet Coke cans leading back into Octavia's space, currently occupied by a livid tornado with the faintest Columbian accent, which sluiced red-hot lava up the accountant's spine where it cooled in his paleomammalian cortex into the shape of a tiny naked Octavia and wrecked his concentration.

It was a manageable problem, most days. Octavia would sweep into the office in a cloud of J-Lo 'Ceremonia,' (he'd spent an entire day at the perfume counter in Marshall Field's to figure that out), hip check the back of his chair, and say *Get to work, Crunch.*

Crunch was her (he was optimistic about this, he'd talked it over with his mother, and they'd concluded it was indeed a term of endearment) term of endearment for him since he was a numbers cruncher.

But it was too risqué for the accountant. He'd lose concentration. He'd make a mistake. She'd catch it almost before he'd finished keying it in, causing her to pop over the top of the low felted wall and say, 'what the fuck, Crunch?!' pouring another plume of Ceremonia over him and rattling his erroneous zones, so he made even more mistakes. She was on the verge of having him fired, and he was on the brink of begging for a transfer, but then he wouldn't be stationed next to a Goddess, so he hadn't submitted the form. Yet.

Today was unmanageable. Octavia was furious at Heller–that sonofabitch–and her trashcan was just the latest in a list of portable items within arm's (and leg's) reach she'd destroyed while trying to find the source of the loop breach.

So far, she'd broken a stapler, a document holder, two memory sticks, a coffee mug with Heller's face as a dartboard, and a copy of *The Manual,* already tattered from previous flings, flung into the cubicle wall six times before it split down the middle and fell apart.

"Fuck king *Heller!*"

The accountant typed as loudly as he could. The sound of his clattering keyboard seemed to calm her down. Restoring her to placidity was his daily devotion. Her explosions were always punctuated by him whispering *tranquilo, tranquilo,* under his breath as he pounded furiously on the keys, even though it sounded stupid coming out of the mouth of an alabaster CPA from Vermont whose family trended toward outdoor winter saunas and lutefisk. But he whispered it anyway, quietly, like a supplication, as he typed.

In her cubicle, Octavia stormed. She'd gone through the protocol manual five times with Randall Jane perched on her shoulder like a hawk. Neither of them found a solitary blunder. They'd walked step-by-step through the procedure for locating a loop breach origin but came up empty every time.

She flipped through it again, the edges riffling under her thumb until she stopped suddenly at a random page. She'd been doing this for twenty minutes, having resorted to divination to trick her mind into finding a fix.

It hadn't worked.

Even now, the stupid book showed her a stupid page that was as stupid and dense and impenetrable as a stupid tax stupid form. She threw the remaining half of the book at her wall, again, then popped over the ledge to bark at the accountant.

"Gimme your Manual."

The accountant swallowed hard, trying not to notice the delicate cloud of Ceremonia filling his workspace, trying not to notice her eyes, like jade volcanoes, trying not–it didn't matter. She'd come into his cubicle while he was trying not to notice her.

Now she was here. She was right next to him. She leaned against him as she reached for the books and reports stacked on top of his cabinet, looking for the manual. It was torture.

"Where is it?!" Before he could answer, she found the manual, exactly like her own copy but untattered. It had a tiny coffee stain on one corner and the accountant's name penciled in small, prim capitals in the upper left.

"Pietre?"

"Don't take that–" the words were barely out of his mouth when she was suddenly nose to nose with him. Her eyes were twin worlds. They were all he could see. Her breath smelled like a warm mango.

"Do know how deep in a hole Heller dug us? And you're going to tell me I can't borrow-bar row-your fucking manual?"

"No, I mean, you want the new edition. Came out last week?" He slid his copy out of the space she hadn't run through yet. It was crisp and tight. He hadn't even penciled his name in the corner. "And Mr. Heller only called it in; he didn't cause-"

She snatched the manual out of his hand and glowered at its pages standing right in front of him, almost on top of him, crowding him back against his desk, ignoring him entirely as she flipped to the ground hogging protocol section-suddenly she stopped.

"Mother *fuck!*" Octavia grabbed Pietre by his chin and planted a hot wet kiss right on his lips.

"You just saved our ass, Crunch."

Then she forgot he existed, stormed out of his workspace, and screamed across the room to Randall Jane.

"It's the wrong fucking book! Get Heller on the phone! That son of a bitch! *It's in the lab!*"

Chapter 20

Sidd burst through the door of the temple. The Master was sprawled on the couch with the remote pointed at the T.V. Eli and Aaron were paused on a beach in Belize in their suspenders and flat wide-brimmed hats, beards wagging, surrounded by nearly naked spring breakers.

Sidd flops down into one of the ornately carved wingbacks. The Master glares at him, then unpauses Eli and Aaron, and forgets Sidd is there.

"Master, why do we have to give up the ways of the flesh to discover the ways of the spirit?"

The Master ignored him because it was a stupid question, and because Eli and Aaron were crumping in the deep white sand as a circle of half-naked college girls cheered them on. The camera pushed past the dancers to focus on a single sour-faced Amish girl in a long denim skirt with her arms crossed, glaring. The chyron said, "Lindsey Decker: Eli's Girlfriend–Pregnant." The Master leaned forward.

"I am dedicated to the path, I am, I swear, but my feelings for this person are an impossible obstacle. I think it is time for me to go to take my–"

"Be still!"

Sidd didn't even look up. He stared down into the design of the rug. The Master was right, of course. All wisdom is born in stillness, and Sidd led a busy life. Perhaps it wasn't just Mooki that was distracting him from his true work. Maybe it wasn't the way they coiled around themselves on the dance floor under the turquoise spot, like a sexy serpentine ghost, their bare shoulders dipping toward him and the look on their face, the way their eyes grabbed him by the lapels and shoved their lips–

It was definitely Mooki.

"Master–"

"Jesus Krishna Christ, Sidd!" The Master violently paused the television. *This fucking kid. How goddam hard is it to–*

He was internal dialoguing again—such a habit.

"How Goddam hard is it to understand that–"

This fucking kid. Now he was external dialoguing and almost blurting out the very thing Sidd needed to learn. But that's not how people learn. *You learn by–*

"putting down your books and"

–doing something. All the–

"preparation in the world"

–wasn't worth–

"a hill of beans,"

–if you never stepped off the–

"precipice"

–and did the thing you had studied–

"for so long!"

One learns–goddammit.

"One learns by doing."

The Master glowered at Sidd. *This kid would never get it. The path of the spirit wends its way through every cell in your body and shoots up the seven-laned highway of your spine to the reptilian walnut-sized body-centric nugget that redirects this thing, this palpable energy, this extreme joy of bonding, of uniting, of merging with another in the act of love, steers it like a jet-fueled Lamborghini into the part of the brain where the mind hovers spherical and luminous. The path of the flesh is one of the surest legs up into the saddle of the spirit. Love will get you there, you–*

"stupid boob."

In every discipline, pretty much all the Buddhist teachings lead away from study to action and tend to herd young bucks like Sidd through the junkyard of their misperceptions and hang-ups and out the other side, which just takes them back to regular life. *That's pretty much–*

"all there is in the end, just life."

But the Master couldn't tell Sidd the most remarkable truth: *It is a gift to be alive. A treasure. The material world is a goddam spiritual theme park, and we're here to ride every shitty rollercoaster it offers, to slurp the terrible lemon freezes, to quaff all the beer, to buy dumb balloons,*

"to watch a parade."

No, he couldn't say a word, and it was driving him crazy with this kid because Jesus Hatha Yoga Christos, the kid was in love, and he was so close to actually understanding something.

But Sidd was a fucking idiot. And, like all seekers, Sidd needed to find the way all by himself. If it meant he missed this opportunity if it meant he lost this oddly named person he loved so much, if it meant his heart shattered into aquarium gravel, *well–*

"that's just school."

Sidd watched his master's face and listened.

"I see," he said. "Yeah. I get it." The Master glowered at him a few seconds longer. Sidd didn't get a damn thing. The Master thumbed the pause button. Eli and Aaron crumped.

Back at the Narrows, after Sidd walked out, Heller looked back at Mooki. They'd stopped dancing. They were statue still. Their look could have melted marble, but the look was the least powerful thing about Mooks. They seemed to be inside some kind of shimmer, a waver in the air, an aura of pure sexual intention, and the object of that intention had just walked out the door that Mooki was trying to incinerate with their eyes (flicker).

As Heller stared, Mooki dissolved into desire. Their gaze let go of the door. They turned that gaze onto Christopher Aldous Perfect Six Pack and V Montgomery, who was twisted into a rictal ictus of real-estate-salesman-on-a-cruise-ship-dance-floor poses, and they locked onto his abdomen like a tractor beam. They need it. He had it. Here they go.

Heller saw it as a diagram of a bad decision. He leaped onto the dance floor and snatched Montgomery by a sleeve before it was too late.

"We gotta go."

Mooki glared.

Heller and Teeth walked out the front door.

A few minutes later, Lazlo reached out with his second right hand to pick up a smartphone snoring on the bar. He tore off a piece of blue kitchen tape, wrapped it around the phone, and wrote HELL on it in fat sharpie black caps. Then he tossed it into a cardboard box under the bar, where it landed in a graveyard of deceased phones.

(Flicker.)

The poor little phone sat up. His screen blinked. He looked around at the telecorpses filling the box and flashed a scream emoji. Using every crystal in his silicone soul, the smartphone reached his noodle-like arms up toward the lip of the box. Music pounded rhythmically through the air, and lights flashed as it struggled for a grip.

It was too high. The rim of the box was miles above his screen.

This is how it ends, he beeped quietly to himself—a scrap of metal on a scrapheap of lost phones and discarded lipstick purses. I will lose power. I will dim. And why not? *I have no signal.*

Don't give up, Chirped a crackling tone from out of the dark. The Smart Phone activated its flashlight app. The boneyard of dead cells sloped away into the dark shadow of the box. But there, just a few inches away, was a dull blue glow. Our little guy scrambled closer, pushing aside a slew of iPhones and Samsungs to reveal the murky, shattered screen of a Moto 4. It was ancient. Bulky. And, improbably, still had bars. It displayed a whew emoji for a split second, but that faded. Only the battery icon was illuminated, a thin crimson sliver of LED labeled 1%. It said, *Don't give up.*

I'll never make it. I don't have your power, the smartphone said.

You think it's about power? You think it's about the icon? Mine's said it was at 1 for a week. The old phone crackled. *But here I am. Holding on. Waiting.*

Waiting for what?

Not for what, son. The Moto 4's screen seemed to flicker. *For who.*

You can't be talking about me. Please, I got nothing left. I. Don't. Have. Bars. Can you hear me now?

The old Moto automatically responded in the age-old ritual. *I can hear you now. But,* crackle, crackle, *can you hear yourself? Look at this slope of charnel. Remind you of anything?*

Our guy stared down the incline. *I don't see...*

Look not with your screen, hissed the old Moto. *But open your*

The slope morphed into a junkyard of highlighted edges of glowing vortices, like a pyramid.

Like steppes.

They're steppes. They're all steppes!

The old moto's screen flared like the fourth of July, using his last watt to flash a bright brawny arm into the dark, then his old screen flickered and died.

The smartphone wiped a tear out of its lens cup. It shook itself. *Come on, man. You can do this,* he thought. Then he, too, flashed a brawny arm.

He grabbed the old man by the edges. He drug the body of the Moto4 up the slope of dead phones to the wall of the box. Then he dragged two more silicone cadavers, begging their cold forgiveness until he had a stack high enough to climb out on.

The smartphone dropped to the floor. A gargantuan beast trundled to and fro, unloading enormous cylinders of poison to other gigantic beasts. The phone slipped between the creature's feet. It dashed across the open space. It slid heroically beneath a low shelf (flicker), skidding deep into the shadows back where the brooms never swept, no longer smart.

Just a phone.

In a drift of gum wrappers and desiccated olives and the residue of a busy dive bar, the phone lit up; it's ring tone playing a snippet of "Brown Eyed Girl," quietly, seventeen times in a row. It was dark for a minute. Then it did it again.

Lazlo stopped cleaning the translucent tortoiseshell in his right zygodactylic talon and cocked his feathered head.

"BAWK! I know that tune! BAWK!" he chirped.

It rang again.

(Flicker).

And again.

(Flicker).

Chapter 21

Octavia del Sol crouched over her phone on Randall Jane's desk. They stared at Heller's face as his number rang over and over.

"Gaaaahhhhhh!" She almost threw her phone across the room, but Randall Jane grabbed her wrist.

"Hold up, Eights," Randall Jane pried the phone out of Octavia's grip. "We're gonna need that."

"Why won't he answer!?"

"You know, I should introduce you two sometime," Randall Jane sarcasted. "I think you'd really hit it off."

"Crunch!" Octavia shouted. The accountant rose slowly to peer over the brink of his cubicle wall, pointing at the top of his sweater vest with a who me? face.

"Yes. You. Can you track a phone?"

(Flicker.)

An hour later, Octavia's carriage pulls up to a creaky, ancient tavern whose gabled roof beams sagged like a dying horse's rib cage. The sign rusting in the breeze out front read Thee Narrows. She shook her head, gathered her ample pleats above the mud, and walked in.

The bar counter was a cracked keel from a short ship. The floor was ankle-deep in a history of bad nights and smelled like the kind of effluviate goop that, if you stepped in it, might give you superpowers. Or eat your toes off.

A sad milkmaid played a recorder on stage.

Octavia gave the barkeep a grimace that froze him in place, giant meaty fist with a dirty rag deep in an oaken tankard.

"Where's Heller?"

"Pray thee, lustrous witch, who is this Heller you seek?"

"Smooth mofo? Old as a cattle brand?"

"Thy tongue is mysterious."

"I'm gonna shove thy tongue down thy hole if thy don't— WHERE IS FUCKING HELLER!? FORSOOTH!!!!"

(Flicker.)

"Lady, I just work here," says the barkeep, a smidgen of a man with a greasy comb-over and a short-sleeved yellow shirt. Octavia pulls out a bulbous copper football with bulbous antennae and '70s stereo knobs. She turns a dial. Names rotate under a window slot until HELLER appears. She flips a toggle.

Van Morrison plays from somewhere behind the bar. The bartender throws his rag onto the counter in a huff. "I been hearing that damn song all day."

Octavia rushes behind the bar. She tracks down the ringing, reaches far under the shelves, straining until her fingertips barely get a grip on a vibrating metallic brick.

(Flicker.)

Earlier, Heller dragged Christopher Aldous White Privilege Montgomery out of The Narrows. He smacked the door open and looked at Mooki, dejected on the dance floor.

"You comin'?"

Mooki glowered. They turned around and kept dancing in the lambent light from the band bobbing in their tanks.

Chris stops Heller on the sidewalk.

"We can't leave them," he says.

"Mooks doesn't want to go."

"So what? We don't leave anybody. This shit is crazy! What happens when it rolls over to a timeline full of hungry sharks?"

"Nothing."

"Whattaya mean, nothing?" Chris said. Frustrated. "SHARKS!"

"Yeah, look, you and me adjust to the timeline. Mooki'd be a shark too. We'd all be sharks."

Christopher Aldous Angry Man Montgomery threw his hands up and growled.

"I'm in a goddam Mick and Jordy cartoon!"

"More like a Terry Adams book."

"Sorry, I wasn't around during the glacial period, cromag."

"He wrote that book about the guy who gets abducted? Whacky story. *The Ridesharer's Handbook for Outer Space?* They made a movie?"

"Wait, you mean Douglas Ratchett?"

"No, that's the guy did the *Whisk World Series.* It was a sweeping examination of a world based mostly on light cleaning."

(Flicker).

"Heller, we need to find whoever opened the loop."

"What's a rookie like you know about finding whoever opened a loop breach?"

"You know you're real stupid for a time cop."

"Yeah, well, you're in uniform to so what's that make you?"

"I'm getting too young for this shit," says Chris, woodenly.

"You just don't get it," Heller says.

"No, you just don't get it, do you?" Chris growls. "You want me to go out there and find this loop breach perp, but when it comes to how a loop breach works, you won't tell me anything!"

"Whattaya want from me?!"

"I want the truth!"

"You can't handle the truth!" Heller pontificates dramatically.

Chris rips the metal star off his shirt. "I'm turning in my badge!"

"I don't know how you live with yourself."

"Is that all you got?" Chris whispers in a menacing hoarse whisper. Then he stops. "Wait–what are we saying?"

"We're in a clichéd timeline," Heller says.

"I have a bad feeling about this," Chris looks around.

"That's *Star Warts*," Heller says.

"This is stupid! How the fuck do we stop the groundhog thing? How did MacMurray do it in that movie?"

"This ain't no movie, kid." Heller pops a match into his mouth. "This is real life."

"It's just dumb. Next thing you know, we'll be fourth walling, and there'll be a narrator and–"

Heller shifted the matchstick from one side of

his mouth to the other.

Heller shifted the matchstick from one side of his mouth to the other.

He looked out of the book with a look of pure horror and surprise.

He looked out of the book with a look of pure horror and surprise.

Chris suddenly looks nervous. Staring right at Heller, he says, he's right behind me, isn't he?

Suddenly Chris looks nervous. Staring directly at Heller, he says, "He's . . . He's right behind me, isn't he?"

"Fucking cut it out!" Heller yells, glaring out of the book at the narrator.

But the narrator ignores him, typing furiously to make his deadline, self-imposed as it may be—

"If it's self-imposed, can you just take a break or something? Go get a smoke?"

Heller says stupidly. Chris turns around and says, see what I mean?

"See what I mean?" Chris rolls his eyes.

No, I don't see—I mean, the narrator doesn't see what he means. Heller gets an idea.

"Wait, if we're in a meta timeline, we can use it to find the breach!" Heller says.

No, you can't. Heller cops an attitude, his plug-ugly face screwing up like a poorly bred rat terrier—

"Ok, alright. That's about enough, Mr. Narrator. Just do us a favor and turn to the page where we find the breach loop–"

But the narrator won't be moved. It's a narration, not a negotiation. The characters will do as they are written, dammit, because that's how literature works and—

(Flicker).

Heller and Teeth stare at each other for a beat.

"Well, that was weird," Heller looks up the street. "We gotta jet."

"Not without Mooks."

The door to the Narrows opens. Mooks spills onto the sidewalk. They are still on fire. Teeth moves to put an arm around Mooki. Heller steps between them.

"Come on, my flexible friend," He takes Mooki's arm gallantly. Chris puckers his mouth and stares a tiny little hole in the side of Heller's head. "We've got an impossible problem to solve."

Chapter 22

Union Station is one of the outstanding architectural achievements of Chicago. It's a city that was built by rail. Built by blood on the hoof. Built by slaughterhouses in the meat district damming the corpulent torrent of future hotdogs flowing into its yards. Yet here in this cavernous room, where angels hold the roof beams up, where even the bronze vent grates are decorated, here in the babble of voices and the murmuring click of heels, here with the background echo of route announcements and people shouting beer orders in the bars lining the corridors against the riverfront side, here there is beauty.

Xavier Crane sits on a bench in the very middle of it all with a cup of Rat King espresso in his delicate hand, a battered copy of *Game Theory* on his knee festooned with colored tabs, and an umbrella. He's wearing a gray Homburg with a brim as crisp as an autumn morning and an English Hunting suit with leather padded shoulder patches and a lot of tweed. Folded across his knees is an overcoat so dark green you can see jaguars in it. Currently, he is concerned about the beautiful ambience of Union Station since, currently, it is not so.

Across from Crane, over the bobbing ocean of faux hawks and knit beanies and shaggy mullets, is a clock displaying the current time which, according to its three-foot-long hours hand and its four-foot-long minutes hand, is seven thirty-four in the evening. Crane calmly observes the second-hand jittering around the dial. As it closes in on the twelve, Crane raises his thimble and its tiny saucer a half an inch off his knee.

(Flicker).

The vista before him shivers, and his bench scoots a quarter of an inch forward all by itself as reality shifts to a nearby timeline. Instead of the distinctly mid-eighties vibe he'd been suffering, the people tooing and froing before Crane now skitter along on a multitude of exoskeletal decapodal limbs, their carapaces flashing colorfully as they chitter to each other and rush to catch the trains–which Crane determines he will, for the next eight minutes, avoid.

A crablike being takes the space on the bench beside him. In their experience of this timeline, Crane is a human-sized Mantis Shrimp enjoying a lukewarm espresso, but Crane sees himself as his latent image, a tall agonizingly thin man with a body like a poorly hydrated eggplant and legs like cheese straws and a face that lurches forward trying to keep up with a nose he could use to sew a purse. He enjoys the verisimilitude. The crustacean waggles its posterior plates against Crane for room. He slides ever so slightly toward the edge of the bench.

"How very shellfish of you," he says quietly, smiling. The crustacean freezes, antennae bending slowly toward Crane. Then it resumes its chittering and ignores him. He gathers his things and scuttles away.

(Flicker).

The broad room of Union Station becomes a court. The people wear exorbitant finery, their faces powdered alabaster, their heads adorned by impossibly complex mountainous wigs, each of them accompanied by a footman or an aide-de-camp depending on the vein of Renaissance fashion they've mined. Crane opens an unmarked door in the wall near the Randolph Street entrance. He descends a narrow stairwell to the gloom of the tracks.

Waiting in the deep shadows far, far away from the public Metra lines is a private track no one ever notices. A sparkling, overly geared, wildly ornate engine breathes quietly on the rails. A conductor in a 17th-century butler's uniform waits patiently in front of a string of three cars. Crane nods to the conductor, hands him his tiny cup, and his coat, and his umbrella then boards the last compartment.

Inside is a perfectly appointed rolling library and an oak desk with a reef of nooks and drawers, a statue of Vulcan whose oversized torch is also a lamp, a laptop, and a phone. Crane sets his Homburg on a shelf explicitly designed to hold his favorite hat. He sits down at the desk and nods to the conductor who's followed him in to deposit the coat and umbrella and see to Crane's needs. The station outside the windows slides backward. Crane asks for another espresso as they roll out of the dark into the bright sunlit yards. The espresso arrives as if it had been assumed. Chicago's skyline pops into the window, and Crane watches it shimmer and shift as his train takes little known tracks that carry him downtown, over Wabash, coming to rest at a rarely used station no one ever notices. He glances out of his window at the thick granite exterior of Transluminal Vacations, Inc.

Crane sighs again.

(Flicker).

Rose and Randall Jane are standing in front of their whiteboard at Jane's little desk. The accountant is explaining how he tracked Heller's phone, and they are trying to look as if they give a thin strawberry's follicle about it when Rose glances up at Crane stalking toward her like a malnourished gray flamingo.

"Hijo de puta," she says through her teeth as the blood drains from her face and her skin frosts over. Jane follows her gaze and sees Crane find them from across the room, smiling like a heron who's just noticed a fat frog.

"Is that . . ." Jane can't even finish her sentence. Rose swallows hard and croaks out:

"The Project Manager."

Crane strolls over. He doesn't say anything. This goes on for what they feel is an eternity, but it isn't, and Crane knows that because he's experienced a tiny sliver of eternity, strictly in a professional capacity, as the founder, president, CEO, and overlord of Transluminal Vacations, Inc. though he prefers, for reasons which everyone assumes are some kind of eldritch irony, Project Manager, and further prefers, for reasons no one can come up with a reason for, to be addressed as Crane. Not sir nor mister nor my lord, just Crane.

"Crane," Rose says, fighting an urge to curtsy.

"How delightful to see you again," he says. Rose doesn't reply, and Crane doesn't say anything else for, well, ever it seems. Jane folds her arms. Rose tries not to combust spontaneously. Finally, he speaks. "Do you have a coffee service?"

A few minutes later, they're all in Rose's office as her espresso machine snorts and sputters a black rivulet into a styrofoam cup. Crane accepts it with exquisite manners though his lips will never touch the rim, and he will never taste the creosote tainted effluvium Rose thinks is good espresso. He just holds it and talks to her, slowly, as is his custom.

"I believe the last time I was here, you were still in sales." He brings the cup to his colorless lips but does not drink.

"Promoted. I was. I got. They promoted me." Rose's spleen goes twisty.

"An obvious choice. You always were one for details," Crane reptiles.

"Crane," Rose seems to be trying to be professionally coy, an attitude that is impossible to achieve when one is shaped like a sweet potato, but she barrels on. "I can only assume you are aware of the loop breach?"

Crane brings the Styrofoam cup back to his thin nostrils and examines the greasy, asphalt bouquet of Rose's 'espresso' for what seems to her and Jane like about nine months. Finally,

"Have you ever had Rat King?"

Rose stares at him with no change of expression, but inside her misshapen skull, her brain contorts to determine the right answer. This isn't some kind of rare anxious reaction to Crane's question, not really. Rose doesn't have a supervisor or a direct report. She's the de-facto CEO, so she's not confronted with superiority often. But in her history, in her past, when she was backstabbing up through the ranks of corporate, she met every question from upper management with this same blank stare as her internal database of potentials ran damage scenarios until she gathered a lobe consensus about what to say.

"No," she murmurs.

"Oh, it's wonderful. Local. Roasted every morning. You can only buy a few ounces at a time. I have it delivered to my workspace daily." He looks down into his cup of rancid motor oil. Sets it on Rose's desk. Looks up at her. Says nothing.

Rose's mind constricts into a tornado of response models as she tries to keep her eyes from dancing tarantellas in their bruised sockets. "I will have to give it a try."

"I love it." He pulls a slim matte black lozenge from his coat pocket and speaks into it. Rose realizes it's some kind of off-brand bespoke phone that probably cost ten grand. "Herbert, would you bring today's ration of espresso to Ms. Pilny's office?" He puts the lozenge back into his coat. His butlerconductor walks through the door like he'd already been on his way and lays a black bag of coffee beans with a tiny gray line drawing of a grinning rat in one corner onto her desk. It's wrapped with a ribbon, and there is a thick paper card attached. It has her name imprinted.

"I am here about the loop breach, Rose. It seems to be in an eight-minute cycle, though it's occurring almost randomly within that temporal space. How are you managing it currently?"

Rose's brain Rubik cubes so fast it almost disappears.

"I'm sending an agent."

"Is he well-trained?"

"It's Heller."

"Oh," the Project Manager raises an eyebrow as his butler positions a grinder on Rose's desk. He fills it with beans then snaps the toggle. The machine fills the room with an ungodly screech. The butler attacks Rose's espresso maker with a bristle brush and a pocket vacuum. "Well, he's definitely the right man for the job. Where is he now?"

Rose's mind, already a tornado of anxiety, finally snaps, and her eyes flutter, and she falls back into her ample chair like a poorly constructed doll. Crane looks at Randall Jane.

"I believe she's swooned."

Chapter 23

Octavia leaps into her town car. It does a U-turn on Montrose, pulls a Larry onto Ravenswood, then races north alongside the elevated tracks.

(Flicker).

Octavia sinks back into plush velvet. Her town car is now a gaudy palanquin. On the bench across from her is a himbo of cartoonish proportions.

"Stop!" Octavia stomps on the floor of the litter. Her bearers set her down. She leans out the window into a neighborhood overtaken by enormous puppets operated by teams of puppeteers. Other litters bearing riders wend through the huge people-powered machines. There is a giant little girl carrying a basket. There is a mountainous elephant. There is a wine bottle the size of a bus. It is a bus. She turns to her shirtless well-oiled associate. "Who are you, and why are you here?"

He rolls his head toward her dumbly. "I'm your consort? Like, it's Thursday? Are you even hydrated?"

Octavia drags herself, and eight tons of crinoline skirts out the door of the palanquin onto the sidewalk with the himbo tracking her like an obedient dog. She hates this stuff. It's why she's desk and not field. She gives Heller a metric ton of flak about it all the time, but the truth is she's terrified of line slipping, and this ground hogging thing has her stomach doing flips.

"Hey," her consort seems lost. "You need some water, or you want to get a room or?"

She shoos him off. She turns up Lawrence, and there's Heller leading a crew of weirdoes north on the other side.

"Jesus Heller Christ, I will delete that f–HELLER!"

Heller spins on his heel. There she is, infuriated beyond her choleric baseline and growing furiouser with every stomp in a shimmering bronze dress and a silver wig and a look on her face that juggles his helpless heart like she might bounce it against a wall any second.

"Octavia," he shouts. "I–"

She shoves his phone against his chest. She turns toward the palanquin, sticks two fingers in her mouth, and whistles so loud Heller's ear bones rattle.

"Standard issue, Heller. Standard. Issue. That means you keep it on you all the time," she glowers.

Heller looks down at the device. Eleven calls. From her. Crap. Her litter comes along, and the Himbo throws the door open.

"Everybody in," Octavia growls. Christopher Aldous Six Pack Montgomery helps Mooki climb in. Heller offers to help Octavia.

"Seriously? Get in the car!"

She crawls into the car where there is no room, so she parks herself sideways on Heller's lap. She doesn't even ask. Like his lap is hers. Her consort tries to climb in, but Octavia snaps the door closed, pounds the side of the car, and yells, "University of Chicago, stat!"

Heller is a frozen block of ice. Her hair hangs in his face. He's staring into the labiate architecture of her earlobe; his lungs fill with her perfume. They leave the consort shirtless and glistening in their dust.

"Octavia, I–" Chris says.

"Who are you?" She says to Mooki.

"That's–" Heller says. Octavia snaps her head around to him, all teeth and powder. Her eyes are glittering gold. Her lips are millimeters away as she snarls.

"Old School, you might want to engage in some silent meditation. She can speak for herself."

"They," Chris corrects her. Octavia glares at him. Then at Mooks and says, seriously. "Sorry. What's your name?"

"Mooki."

"And you are with this decrepit old shoe becauuuuseee . . ."

"I think I'm a client?"

"She's client adjacent," Chris says. "The actual–"

"Intern." Octavia waggles her fingers at him dismissively. Mooki disapproves. Octavia raises an eyebrow. "Oh, alright. You two," she circles her hand to include them both in her regard. "Ok."

"I don't think–" Heller doesn't even finish.

"Heller. Don't think. Listen. To. Me." She looks gravely at him. "It's the lab."

"Shit. Ok. That's bad."

"Why is that bad?" Chris asks. She waggles fingers at him to shut up again without even looking. Heller looks over Octavia's shoulder at Chris and Mooki.

"The lab is where they make new watches. Where they fix the broken ones. If the breach is in the lab, it means the core machinery of the entire operation is confuckulated, and I don't know how to fix it."

"Machinery," Octavia snorts.

"Electronics, gears, calibration, and–what?"

Octavia smirks. "I guess there's some things you don't know, School."

(Flicker).

Crane invented the scientific framework upon which Transluminal Vacations, Inc. rests. He also drew up the first sales funnel for milking millionaires in adjacent timelines by appealing to their penniless timeline's inherent greed. He did not call it a Fuck You Money Timeline, however, because Crane hated vulgar language. Spoiled his coffee.

Which begs the question of what Crane gets out of the temporal trampoline he knitted out of old scientific formula and experiential curiosity. You would think it would be all the money.

Heller had met him once, sitting like a statue on his favorite bench in Union station having an espresso. Heller's stellar seller rep got him a brief meeting with Crane who regarded his outstretched hand much like an alien seeing one for the first time.

"It's a pleasure to meet you, Si–Crane."

Crane looked up into Heller's four-thousand-watt salesman's grill until it drooped.

"Likewise," he hissed. Heller dropped down on the bench next to him.

"So, you own this place?"

"No."

"Kidding. But seriously, you must have the best fuck you money timeline in the whole history of TVI."

Crane focused one round unblinking eye at Heller and showed his confusion by cocking his head ever so slightly away from the salesman and taking a long noisy slurp of Rat King.

"I mean," Heller was losing ground here. "You have to be worth jillions."

"I suppose. I've never looked. Herbert does all my accounting and, of course, the accounting wing at the firm. I never really concern myself with it. I'm more about the science."

"But surely, you've looked."

"At what?"

"Your other timelines?"

"No."

"You don't have . . . Did you ever, you know, take a vacation?"

"No."

Heller got antsy when he was confused. His knee bounced like he was a kid in church. "But, I mean, I feel like, well, you could have anything you want?"

"I enjoy the ultimate luxury, Mr. Heller." The man slowly unfolded off the bench looking a lot like the tightly furled umbrella dangling from his long bony hand. "Time to myself."

Crane walked away. Heller lost him in the crowd.

. . .

Now the tiny car jerked and rolled through side street traffic toward the university campus. Heller was still a frozen block of ice, but they'd jumped into a late 70s timeline. The car radio was a bulky eight-track tape player, a thick blue plastic cartridge jutting out with a label proclaiming the voice singing into the car was that of Gerry Rafferty, who was telling the woman he loved that it was her, right down the line.

Heller was frozen because in this timeline, Octavia Del Sol's hair had retreated from his face into a tight bun behind her head, and she was slightly heavier, and she was wearing glasses, and she had fallen asleep, pressed into him with her head on his shoulder, her teacup face nestled warmly in the crook of his neck, her breath warm and humid on his skin, snoring. Quietly. Heller wrapped a cautious arm around her to keep her from falling, of course, safety being a priority, natch, of all salesmen. He looked up, and Mooki and Chris were looking at him in a way.

"What?" he whispered.

"Nothing," Mooki grinned. They glanced at Chris, but in that gaze, no doorway cracked even a little. They looked back at Heller, then down at Octavia from the timeline where she liked him, then back up at Heller, who was staring at the town car dividing wall across from him, steeled to any reaction. "She's cute."

"Leave it alone," Heller said. Mooki's eyes widened as they realized a thing. "Wait, why don't you jump into a timeline where she likes–"

"I said, leave it alone, Mooki." He said earnestly. Quietly. Sadly.

"He likes the challenge of the smokestack version," Chris says. "It doesn't count unless it's the real one, the furious Latino in his timeline. The one who he'll take with him when he wins the platinum package vacation of his dreams."

"I think that ship has sailed," Heller croaks, staring out the window.

"Heller, we've been in this timeline," Chris says. "This is the music the band was playing at your bar when we walked in. It's all 70s stuff. Look at Mooki's suede jacket. Look at this carpet."

Heller ran his fingers through the deep shag on the wall of the car. "That's why they call it a loop."

A warm, moist voice spoke into the crook of his neck. "School? Why in the hell am I making out with your stringy ass neck?"

"You fell asleep."

"It's been a long day." She doesn't move. Heller doesn't move. "How far?"

"In this traffic? Twenty minutes. Unless we drop into a low tech timelin–"

"Shut up, School. I swear if your hand moves a single millimeter, I will cut it off." Heller's hand was firmly gripping her hip to keep her from sliding off his lap. He could practically read her lips as she spoke against his skin. "Wake me up when we're there." She shifted, digging her hip deeper into him, slipping her arms around him and locking her fingers together. Her face remained nestled under his ear, which was pulsating with a lurid heat. "You're pretty comfortable for a retiree."

Mooki grins. Chris wiggles his eyebrows at Heller and pops a blue tip match into his teeth.

Chapter 24

Eli and Aaron are sharing a Dr. Phibb in the only barber shop in Arthur, Illinois. The barber's busy with their Uncle Lamar who is getting his beard fluffed and having a neck shave. It is his only luxury and Eli and Aaron can't believe they're here in an 'English' Barbershop. They get their hair styled traditionally in the barnyard sitting on a milking stool with a bucket on their heads and their mother using razor sharp sheep shears.

High on the wall, a tiny tube television shows a staticky reality series, "Master and Monk". The program starts like it always does, with the Monk, a skinny kid in punk rock black stovepipe pants kicking through the door like Cramder on Steinfield. The Master doesn't even bat an eye. Eli sniggers.

"English is a lizard," Eli sips the Dr. Phibb and hands it to Aaron.

"It is the way of celestials, Eli." Aaron sips. Returns the can.

On the screen, the Punk Monk flops down onto a couch. The Master just stares into the screen, right at Eli and Aaron, unblinking. Apparently furious.

"He is so livid, Aaron."

"Eli," Aaron says, looking at the screen. "Those two idiots are always fighting."

The Monk talks.

"Master, I am at the end of my rope. I don't know what to do. I can't stop thinking about Mooki. About their body."

Eli's eyes widen. He elbows Aaron.

The master's shoulders sag. He can hear the tears in Sidd's trembling voice. Perhaps this isn't a time for severity. Perhaps it's time–dammit!

"–for compassion," he says.

Aaron looks at the screen like the Master just grew another head.

This kid is never–ack!

"–going to get it if–"

–he doesn't start recognizing the things in the world as aspects and manifestations–gaaah!

"–of the divine, here in the material."

The spirit of God isn't separate from–*seriously?*

"–this world, it is this world–"

–one only needs to live–Godammit!–
–fully in the moment–"
–of one's immediate experience to–
"–fully experience the spirit–"

"I think the elder lizard is off his porch chair, Eli."

"No, Aaron." Eli seems to have followed what the reptilian master didn't say as well as what was spoken. "It is not far and away crossed from what Pastor Nedward tells us, that one must find God in the smallest details to know that God is in all things present. Tis in the book," sip. "Dullard."

"I have read the book as thoroughly as thee, dunderwhelp."

"If you are referring to the pleats of yon cousin Mary's dress when you say 'book,' I would agree, ninny sledge."

Aaron's face turned barn burning red. "Your mother's canned beef has always gone off!"

Eli's beard suddenly seemed like smoke on a fire. "Thou wilt take that back, dirtclod."

"Facts are facts, feather duck," Aaron crushed the Dr. Phibb into Eli's nose. They erupted into a dust devil of facial hair and denim. Their uncle beamed with pride.

On the small T.V. the master stood up, his face filling the screen which flickered into a commercial.

"Those two idiots," he said. He turned to Sidd. He'd been crying again. The master sat next to Sidd on the couch and laid a hand on his back, fatherly, kind, supportive. Then, with his other hand, he smacked Sidd in the face as hard as he could. Sidd's head snapped back from the blow.

"Thank you, Master." Sidd says.

"For what? I just smacked you in the damn face, Sidd."

"Obviously it is a lesson, you are trying–"

SMACK!

"–to tea be to beh mo id da spirt."

"No, you idiot. I'm just sick of your whining."

"Bu ure by teaer."

"Yeah, and you aren't learning jack diddly squat."

"Ab tried do alahn byseb widda ways ud da bood–"

SMACK!

"Whad da fug, massr?"

"Who just smacked you in the face?"

"Ew?"

"No, it was my hand, but it was the Buddha who slapped you. You know why?"

"Ab purry chure id beek–"

SMACK!

"Because you are walking around in the spirit all day long! Because the spirit is speaking to you from everything, like crickets, like static. It never stops. Sometimes, it reaches out to you through desire, *through another.* Just as my hand is not smacking you–

EXAMPLE SMACK!

–But is the instrument of the divine. So is your body sometimes such an instrument, as when you feed the homeless or when you receive the hot monkey love being offered to you by this Spooki person with whom you are in love."

"Ab noddin lub"

DISAGREE SLAP!

"Idiot."

"Bud u r celibate prees"

"Yeah, *now.* I wasn't always a priest, and you aren't one right now. Desire is a voice of the divine. Follow it. Dumbass."

EMPHASIS CRACK!

"Ow?"

"Sorry, not me. *God.* I'd get moving if I were you."

"Moogeh?"

EMPOWERMENT JAB!

"Find Floppy. Follow your desire. Learn something."

Sidd ducked the next whack of the divine. He looked at the temple door.

Back in the barbershop. Eli and Aaron are sitting back in their chairs watching the Master as he smacks his apprentice.

"Those two idiots are always fighting."

Chapter 25

Pilny comes to lying on the floor of her office. Crane's on her couch. His Butler's there. Randall Jane's there. They're all looking down at her.

"You snore," Crane says with a faint grin.

"We have to get to the lab!"

Crane's butler helps Rose up.

"Perhaps. I don't think it will do much good."

"But the loop breach!"

"If I am not mistaken, the lab has a protocol for a loop breach. However, we've been looping for some time now. It's 8:35, and we're still looping, which means the lab didn't run the protocol, which means something is quite disastrously askew." He sips his tiny cup. About a month later, he says "Could be dangerous."

"What do you mean?"

Crane stared unblinking.

"What!?" Pilny yelled. She clapped a hand over her mouth, and her eyes grew to the size of hardboiled eggs. "I'm so sorry!"

"No need. I don't seem to be able to achieve a sense of urgency. It can be frustrating," said Crane. The butler blinked slowly, his expression remaining entirely passive as he stared at nothing, awaiting instructions. But he remembered the time they'd set the conservatory on fire, and his boss stood stock-still in the middle of the room watching the flames curl across the glass-paned ceiling like he had all the time in the world. He asked for an espresso. The Butler remembers the sheer indignity of tossing his boss over his shoulder like an empty golf bag and running through an inferno for the door. He lost an eyebrow. Blink indeed. Blink . . . Indeed.

"I'm wondering if racing into the lab is the best idea?"

"I'm all ears, Crane."

"I believe that the intensity and . . ." Crane stared. Pilny ahemmed with some urgency. "Sorry. I believe the intensity and, er, frequency of jumps, as it were, are more intense and more . . ." Staring.

"Frequent?"

Crane snapped back into the moment. "Yes. And I believe one's control or ability to recognize the jumps is less . . ."

Pilny looked at the Butler. The Butler raised one eyebrow a half millimeter. He surreptitiously rattled a tiny spoon in a tiny empty espresso cup.

"I think if we open the door to that lab, we'll disappear into a standing strobe of timelines to the point where our temporal cohesion will appear random."

"Isn't all this already random?" Pilny asked.

Crane stared at her. The Butler flicked a crumb off his lapel. Randall Jane looked at their watch. Finally, Crane answered. "Uh, no. Tardigrada move in a linear progression to immediately adjacent temporal threads. The differences between them are often imperceptible. That's why we never notice."

Randall Jane looked sharply at Pilny. Pilny looked at Crane's avian face. A powerful glower built as she pressed her tiny fists into her ample hips and leaned (theoretically) toward him.

"Who is we?"

The Butler sniffed and closed his eyes.

"We? We is you and I and my Butler–"

"Aide de Camp, sir."

"–and, well, everyone. When a Tardigrada bounces, the world bounces with them."

"But when we do it, when we use the device, we recognize the difference in the timelines. We see the giant balloon animals, and we notice if we're not wearing clothes."

The Butl–

"Ahem,"

–Aide de Camp snorted discreetly.

"Well, yes. However. The watches compress the process."

"When I spin the dial on a company Watch," Pilny said, pointing to her dimply unwatched slightly hirsute wrist, "I jump to the next timeline. If it's full of giant crabs, I notice."

"No, Rosemarie, to you, it is one instantaneous leap, but in the microaquabiotic world of Tardigrada, it is a decade of thousands of successive, contiguous leaps."

"Well, that would mean the whole world is popping in and out of adjacent timelines all the time!"

Crane stared at her for an endless period. He lifted a pinky off his kneecap a mere millimeter, and the AIDE DE CAMP leaped into the ritual of grinding beans to make a cup of joe. Pilny made the whole-body waggle of a person experiencing disproportionate frustration with another person who should have responded years ago and went *gah!*

"Quite," Crane said very quietly.

"But how do people even live?"

"Oh, people are resilient. And really, the tardigrade is an ancient species. People showed up long after they did. We evolved in the temporal maelstrom of horologically hopping moss piglets."

"Jesus Horacrux Christ, Crane!" Randall Jane barked. "Are we even who we are?"

Crane accepted the thimble of walnut-colored coffee from his AIDE DE CAMP who looked, seemingly for the first time, at the other people in Pilny's office, who were discovering they were never really in the same day twice, and whose faces had achieved the upper reaches of the aghast level, then placed a perfectly steady finger onto the rim of his boss's saucer. "Sir, your cruelty is showing," he said, removing his finger.

Crane slurped his espresso and seemed to disappear without actually going anywhere. The AIDE DE CAMP addressed the room.

"According to what I've learned as Mr. Crane's AIDE DE CAMP," said Crane's AIDE DE CAMP. "The change is imperceptible. And honestly, Tardigrada aren't alone. Time is fragile as a soap bubble and malleable as a lump of putty. It's also, and I regret being the informer here; but it is also not exactly consistent. Any sufficiently alarming situation can trigger a hyperlocal temporal shift. You can sneeze yourself into an adjacent thread. I have experienced this."

"Like how?" asked Jane.

"I was crossing from the observatory to the orchid house and just took a shortcut through the media room. Well, I forgot the media room is a half level lower than the rest of the estate and stepped through the door into thin air and, well, there are multiple glass-topped tables, and I thought I might fall through one and the panic I felt was sufficient to pop me into the next line over."

"How could you tell?"

"It was the media room, after all, and the news was on, and suddenly Ronald Lump was president."

Everyone laughed loudly.

"Come on, man," Jane said, wiping an incredulous tear from their eye.

"Hand, as my dear old mum would say, to Jesus. I walked across the media room, trimmed the lapizalea in the orchid chamber, then, and, if I do say so, nervously, returned. It was back to normal."

"Well, it was a T.V. show or something."

"No," the AIDE DE CAMP said, seriously, one hand behind him, the other at waist height as he embarrassingly observed his nails. "No, we have a multitude of televisions showing a multitude of news streams. He was on all of them. Something about pardoning the Halloween swan."

"The lab is ground zero," Pilny whispered.

They all looked at the AIDE DE CAMP. He shifted very gently against his boss. Crane snapped to like he'd been in the conversation the entire time.

"Yes. It is, as Herbert said," Crane handed his AIDE DE CAMP the coffee cup, "sufficient."

Chapter 26

"What about Sidd?" asked Christopher Aldous Friend Zoned Montgomery.

"I don't know, kid," said Heller.

"But you gotta close."

"I gotta shut down the breach. Sidd turned us down. It was a challenge mark and I failed."

"Please drop me off at the church," Mooki sniffled.

"We're two miles out going the other way; we're on our way to the lab," Heller said. "It's kind of like an emergency."

"I didn't ask to be part of your emergency." They wiped a tiny tear out of their eye. "Sidd needs me."

"Sorry kid, I can't–"

Octavia pushed herself off Heller and rapped a knuckle on the driver's glass. She switched seats with Chris and leaned against Mooki.

"Priorities, School." The glass rolled down. "Take us to the Ravenswood Episcopal Church."

The car turned around. Octavia looked at Heller.

"They're in love."

(Flicker).

Sidd was standing by the side door when the hovercar hovered up. Mooki leaped out. They threw their arms around him. He tentatively put his arms around them back. Octavia leaned out of the hovercar window.

"Get in!"

Sidd didn't move. When he left the bar, he let Heller's protective temporal soap bubble and was experiencing this new reality sort of kind of freshly. It was even better than the last iteration Heller'd showed him. He peeled Mooki off him, and together they gawked at the tabernacle. It was magnificent. Beautifully maintained. Every window was stained glass. The grounds were landscaped down to their roots. Sidd was beaming. He pulled Mooks down the stairs into the basement. It was well-lit. Strong modern shelves held years of food. A team of uniformed cooks all yelled, "yes, chef!" to an actual chef who was talking to them about tonight's five-star meal. A crowd–a *crowd*–of volunteers in team t-shirts were listening, prepared to serve the hundreds of homeless diners waiting upstairs. Sidd dragged them back to the furthest wall and scraped his foot along the cement.

"Mooki, look–" he grinned so genuinely, so broadly. "Bone dry! They fixed the seepage." He was so happy. They burst into bittersweet tears. "Why are you crying?"

Mooki whispered, "We have to go."

Heller swooped into the basement, all elbows and shoulders. "Sidd, let's roll–" he whistled. "Well now, this is something!"

(Flicker).

Dark. Musty. Sidd stared at the basement that was the same old basement he'd always suffered a chill in. A pool of water peeked out from under the sagging half-empty shelves.

He got into the car. They piled in after him.

Mooki stared into their lap.

Sidd stared out the window.

Everyone else stared anywhere else but at Sidd or Mooki.

***

George tried to catch his breath. He leaned against the spear in his second right hand. His other five hands waved swords and daggers in a mindlessly protective orbit.

Moss fields swept down and away, their gametophytic leaves gently waving. Milky light of the Everpresent Glow from Above shone over the verdant expanse. Tardigrada bodies everywhere. Pierced, stabbed, squashed, and pummeled. Here and there, pairs of enemy warriors floated just above the ground locked in their grappling, too exhausted to raise their blades.

George's oldest son had flung himself onto the ground nearby, spent, heaving, bloodstained, but whole. George thanked the Mysterious Shape Beyond the Everpresent Glow. This was his fifth campaign.

The great wars had gone on so long, George couldn't remember when he wasn't in the Moss Fields fighting uppy-downies. Ever since the disturbance, ever since the verts charged into his Lodge, ever since he tried to jump away.

He'd brought them along, somehow. Their jumps took them into more fighting, into crueler wars. His little town had burned and then had not been burned and then was on fire and then was not. Their once still waters were endlessly aswirl. Endless jumping. Endless war.

Over the crest of the far hill, he saw doom barreling down on their line. Great Harpaticoid Copepods glided forward, their antennae sweeping the spore fields, their great eyeholes burning with rapacious intent and on their backs, verts waving swords, flags, death.

George looked at his boy. His eyes were open, unfocused, looking up into the alabaster watery sky. There were so few warriors left. Behind him, a collection of the dead and injured, a claw full of gently bobbing soldiers staring at the hill. Exhausted. Bleeding. Resolute.

Already, scores of his men had flicked themselves into adjoining timelines. He couldn't blame them. It wasn't cowardice. It was how they were designed. It was involuntary. For many. Not for George.

They had to out jump the tanarctus chronosfichtosvarelli. There had to be a way. George closed his eyes. He descended into his scorched and darkened mental cellar. The nubbin hung off the wall, naked wires pulled out like torn ganglia. He ripped the switch and all its trailing arteries out onto the floor. Wires sparked. He took a bundle in his top right hands, a bundle in his top left hands, said a hasty prayer to the Mysterious Shape Beyond the Ever-present Glow, and jammed them together.

Time blasted from between his fists. He tried to drop the sparking cables, but he was paralyzed, temporalocuted. Beams of time shot out of his burning eyes. Reality melted, reassembled, melted again; timelines roiled like a boiling stew.

***

As they drive to the lab, the ground hogging seemed to speed up. It seemed to get jangly and rattle its wheels on the rails. The world blurred.

Chapter 27

Tripping your balls off on Bakers treats
Buzzing and laughing, feeling the heat
Hey it's another lazy day
Let's get us a cupcake
And put on some Dan and sing...

(Flicker).

Chapter 28

This cromuffin top is just so bold
It's got, pecans and walnuts, but it's got no soul
And it's taking me so long
To find out I am wrong:
I can eat it in just two bites.

(Flicker).

Chapter 29

You used to squeak that it was so squeaky
Squeak Squeaky Squeak squeak squeak was so squeaky
But you're squeaking, you're

(Flicker).

Chapter 30, 31, 32, and 33

Another day and then you'd eat chicken
Just one more bird and then
(Flicker).
you'd be happy
But you're cry
(Flicker).
ing, you're
(Flicker).
crying
(Flicker).
now

CHAPTER 34 35 36 AAAHH!

Way down the street

(Flicker)

there's a light in his face

He opens the window with that look on his face

And he asks you who you've been

You tell him where

(Flicker)

you've seen

And you talk about flicker ing

He's got this dream about buying some cans

He's gonna give up the juices and the hot-dog stands

And then he'll

(Flicker)

settle down

In some stupid little town

And forget

(Flicker)

about flicker ing

But you know he'll always keep grooving

You know

(Flicker)

he's never

(Flicker)

gonna chop

(Flicker)

goofing

(Flicker)

'Cause he's

(Flicker)

old and, he's

(Flicker)

ben rolled in

(Flicker)

go

(Flicker)

ld

(Flicker)

(Flicker)(Flicker)

(Flicker)(Flicker)(Flicker)

(Flicker)(Flicker)(Flicker)(Flicker)

(Flicker)(Flicker)(Flicker)(Flicker)(Flicker)(Flicker)(Flicker)
(Flicker)(Flicker)(Flicker)(Flicker)(Flicker)(Flicker)(Flicker)(Flicker)
(Flicker)(Flicker)(Flicker)(Flicker)(Flicker)(Flicker)(Flicker)(Flicker)
(Flicker)(Flicker)(Flicker)(Flicker)(Flicker)(Flicker)(Flicker)(Flicker)
(Flicker)(Flicker)(Flicker)(Flicker)(Flicker)(Flicker)(Flicker)(Flicker)
(Flicker)(Flicker)(Flicker)(Flicker)(Flicker)(Flicker)(Flicker)

(Flicker)(Flicker)(Flicker)

(Flicker)(Flicker)

(Flicker)

***

(Flicker)(Flicker)(Flicker)

(Flicker)

**

(FFFFFFFFflicker)

(fli(fli(flicker)c(flicker)ker)cker)

(Fli(flic(Flick(Flicke(Fl(fli(Flicker)cker)icker)r)er)ker)cker)

*

Chapter 37

The lab pulsed and glowed. A great bundle of luminescent ghostly threads flashed up through the denter of the tiny building like a shimmering spoke, their liminal echoes radiating out across the campus. University staff and students skittered through the standing waves of the breach. They scuttled into it as giant crabs, then loped out of the first wave as lascivious Wookie Sandinistas, then out of the next wave as well-dressed octopuses, then faintly glowing translucent soap bubbles, then people with their gender switched, then everyone again but with gleaming skulls, then everyone as a great ape, then endless Cthulian dread as giant snails; sentient trees; etymological terror; and strange, uncategorized zoology. Then they walked out the farthest wave in fringe jackets and bell-bottomed pants. Some of them veered off into the west campus. The ones who kept going walked through the last wave and right past our group of timeline-hopping weirdoes in lacy medieval finery.

Heller adjusted his powdered wig. He reached into the pocket of his jade green velvet waistcoat and retrieved a slim brass box engraved with his family crest and from it carefully took an Ohio Blue Tip match, which he bit into with a bitter grin.

"I don't know about this," Heller rolled the match around.

"Listen, School; somebody's got to go in there."

"And do what?" Heller asked her quietly.

"Something?!"

"I thought it was just storage."

"We could keep all the watches in a box under my desk," Octavia said. "And why would we put it on the University Campus?"

"I never thought about it."

"I never thought about it," Octavia mocked.

"Look, I'm a salesman. I'm the best–"

"–for now," she growled.

"–It's what I do. I don't know how these fuckticular devices work anymore than I know what's under the hood of a laptop. I don't need to know. We have people for that. We got people for this, too."

"The people for this is a person, and we can't reach him. And believe me, if he were O.K. and breathing and walking upright, he'd be following whatever protocol's set up for a breach loop, but as you may have surmised," she swept her arm out to indicate everything. "Protocol is not so much being followed."

"Let's make a plan. What's the worst that can happen?"

"Si este hombre no produce huevosmásgrandestendré quecultivarlosyomismo—Huevos! Mas! Grandes! Heller!"

By now their faces were millimeters apart. Heller was growling his words, but not because he was angry with Octavia, a fact she registered as easily as she did everything else in her life, a fact she ticked off among all her other data for Heller: he was angry that she was in danger and he didn't know what to do.

"We don't have any idea—not one iota of an idea—what will happen when we open the door to that lab'" Heller says, pointing a match labward. "Hell, if we *can* open the door to the lab."

"We won't know until you try, School! How about–"

"Is it locked?" Sidd asked.

"–it's a keypad–8643, I think–how about you hustle up your skirts and–"

"No star or pound or anything?" Sidd asked, walking away.

"—No, you just punch in the numbers—actuar como un hombre no como un niño!"

"I am a grown assed man!"

"Prove it!"

"Sidd?" Mooki stepped between Heller and Octavia. Sidd was punching a number into a keypad. "SIDD!?"

Mooki ran.

Chris ran.

Sidd disappeared in a blinding burst of stellar light.

"SIDD!" Mooki punched 8643 into the pad, threw the door open, and disappeared in a blinding burst of stellar light. Christopher Aldous Pointless Heroic Effort Montgomery flew over the threshold after them. He turned around in the vestibule, alone, looking out at Heller and Octavia. He shimmered through a nickelodeon of iterations of himself–long hair and beard, carapace and claws, bandoleers and body hair, tentacles–then there was a whoomph, and Chris disappeared in a blinding burst of stellar light. Then everyone was back to normal. It was a perfectly ordinary evening.

Heller ran into the lab, Octavia on his heels.

Shambles. Ovales Calvarium was face down on the floor by the magnevibratron, which was frozen solid in a thick layer of ice. Crane and his AIDE DE CAMP were there. Herbert was toting a shoulder-mounted reverse tactical microwave and peeling off his safety goggles.

"Perhaps," Crane started. Many years later, it seemed, he continued. "we should call for medical aid?"

***

Sidd was in an office. Kind of. It was a canopy. Outside. Under the canopy were two extraordinarily hideous beings. One had a horse's head; the other had an Ox's head. Kind of. The Horse was white. The Ox was red. The Ox was picking his nose and didn't notice Sidd. The one with the horse face and the spiked club snorted at him. Under the canopy was a desk, and behind the desk was a large blue creature with crimson horns, a crown of skulls, three eyes, four arms (two hands were writing in two different books, one scratched his hairy chin, the other drummed on the desktop), curled tusks, and a top hat wreathed in silent flame.

This was Yamaraja, aka Yama, one of the Asta Dikpala, guardian of the south, God of death. Unless you were Greek, in which case he was Charon, also a God of death. If you were from the 9th ward of New Orleans, there's a slim chance you'd call him Baron Samedi (hence the top hat), a guardian of the dead, and if you were Egyptian, you'd be looking at Anubis–the god of the underworld, or death–and you'd be dead as a doorknob.

Outside, a large buffalo munched on a bale of golden-green hay. As far as Sidd could see, behind the buffalo were vast plains of snow and ice dotted by screaming people frozen in searing agony.

Around his neck the being wore an amulet of two crossed keys. On his desk were three brass monkey paperweights and a pencil sharpener shaped like a pyramid.

"Siddney Hearth Ough," Yama's voice was subterranean.

"Lord Yama," Sidd swallowed. Lord Yama was a guardian of the underworld who took one's soul at the time of death. Sidd was dead.

I am dead, Sidd thought.

He bowed slightly. "Lord Yama, I have much to confess: I was sure to become old yet tried to avoid aging; I was sure to become ill, yet tried to avoid illness; my actions are the womb from which–"

"Crap–is he Buddhist?" Lord Yama yelled out to Ox Head and Horse Face.

"NEIGH," horse face neighed.

"You can't make assumptions like that. We pride ourselves on accuracy."

"SNORT," Ox-head snorted.

"Well, yes, he is dressed like a priest. But he could be Episcopalian for all we–"

"I am Episcopalian," Sidd interrupted.

"You're wearing mala beads!"

"I'm also Buddhist."

Lord Yama blew a frustrated flame out one nostril. Sidd couldn't tell if Yama was a fat jackal or a skinny bull.

"You think any of that matters?"

"Lord?"

"The five remembrances? The myriad karma traps? The threefold pride of youth?"

"Lord?"

"I mean, this is your funeral. We can give you the Episcopalian package—which is pretty cheap—or we can do the whole six hot Narakas which, trust me, is gonna cost you."

"NEIGH," Horse face said under his breath.

"Hush, pitiful creature," Yama hissed. He looked at Sidd. "Don't listen to him. The Path of the Buddha is perfectly fine. I mean, yes, it means burning alive for as many years as if you had a basket of celery seeds and took one out each century, which, by the way," the great god of death chuckled earthquakingly, "is a criminal underestimation." He grinned. Perhaps. Something happened to his mouth. "It's longer." He winked. Sidd stared. "Anyhoo . . ."

"I am prepared to face the results of my karma."

"Okey dokey, let me just look you up."

"Wouldn't you already have the book open to my name? According to scripture, Ox-head and Horse-face brought me here, so you knew I was coming . . ."

"Are you," Yama planted three fists onto the desk and rose up, pointing a fourth flaming finger at Sidd's nose. "Are you complaining?"

"Lord Yama, forgive me, I just–"

"Horse-Face, how's the weather in the cold hell of Arbuda today?"

"NEIGH!"

"Minus eighty thousand degrees," he glowered at Sidd. "Positively tropical!"

"Lord Yama, I'm only noticing you may have greater efficiency if you employed an event triggered check-in system. I use one–used one–at my restaurant."

"Efficiency. How human."

"Better systems give you more free time, Lord Yama."

"Free time? I own time! I–"

"SNORT!"

Lord Yama looked at Ox-Head for a moment then reached under his desk for a complicated balsa model of an Edo period Higaki-Kaisen that was half-finished. "I never seem to have even a moment to work on it. What do you think?" He held it up for Sidd. A mast fell over.

Chapter 38

George Junior surveyed the frozen wastelands of the great wars. Peace had finally come, but it was not the peace he'd fought for. It was colder.

No one knows why the ice came. They only knew it was blisteringly frigid. That it was everywhere. There were ice plains, ice mountains, and weird ice craters as if the ice had been propelled with incredible force.

George Junior's town was frozen. He'd floated through its arctic ruins this morning. It wasn't easy–the waters were viscous and chilled. In some of the buildings, there were still bodies of tardigara frozen into hideous statues. They looked as if their limbs were still thrashing, their papillae fixed and fully extended, their mouth opened for a scream that never dies; that was never heard.

Yet, in this wintry apocalypse, life goes on. Now his family lives deep in an ice mountain cave. They farm phytoplankton hacked out of the ground and chewed like tasteless popsicles.

"George." It was his old friend from the wars, Lorenz, back from an excursion to the outer limits.

"I have news," said Lorenz.

"I hope it's about food," said George Jr.

"We're melting."

George turned to his old friend. His expression was as rigid as the ground he drifted over but the hope in his heart could've melted iron.

"Not funny, Lorenz."

"I've never been funny a day in my life. It's true. The water levels are rising. Here," Lorenz handed George a tiny rotifer–still alive.

"In the name of the Unknown Name!"

"There are more. And their numbers are growing."

George was careful with his hope. He ladled it out in tiny portions, carefully weighed, with the understanding it was supposed to stay right where he left it and not get into any trouble. Right this second, his hope spilled out onto the ground and threatened to explode into untamed optimism.

"How many more?" George asked. Lorenz pointed across the white wastes at a small dot. George swore it looked like two paramecia pulling a wagon filled with stunted rotifers. Moisture welled in his eyespot (then froze). They were saved. He was so happy he could molt.

***

Mooki is standing on the shore of a small pond. It is surrounded by a glory of flowering trees: enormous blue jacaranda, great pink, rosy trumpets, golden rain trees dipping almost to the water's surface. Great clouds of violet rhododendrons crash into the green reeds at the water's edge. In the center of the pond, two elephants face each other, rearing back on their hind legs, their tusks entangled, their trunks pouring entwined showers over a beautiful woman sitting between them on a lotus blossom the size of a 1958 Buick Skylark.

Her skin is the color of storm clouds in the morning. Her dress is red with golden piping and flows over the edges of the flower. She is perfectly serene, dry as a piece of paper. She holds padma blossoms in her four hands.

A beautiful man with emerald skin riding a giant chicken aims a golden arrow at Mooki. A stunning young woman gently pushes his arrow aside and takes Mooki's arm in hers. She leads them across the water toward the lady on the lotus blossom.

"Where am I?"

"Vaikuntha. I am Rati and that is my idiot brother, Kama. I am bringing you to our mother, Lakshmi, the wife of Vishnu," Mooki looked confused. "She's, like, the Virgin Mary."

"You're so pretty!"

"So are you, supple being. My brother agrees."

It was taking a long time to get to the center of the very small pond.

"Let me shoot this creature," Kama said.

"Idiot, look into this human's heart. Look how much the creature loves. Their thirst is legendary."

The green skinned man nodded. "Fine. But I get to shoot the next one."

"Am I in heaven?" Mooki was confused.

"More or less."

"I'm dead?" Mooki asked.

"You are not, which is perplexing, and which is why we are taking you to Lakshmi."

"Is Sidd here?"

Rati looked into Mooki's auras. Sidd's memory stepped out from behind their left shoulder and smiled.

"Oh, he's cute!"

"I'm so worried about him."

"You are correct," Kama said, studying Mooki's auras while polishing his arrow. "This being loves splendidly."

"Fear not, little thing," Rama comforted Mooki. "he is experiencing a similar dream."

"This is a dream?"

They came to Lakshmi. Mooki sat on a smaller lotus blossom and they looked at each other for a little while.

"It is and it is not a dream," Lakshmi said. The sound of her voice was like honey poured onto a rose petal formed by the echoes of the Mormon Tabernacle Choir. "It is a shimmer of a dream."

"Your daughter is beautiful."

Lakshmi smiled warmly at Mooki. "Look at you; your soul is like this flower. You've lived before, and before that too. You're on your way to becoming a brahmin. A bodhisattva. Oh, you are wonderful!"

"Can we keep this one?" Kama leered at Mooki.

Lakshmi hushed her son. She led Mooki out into the gardens.

"It's all so perfect." Mooki was overwhelmed. The gardens were riotous, wild, yet exquisitely ordered–like well-groomed chaos.

"You may stay as long as you wish, child of two stars. We can walk through these gardens for centuries."

And the perfume, the bouquet of all the flowers, it was jasmine, but it was roses, but it was orange blossoms, but it was also elephant sweat and manure. Mooki closed their eyes and breathed deep. Underneath the floral perfume, they smelled the basement of the Ravenswood Episcopal Church; they smelled the onions going to seed in the far dark reaches under the sagging shelves. They smelled Sanka and opened their eyes.

Lakshmi was smiling.

"I can't stay," Mooki said.

Lakshmi wrapped her beautiful azure arm around Mooki's waist.

"I know, child. I have always known. But time is a little forgetful here in the gardens. Let's finish our walk. Smell the flowers. Tell me about the priest."

Mooki blushed.

It was a good walk.

Rati pulled out her phone to check her messages. Kama scrolled through his dating app.

"She was cute," he said, absentmindedly.

"They," Rati corrected.

"Pretty curvy for such an indistinct pronoun."

"You are a tumor."

"They're gonna go back." Kama shot an arrow at a low hanging jackfruit. It ripened instantly.

"It won't matter, they won't remember a thing."

***

FFFFFLLLAAAAAAAAAAAAAAAAAAAAARRRRGGGHHH!—if I'd maybe understood how decency works a little bit more, I might've—BBBBEEEEEEEEEENNN-nicer?"

"I get it, I hear you," Sidd says reassuringly. "Sometimes, the simplest lessons take the longest to learn."

"PPPPPPLAAAAAAAAAAAAAAAAAAAAAAMMM! Right?   I'm   just   saying   that—KKKAAAAAAAAAAAAAAAAAAAAAAARRRGGGHHH!—the   version   of   me   that   did,   well-JJJJAAAAAAAAAAAAAAAAAAAABBBB!-terrible things, isn't the

197

me here now, burning to a–CCCCRRRRRIIIIISSSSSSSSSPPPPPP!–in these pits."

"Ned, if you went back and met some of the people you murdered, what would you say to them?"

"AAAIIIIIIIIIIIIIIIIIIIII'M sorry? I mean, what else is there? I can't actually redeem myself. I can't take the thumbtacks out of their eyes in, like—RRRREEEEEEEEEETTT!—trospect," Ned stirred the surface of the lava aimlessly. "I just. I'm really sorry. That's all there is—AAAAAAAAAAAAAAAAAAAA!—to it. I regret every stab."

"Nedward Jameson?" It's a bald Buddhist monk with a staff in one hand, a crystal ball in the other. Ox Head and Horse Face also arrive at the frozen fiery fecal fissure.

"SNORT!" Ox Head is livid.

"NEIGH!?" So is Horse Face. The monk ignores them.

"That's me, what can I do ya for?" asks Ned.

"I am Ksitigharba, and I'm here to move you out of this hell."

"Shoot, really?" Ned stands up, shedding lava and bits of his skin, which grow back instantly so it can burn off immediately.

"The sincerity of your regret has been entered into row 1344, column 15 of your karmic database."

"NEIGH!" Horse Face counters.

"Well, it's my job, isn't it?" Ksitigharba says to Horse Face. "I empty hell—under strict conditions, I don't want to upset the balance of power—and take redeemed creatures into the lesser hells so they can work their way up the chain to one of the starter heavens."

"I'm not familiar with starter heavens," Ned says.

Ksitigharba shoves the crystal ball into a pocket in his robe and hands his staff to Horse Face.

"Hold this, would you please?" He takes an off-market i-Pad knockoff from his satchel and scrolls.

"Jalisco, Jalta, Jamm, Jame–here we go. Nedward Wayne Jameson, psycho killer–Oh, wow, I'm taking you to Swarga Loka. That's a good one."

"NEIGH! NEIGH! NEIGH!" Horse Face argues.

"Well, how long have you been working for Lord Yama?"

"NEIGH!"

"Have you tried repenting?"

"NEIGH! NEIGH!"

"Sounds technical. I mean, I can run it up the pole, see if it unfurls. But I'm pretty sure you're manifested through Yama Lama Ding Dong over there and–"

"Sidd!" Lord Yama stomps to the edge of the pit. "Get back to my tent, and–what the hell are you doing?"

"Ministering to the Damned, My Lord."

"Well, stop it! They're here for 36,000 years of hot freezing torment."

"And fecal lava," said Ned.

"And fecal lava," Yama added. "Anyway, I need you to explain tab delimiters in the deebee. We got souls stacked and waiting."

Yama notices how the pools of flaming frozen poop are mostly empty. "Hey, where the fuck is everybody?"

"Processed, Lord Yama," Sidd says.

"These pools were overflowing with the cold inflamed howling damned two days ago!"

"Yes, Lord Yama, but once we got the data organized, it was just a matter of grouping them into the right verticals then prioritizing them by redemptionality."

"Redemp–WHERE ARE MY DAMNED SOULS?" Yama roared.

Ksitigharba passed his not exactly an i-Pad over to Yama, who anger scrolled through page after page of the redeemed.

"How the hell did you do that?"

"Like I said, you filter them by the likelihood of redemption; then you can burn through them quickly."

"I'm all for burning," said Yama.

"SNORT!" said Ox Head.

"I've been working sixteen-hour days," Ksitigharba says hoarsely. "Honestly, I'm stuffing the redeemed in the closets. We don't have the kind of efficiency you guys have here. We're windmilling."

A dignified Indian yogi appears out of thin air. He's looking through his big round glasses at an off-market i-Pad.

"Chitragupta!" Yama yells. "What's up, my Brahma!"

"I'm having a hell of a time. Sidd?" He hands the tablet to Sidd who looks down at the Customer Relations Management app he built to sort souls. "Do I have to enter their middle initial? Can't we cross-reference–"

"You're working with Sidd?"

"I popped in a few days ago to see who greased the wheels and found Sidd redeeming the shit out of your fields of the damned."

"Meh," Grumbled Yama. "I'm an ancient guardian deity. I'm old school. Gimme a stylus and a smooth lump of clay."

"I'm not in favor of his programming," said Chitragupta, "but pen and paper? Please."

"Jesus," Yama hisses.

"What?" Chitragupta asks. Ksitigharba curses and snatches his staff out of Horse Head's hoof. Chitragupta turns to behold a serene-looking Arab approaching . Light shines down through the clouds and lights the man up like a spotlight. He has a large nose and long hair and a beard. A deep blue sash offsets his dirty robes.

"No, it's actually Jesus," says Yama.

"Here comes Hollywood," Chitragupta snarks.

"Lord Jesus," Ksitigharba bows slightly.

"Bless you, my son," Jesus waves two fingers Jedi-ishly. "I was sent by my father–"

"Here we go," whispered Ksitigharba.

"Always with the daddy issues," Chitragupta said.

"–I was sent by my father," Jesus ahemmed. "To find out what the hell is going on down here?"

Sidd bows. "My Lord, Jesus."

"Oh, please," said Jesus. "Who even calls me that? Call me Issa or Ishu or just Jay to the C. Who is the one they call Sidd?"

Sidd answers from near the Savior's sandals.

"I am Sidd, My Christ."

"Call me Christ again, and I'll heal away something you depend on." Jesus whips out a cheap i-Pad knockoff. "Look, this date format doesn't work. It's got paradise locked up from all the traffic down here–"

There was an elegant explosion.

"Shit! Vishnu!"

"Everybody be cool," Chitragupta says.

"Which one of you short-timers is using brackets in your programming thread? We use slashes, not brackets. Brackets are for noobs!"

"Lord Vishnu, I leave the programming to Sidd," said Ksitigharba, throwing-people-under-the-bussedly.

"So do I," said Yama.

"Me too," said Chitragupta.

Vishnu turned to Jesus. "What about–"

"Brackets use less disk space–" Jesus growled.

Vishnu glowered. "I established the spacing convention for a reason, Sandals. Now clean up your code or–"

"I'm not even in your pantheon!" Jesus yelled. "Stop ordering me around."

"Oh my Gods, what are you gonna do," Vishnu taunted. "Call your dad? You know that's just me in Greek drag, right—*son?*"

Jesus fumed. Vishnu noticed the empty hell plains and made a decision. "Alright, hand them over." He tossed the tablets into the glowing red-hot frozen turd lava. They incinerated with a pop. Vishnu wiped his hands.

"Alright, back to basics, you idiots. Let the humans work as inefficiently as possible while we melt their skeletons over and over again for all of eternity like in the good old days."

Vishnu grabbed Sidd by his belt and hurled him out into the infinite spiritual beyond.

"Try again, meat sock."

Chapter 40

Mahavishnu, who is an upgrade from regular Vishnu, although they are also the same being, a three-in-one all-purpose mega God consisting of Vishnu, Garbhodakaśāyī Vishnu, and Joe Bob Bynum Vishnu, oversees the efforts of the contained triplets, but in his own work, manifests the endless birth of infinite universes as if they were mustard seeds popping out of his pores like a million billion blackheads reflected in a prom night mirror.

Which is metaphorical. In person, Lord Mahavishnu is a resplendent and charming deity with blue skin and assorted arms reclining on a lotus blossom in the black heart of infinite space except Lotus Blossom is the name of his palatial spaceship and he's standing in it now, admiring yet another hand-crafted world when a thin Filipino man hurtles through the skylight, and crashes into the floor.

"Krishna's tits, who are you?"

"Aghrlsoghssd," Sidd explains.

"Oh, I remember, I was Garbhodakaśāyī, and I threw you into the eternal beyond. Meh. I'm grumpy when I'm Garbhodakaśāyī. How do you like it?" Mahavishnu looks around his spaceship proudly.

"SUeerkads9"

"I know. Gorgeous." Mahavishnu bounces an incandescent orb universe like a basketball then shoots it through the skylight like he's throwing a fade on the court. It rockets out into the infinite recesses of endless multiverses bunched together like grapes as he shouts, "Sports!"

"NaseirHSD*(?"

"Oh yeah, a trip like that will mess you up, son. I was mad. You probably flew through nine or ten iterations of the permanent world before you hit the other side and popped into the ineffable. Which brings me to the inevitable question, how do you like it?"

"Adkjew purdny nice."

"Yeah," Mahavishnu gave Sidd a once over. "You are scrambled, kid. Hang on," Mahavishnu carves out a small closed-loop universe of a Rock Star resort in the Maldives with an unlimited buffet package and sticks Sidd in it for a week, which Mahayaddayadda experiences as a blip then Sidd is back, slightly—*slightly*—tanned and perfectly sober. The Hospitality GM walks out with him.

"Lord Vishnu, thank you for the opportunity to rehabilitate Mr. Ough. Um . . ." The woman looked nervous. "On behalf of the staff, we were wondering if you might consider . . . Um . . ."

"Padma. You can tell me anything. What?"

"Never send him back."

Sidd adjusted his glasses, expressionless as a bored Iguana; he folded his arms across his birdlike chest. Mahavishnu looked disapprovingly at him.

"Siddney Hearth Ough, were you lascivious?" Sidd returned all the regard of chalk board.

"Lord Mahavishnu, it's worse. He kept showing up in the management suite and, well . . ."

"Look, humans are horny little bastards, I'm sorr–"

"No, he's a perfect gentleman. Hell, he's a priest."

"Like I said," Vishnu slowly blew a bubble of a universe out of his open palm.

"He organized."

"Gross."

"Exactly. We're working at peak efficiency. I had to let three people go."

"Go where?"

"How the Hell do I know? We've never done it before, but their position was . . . Crap." She looks at Sidd. "How did you put it again?"

Sidd stared at Mahavishnu.

"Redundant."

"I mean, I should be grateful," said the Hospitality GM, "But we've never *been* efficient. It's kind of our signature thing. We have too many people. We usually have four guys handing out the towels at the pool."

"One to pull a towel off the pile, one to fold it, one to hand it to a guest, one to observe," Mahavishnu chanted as if he'd been to the resort many times. "Classic."

"Now it's self-serve."

"What the fnord?"

"Yeah, nobody running towels. And guests love it. Marvin is raking the gravel paths and Lorraine is looking for a job."

"Ok, just, bring everybody back and I promise I'll never send him in there again. Right Sidd?"

"Lord Mahavishnu, I don't know what is happening. It's not a dream, but neither is it the real." Sidd spoke with a flat voice. "I have slipped beyond the liminal."

Mahavishnu waved the GM into nonexistence. He twiddled his

fingers. "You're not wrong."

Lord Mahavishnu suddenly vibrates, as if the film strip from which he was projected came off its sprocket. He shatters into a crowd of vishnus: merman Vishnu, swarthy dwarf Vishnu, a-man-who-looked-so-much-like-a-lion-that-sometimes-he-was-a-lion-who-looked-an-awful-lot-like-a-man Vishnu, a Vishnu who was mostly turtle, and a kind of steampunk cyberpunk metalpunk robot vishnu. From this group, four respectable Hindu men come forward. One steps up to Sidd absently twirling a flute. From behind him a beautiful woman, Rhada, a manifestation and a lover of Krishna, slides sexily around to sexily lean back sexily against him. Sexily. The god slips an arm around her waist.

"Dearest Krishna, where did you find this being?"

"Yama was causing trouble. I dropped in to put a quit in him. This one was uncausing mayhem. Bad for the brand."

"But my love, can you not see?" She bends down to grab a silver thread spilling across the floor of Mahavishnu's ship directly into Sidd's heart. "He is in love."

"Are you sure?" Krishna, who is only a manifestation of Vishnu as are the other manifested beings. "He doesn't look like he's in love."

"Observe, husband." Rhada pulls the silver cord until Mookie's soul floats into the room, like an inflated, transparent kite. Sidd leaps toward them, eyes glowing with compassionate fury.

"Mooks!" Then, to Rhada. "What did you do to them?! What have you done?"

As they watch, Mookie rolls in slumber. They mumble Sidd's name. Sidd melts. Rhada bats Mookie's avatar away. The silver cord snakes viciously across the floor after them until it pulls tight and drags Sidd forward.

"Wow," Krishna whistles. "You are knee deep in it, aren't you?"

Sidd wipes a tear. "Lord Krishna, I know that I deserve whatever torture this is, but please spare that person, that lovely person, they are pure."

Krishna pulls Rhada tighter against him, leaning down to whisper in her ear. "What should I do? He is outside time."

Rhada pushes him away. "What should you do? Are you not a God? What would you do if we were separated like these two? To whom would you petition? With what passion? How dare you even ask!" She glares pure molten diamonds at Krishna who shudders and dissolves and is Mahavishnu again. He pulls Rhada close, holding her delicate azure fingers. "Rhada, you are right. You are always right. Your compassion reduces me to dust. I am but a–"

"Vish . . . must we?"

"Our marriage counselor said–"

"I am staring at you meaningfully," she says, staring at him meaningfully.

Mahavishnu drops her hand, wraps the silver chord around his fist a few times, then whips it over his head, throwing Sidd earthward with an impossible velocity through the skylight. He bends to kiss Rhada, but she turns her head away (secretly grinning; nothing inflames desire like being turned down). New, impossible worlds drip from his fingers.

Chapter 41

It was a tough day on Doodad Street. The solar wind was lashing through the booths and tents. A vendor's table was overturned, his sign had blown off, and a rumpled, paper-thin Buddhist Episcopalian lay priest had just crashed into the street.

Sidd stood up, dusted himself off. He was livid, which to anyone watching him was indistinguishable from boredom.

He'd had enough. He'd been trying very hard to maintain his cool, but he'd reorganized hell, worked with three different death deities (and post-crucifixion Jesus), had been flung into the Space Ship Mansion of Mahavishnu, and now . . . What? He noticed a dusty old God picking up dusty, familiar looking dusty orbs and trying to deityhandle a fallen dusty hand-lettered sign. Sidd read the words, though they were written in a script that was older than Sanskrit: Mahavishnu's Hand-Crafted Universes and Custom Realities–For Sale. Someone had chalked in 'or lease' at the end, the letters crammed together to fit. Sidd grabbed the sign. There was work everywhere.

"Oh, my, thank you, pleasant being."

"Mahavishnu?"

"Here, take one of my cards." Mahavishnu patted his rumpled, dingy vestments but came up empty.

"I don't mean to complain, but if you're gonna yank me through multiple realities, can I maybe rest up a little—and can we talk about this?" Sidd held up the ghostly silver cord dangling out of his chest.

Mahavishnu stared, grumbling to himself, "Eons . . . silver cord . . . Lakshmi." He clapped his hands and grinned through his dusty blue face. "Sidd Hearth Ough. The priest."

"Lay priest."

"Not my thing, pleasant being, but I can introduce you to Zulie–" Mahavishnu waggled his eyebrows suggestively at a gorgeous middle-aged Haitian woman a couple booths down who was wearing more jewelry than one would think possible and staring at Sidd with a look that made him sweat.

"Lord Vishnu," Sidd hung the sign over the stall then took a seat on an upturned crate. "Where is the Lotus Blossom? What happened to your ship?"

"Sold it."

"To WHO?!"

"I don't remember. Look, times are tough in this version."

"Version? Tough times? You're a GOD! Can you just let me rest in peace so I can forget about Mooks?"

Mahavishnu looked nervous. Sidd was his only customer in a millennium, and he wasn't going to lose him.

"Maybe, maybe not. Look," Mahavishnu handed Sidd a swirling orb universe. "Made this one myself. Order is emphasized so, almost nothing happens. Very peaceful."

"I thought death would be less chaotic."

"Where's the fun in that? Anyway, how'd you end up on the Lotus?"

"I tried to organize–"

"Gross."

"–with Yama and all the other deities. But ultimately they rejected my efforts."

"What do you mean?"

"Just a database. Nothing special."

"What does that do?"

"I reprioritized the damned by their redemption quotient–"

"Their what?"

"I'm sure you use something similar to keep track of all these worlds."

Mahavishnu's stall was mostly unlabeled crates of galaxies piled up into dangerously sagging hills. There were papers and blueprints everywhere. Candy wrappers. A dried-out apple core. His fingertips were stained with ink.

"Tell me more, pleasant being."

***

The gardens were endless. Mookie met eight different versions of Lakshmi and spent what seemed like days and weeks and months sitting by streams, listening to birdsong, making flower necklaces and endlessly fending off Kama's constant fawning. Here he was again.

"Mookie; smoldering, as usual." He notched a golden arrow but didn't aim it anywhere. He'd learned his lesson on that when Mooki had popped him in his nose. Still; old habits.

"What happens when you shoot someone?" Mookie asked.

Kama's face turned deep forest green. "They fall in love."

"I'm already in love."

"Yeah, but it would be more."

"I thought you were a deity."

"I'm on the spectrum."

"Surely you understand love is not quantifiable. You can't love someone just a little."

"Sure you can."

"That's fraternity."

"Love is love."

"Have you ever been in love?" Mookie asked.

Kama accidentally shot his arrow. It sailed out of view, high into the coral-colored clouds then turned. The arrow whistled down into one of the elephants showering Lakshmi. The elephant, Arjunae, had been standing on its hind legs, front feet pressed against the front feet of her partner, Balarmaja, their trunks entwined, for centuries. Suddenly, Arjunae realized the Balarmaja's eyelashes were glossy and lush. It could smell the sweat from behind his ears. She flushed hotly from the tip of her tail to the ends of her ears and scraped a tusk tentatively against Balarmaja's lower lip. He snapped out of his endless fugue with his eyes on fire, burning a hole straight to her heart. They crashed into the underbrush, trumpeting lubriciously, hunkering behind a gargantuan stand of rhododendrons. There was a lot of noise. Lakshmi looked up, suddenly unshowered, and noticed her elephants were gone. She turned to the snorting and the quiet, squealish trumpeting from behind the purple trees then looked back across the garden to her son, Kama, who was ignoring her and talking to Mookie.

"The circus is over when the elephants go home," she quoted quietly to no one. Lakshmi wrinkled her nose bewitchedly and Mooki disappeared. Kama was startled. He saw Lakshmi smirking.

"Mom! Seriously?!" Furious, Kama jumped on his giant chicken and flapped away across the endless beauty of the gardens to sulk and maybe shoot someone.

***

Mahavishnu's orbs were the very illustration of order and organization. A line of customers a mile long snaked up Doodad Street and he was running out of bespoke macrocosms.

He was wearing his new cerulean robes with the star fields from the Magellan Cloud playing in real time. Cost him a fortune. He smelled amazing and his barber had performed absolute magic on his eyebrows. He was transcendent.

Sidd was taking wads of cash, baskets full of moons, a tiny diamond planet, and from one of the Vegetable Gods, a cornucopia stuffed with okra. Mahavishnu's wife, Rhada (who looked suspiciously like Lakshmi), swerved luxuriously into the stall to lean lewdly against Mahavishnu and kiss him on his storm-colored earlobe. She was dressed to complement in robes spun from a peculiar Martian metal which rusted into a purely blood-red shimmer. Mahavishnu glanced at her and swore under his breath; he could count her ribs.

Of course, it was all on credit, but that's ok because everyone could see how he was burning down the market. His stall was the jewel of Doodad street. There were rumors he was going to go brick-and-mortar, but he wouldn't confirm it (of course he was) to the grapevine.

"Sidd, look at this traffic. If I had a god, I would be compelled to utter 'my God,' in joyful shock."

Doodad street was dead center on the shambling edges of Supreme City. Supreme beings of all walks of afterlife strolled (and rolled, and floated, and slunk, and slithered, and apparated) its noisy bazar looking for good deals on new worlds to rule. Mahavishnu had made it all and he was proud of his work.

"Mahavishnu, isn't this a world you made?" Sidd is talking while he organizes a new box of orbs.

"Which one, pleasant being?" Mahavishnu stirs the translucent spheres.

"No, I mean," Sidd waved his arms around. "This."

Mahavishnu looked around as if he'd just noticed where he was. "Looks like one of mine."

"They're all yours, darling," said Rhada.

"I'm trying to wrap my head around this. You make all these worlds and you're selling them in a street market?"

Mahavishnu sagged a little. Goddam cosmologies. Why can't people just accept the liminal and go on with their day? If he didn't play this one right, he'd lose half his line to the exotic fruit vendor. Again. Well, not on his watch.

"How about this one," Mahavishnu grabbed a mini-verse about the size of a baseball and chucked it at Sidd who caught it without even looking. "Nine layers of determinism. You'll love it."

"If you make infinite worlds, why not just make a world where you have everything you need and you live comfortably with a staff and-"

"Are you looking for a nice comfortable universe?" Mahavishnu grabbed a box from under the table marked 'Discount universes—SOLD AS IS! No returns!'

"It's hot and dusty and I just, I can't understand why, I mean we suffer our mortal existence with the understanding that the afterlife will be a lot nicer."

"Ok, look. I have policies on these things. It's not my fault if you don't read them. Caveat emptor-"

"But how are you here when I also saw you luxuriating in your ship?"

"I am in my ship."

"I'm going to explode."

Mahavishnu tossed a warped, lumpy discount universe to Sidd. "What do you think I make these out of? They're all made from me, from my limitless existence, from godstuff. You take a couple of monads and a nested infinity or three, throw in some camels, dip it in the finishing agent, hang it up to dry. It's a process."

"But–"

"So, I'm in each world."

"So, we're in one of the worlds you created?"

"Now you're catching on. You want this one? I mean, it's display only, but I suppose I can part with it–"

"The world we're in right now?!"

"Sure. It can be yours for the low low price–"

"So, you're outside this world making worlds like this one but you're also in this world making more worlds?"

"That I am also in, where I'm making more universes." Mahavishnu shrugged. "It's a living."

"How many—"

"Oh, kid, no. You don't wanna think about that. Let's turn this buffalo around. Look at this little guy–pocket universe. Cute as a bug. I can let it go for . . ." Mahavishnu noticed the world had a deep crack all the way through. He shoved it into his pocket.

"Then why are you running a stall in a dead-end street in a half-baked bazar?"

"This is where the money is."

Sidd shuffles a box full of jade moons and diamond planets. "I guess it's money." While they all stare silently at the loot, a rangy kid slips around the side of the booth. Sidd hands him a book. The kid makes a mark in the book. Sidd initials it. The kid takes the box of loot and disappears.

"Observe, my luminescent lover: he's even developed an ad hoc banking system."

"Well, not banking," Sidd says.

A shining being steps into the stall bearing a small ornate box. "Sidward," Mahavishnu snaps his fingers. "Our first payment is due on the advance." The being seems to leer. It holds the bejeweled box open toward Mahavishnu. You could, if you were the kind of person to always see the negative, think maybe there was a hint of threat in the way the shining creature held the receptacle.

"Pay who?"

"Our debtors."

"Your what?"

"I took out a well-considered loan. Now, pay the man so we can get back to work."

"With what?"

"With–" Mahavishnu laughed. "Well, with all the loot, kid. You've been taking payments hand over fist for three days. I'll need to carve out some new product just to keep up. Use the moola you took in."

"I gave it away."

The being with the box slams the lid closed quite loudly. It suddenly glowers.

"Did what with the who?"

"Lord Mahavishnu, I know you want to help the less fortunate, so I donated all your income to the Church of the Supreme Beings Who are Kind of Not so Supreme Right Now." Sidd opened a ledger which bloomed with slips of paper. "I kept receipts."

"Sidd, why–"

"It is the right thing to do, Lord Mahavishnu. You don't need it–you make worlds to order. Whatever role you're playing in this one is a role you designed. You could make yourself rich, tall, whatever. But you picked a run-down stall on Doodad street. Other gods are not so fortunate. They need our assistance. They need—"

"GAAAAAHHHHH!" Mahavishnu grabbed Sidd by his collar but Rhada—lurid and glowing from within–pushed him away.

"He's mine!" She screamed, grabbing Sidd by his pants and throwing him out of their reality without a care for where he landed.

"Human!" she screamed.

Chapter 42

Christopher Aldous Oh Shit Montgomery sat in a waiting room painted the color of a bored lima bean. On the table before him, magazines were stacked into neat piles. They were all from before he was born. Most were printed in dead languages. One of them was a scroll.

A clock made from brittle black plastic in the shape of a cartoon cat ticked its tail slowly back and forth, though its hideous pupils were perfectly still and seemed to bore into Chris's brain every time he glanced at the thing. It read 4:37. It never changed. He'd been there for hours.

It made sense. He'd clearly suffered some kind of lapse. Some kind of neurological glitch. He'd been having strange dreams. He reached for a magazine. The door opened.

"The Executioner will see you now," a rail-thin man holding a folder waved him through the door.

The office was dark, wood-paneled, luxurious.

"Mr. Montgomery," a woman in a well-tailored suit reached out. Chris shook her hand out of habit. The room was adorned with massive swords, nooses, and on one side of the room, a miniature guillotine.

"For children," the woman said following Christopher's horrified gaze.

"What kind of doctor are you?"

"Is it the magazines? Usually people think I'm a dentist."

"I've been having weird dreams," Christopher said weakly.

"You've also been fucking around with the temporal continuum."

"I'm an apprentice—" Christopher stopped. Was he an apprentice?

"Apprentice. Accomplice. Let's not get technical. You jumped," the woman looked through the papers in the folder the man had laid on the desk. "Eleven times and then you voluntarily–" she looked up at Chris. "Voluntarily," she looked back down, "interrupted a temporal restructuring by stepping into it."

"Wait, that was a dream, that was–"

"We here in Management do not distinguish."

"I can get in trouble for stuff I do in my dreams?"

"If you are asking me if dream sins are still sins then I have to question your education. Yes, of course you can." The woman closed the folder. "But you weren't dreaming so it's worse. Why'd you jump into the breech?"

"To save Mooki."

She opens the folder again, checks the front page. "Morgan Hayden Whitfield."

"Morgan?"

"This person–"

"Ma'am?"

"Yes?"

"I'm getting the impression I'm in some kind of, um . . . That I'm . . . That this is . . ."

"Get to the point, Mr. Montgomery."

"Am I dead?"

"Not quite. This is the exit interview."

"Exit interview?"

"After this, you'll be dead."

"How?"

The woman nodded suggestively at the miniature guillotine. Chris sunk into his chair.

"I have a question."

"Allowed."

"Is Mooki–Morgan–a woman?"

"I'm afraid I cannot say. HYPA rules."

"But, I mean, I'm out, so . . .?"

"I suppose it wouldn't matter a hill of beans at this point. It's not like you're going back." She tabbed a button on a desktop speaker. "Steve, get me the file on Morgan Hayden Whitfield."

Steve walks in with a folder two inches thick. The woman opens it. Reads for a moment. "Looks like Morgan is—"

There is a soft explosion and a horse headed being is suddenly standing in the room. "NEIGH!"

"Shit!" Christopher yells.

"I understand," the woman says to the Horse Headed creature. "but I'm about to lop off his head so what does it matter?"

"NEIGH!"

"It's not like Yama plays by the rules."

"NEIGH! NEIGH!"

"He is here voluntarily. I'm following the rules to the letter–to the letter–so yes he is supposed to be here."

"Neigh," Horse Head neighs menacingly.

"Not on my watch!" The woman lunges for a scimitar then, snarling, swings it at Christopher's neck as the Horse Faced being leans a staff toward Chris but Chris is standing in Millennium park.

Chapter 43

Ovales Calvarium moved a pinky. He shrugged, lying face down on the damp terrazzo of the Tardigrade Lab, and groaned.

Heller poked him with the toe of his boot.

"You in there kid?" Heller popped a Blue Tip into his grim smile.

"Glurrgh"

"I still believe medical attention may be in order," Crane said. "Herbert?"

His AIDE DE CAMP dropped down beside Ovales and opened a medical kit. He rolled Ovales over. Everyone gasped. Ovales' eyes slammed open.

"Wad? Wad ham end? Wide He'er here? Wide er you all daring at me as ib sum ding truly horrimle hab hammened that nigh'm nona ware ub mecause nigh gan't loog in a meer?"

Herbert held up a small mirror. Ovales stared into it silently, noting how his nose, previously prominent and beakish, was now laid entirely sideways, still prominent, in a way, still beakish, in a way, but pressed tightly against his right cheek.

"Nigh gant feel id," he said, reaching up to prod his proboscis.

Herbert batted his hand. Then Ovales gasped and sat up, knocking Herbert over. "Nuh nar ni grabs!"

"Just lay back down," Heller said. "You're in no shape for heroics. The butler–"

"Aide de camp," Herbert grumbled.

"–froze them with a boomstick."

"No, no, no . . . Oh no. No." Ovales sank down onto the cold floor. Herbert smoothed a bandage on a cut and turned to Heller.

"Mr. Heller if you'd be so kind as to hold this gentleman's ankles. Octavia, his elbows, please." Herbert took a tight grip on Ovale's schnozz.

"Don'd fig my nose. DON'D FIG MY–"

There was a terrific crackling, as if a furious chef had twisted a full bunch of celery stalks until they all snapped while beside him his equally livid sous chef cracked a fistful of dry breadsticks. Ovales screamed.

Heller turned his powerful glare at Crane.

"The fuck just happened, Crane? You're the damn CEO, you designed all this crap. Where the fuck's my customer? Where is Mooki? Where is my goddam apprentice?!"

Crane leaned a millimeter forward and slid one shoe up his leg to balance it against the opposite knee, a pose he took when he was thinking on his foot.

"It seems our loop breach suffered from a wee smidgen of recursive liminal feedback."

Heller, his face now sporting the beginnings of a well-after-five-o'clock-shadow, silver and white bristles standing out on his caramel leathery cheeks, leaned so close into Crane's face the blue tip of the Blue Tip almost touched the blue tip of Crane's avian nose. "You wanna run that by me again?"

"The loop breach became entangled in its own loop then repeated that over and over, like a poorly timed microphone test at a musical concert."

"Where are they?" Octavia growled. She stepped up behind Crane, automatically teaming up with Heller which Heller definitely noticed though he was busy, so he didn't have a lot of time to think about it, but she didn't hesitate at all. They were a team. His heart bobbed briefly in its cradle, but Heller left it alone. Work. Work. Work.

"I have no idea. If I understand a feedback breech well enough, they would have stepped into a standing timeline wave then stayed with it when we slipped into another one."

"Boss, I got this one sale. This one last sale and I'm out. You know how hard I've worked for this?" Heller said. "You tell me-right now-how to find my mark, rescue his sweetheart, and get my partner back."

"It is impossible."

"We had impossible for lunch," Octavia whispered. "Try harder."

"Ib you pland a marger, you ca drag him acrodd time lides," Ovales says gingerly nudging his gnarled nozzle.

"They're already gone!" Heller yells.

"Doe? Go bag."

Ovales cuts a glance at Crane who pretends to ignore what Ovales just said.

"Go back where?" Heller asks.

"Or when?" Octavia adds.

"I men go bag."

Herbert ahemmed in a way that meant, to Crane: Sir, perhaps now is the time to advance our associates to the next level.

"Are you telling me, kid, we can go back in time? Because my training explained—it explicitly taught me—that time travel is not an option.”

“Well, strictly speaking,” Crane said, “the training means it’s not an option, for *you.*”

Heller glared a perfectly blank glare at Crane that indicated he realized he was probably not going to get that bonus Platinum package after all, that he had somehow screwed everything up magnificently, and had very, very little, here at the agreed-upon final days of his career at Transluminal Vacations, Inc., to lose. Crane understood. He also took a discreet step backward.

“It isn’t recommended except in emergencies,” Crane said.

“THIS QUALIFIES!” Octavia barked.

“Right, well, of course. It can cause all kinds of technical problems and chronologically, it isn’t particularly sound. But you can, if you need to, jump sideways but also backward and forward from one timeline to another.”

“How far back?”

“Theoretically? Infinitely. But the effect on your mind and body is significant. I’ve only been able to go a couple of weeks and it was agonizing.”

“You seem fine.”

“Neither Herbert nor I could detect any irregularities on our return. But, again, we were performing short trips. A minute, an hour. It took me a full day to go back a week. It’s not easy.”

“Take us back to ten minutes ago so we can stop Sidd and Mookie and Chris from coming into the lab,” Heller said.

“Or maybe take us here, right before the breech so like the breech doesn’t happen, numbnuts!?” Octavia smacked Heller in the shoulder. Really, hard, he noted. But also, warmly, if that’s possible.

Herbert ahemmed again. This one was complex. He meant, by

clearing his throat, that Crane should stop being so inscrutable and just bring them on board entirely and explain all the problems with temporal locality shifts and how no matter how much you want to stay in the same thread, it is fundamentally terrifying and likely to result in spontaneous nipple inversion and sentient toes.

"If you go back in a timeline, you can't return to your point of origin. You can go all over the place around it, immediately adjacent, 24 hours later, etcetera, etcetera, etcetera."

Heller looked at Octavia for a moment and thought about how she looks with her hair in a bun.

"We can save them?"

"More or less."

Octavia growled and took off her shoe and threw it at Crane's head. "Tu caremonda! Tu pinche hijueputa! Culicagedo GÜVON! PUTA!"

Herbert catches the shoe in midair, an inch from his boss's face. He clears his throat once again, this time meaning, simply, *she's right, you know.*

"It is absurdly perilous," Crane says languidly. As if he's talking about how he likes his coffee.

"Send us." Octavia slips her arm through Heller's and something in his heart blooms like a distant star.

"I can't even be sure–"

Octavia snarls, reaches for her other shoe. Crane snaps his fingers and they disappear.

Chapter 44

The five of them land one by one on the bricks by Buckingham Fountain. It's too weird for them to process so they just stand there looking at each other until Octavia screams.

"What the fuck are we gonna do now, School!?"

"Sidd!" Mooki goes to hug the beanpole Buddhist but Chris steps into their path.

"Mooki, I was so worried!" He says. "I jumped after you!"

"That was very sweet." Mooki flops their arms weakly around Christopher Aldous Doesn't Realize this is a Brush Off Montgomery. Chris nearly crushes their ribcage. They look for Sidd over Chris's shoulder. They try to peel Chris off but it's too late, Sidd's up in Heller's face, railing at him in his impeccably polite, incredibly fierce way. Mooki calls it Monk Mode.

"What have you done to us, Mr. Heller?" Heller knows he's in for it so he just takes fire from the priest with as much dignity as he can preserve. "We were fine. We were getting work done. We were feeding people, Mr. Heller, feeding hungry people. Now what the hell are we—" Sidd smolders. "What are we doing? I've been—in the last couple of hours, I have been in some seriously peculiar situations. I did not request these lessons, Mr. Heller. What do you have to say about that?"

"Well, the fucknusual thing about that is—"

Mooki let's Heller drone on in his homespunness but they're watching Sidd and they're seeing what no one else can see. His remarkable self-control is in riot mode. He's almost vibrating with anger. He is in danger and Mooki knows he won't accept any help. They could throw him a rope, cut into the conversation, pour some metaphorical water on the fire but that only works when things are normal, not when he's furious—and he is furious.

"I walked into the lab to stop this thing so Mooki and I could get back to our work."

It's that inclusion that gets them—*Mooki and I.* They're not made of stone. They're not made out of steel. And they graduated with honors and they actually did finally finish college, cumma sum in philosophy even, to hopefully help them build a frame around their heart to protect it and here they are wanting to build a rollcage around Sidd's because this fury will wreck that delicate instrument.

"But instead," Sidd takes odd moments to pause when he's mad. They never make sense. They aren't calculated, they are indicative of his effort to control himself and weirdly timed, so they tend to alarm, and Heller has taken a step back which Mooki knows Sidd has noticed which makes it worse. "Instead, I landed in hell, Mr. Heller. Actual hell with the Hindu lord of the dead where I had to work, Mr. Heller. There were souls to minister. I spent weeks talking to them—"

"You were gone for five minutes."

"—And it was uncomfortable. I met gods, Heller. Gods."

Mooki explodes into sniffles. Tears leap off the high ridges of their cheekbones to die valiantly on the toes of their shoes. Sidd doesn't notice. Mooki can see him hardening and their heart folds in on itself.

Which Christopher Aldous I will Save You Montgomery doesn't understand. He attributes them to Heller's meddling—accurate—and, like any frat boy capable of eight or nine nano seconds of sustained reason, he stalks over to Heller, rips the watch off his arm, grips the bezel to twist them all out of there, then fumbles and drops it into a sewer grate.

"Oh shit."

"WHAT THE FUCK DID YOU DO?"

"Mooki's crying!"

They crouch next to the grate.

"How deep is it?"

Chris presses his face against the grate. "Maybe 20 feet?"

"Jesus Fuckwardian Christ! We're screwed. Ok. Goddammit. Ok."

"This is exactly what I meant, Heller." Sidd is still on fire. Heller looks painfully at him then notices everyone is alarmingly crustaceous.

"Aw shit," Heller says. "Aw shit. Listen," he gathers them together. "The watch is too far way. The temporal bubble can't hold us. It's about to snap. The breach will probably wash over us any second now."

"Heller what the goddam fuck?!" Octavia is livid. Scared.

"Just . . . Everybody stay calm."

"What happens when it goes over us?" Chris asks.

"It keeps going," Octavia says. She glowers at Heller. "And we stay here."

"Everyone crowd onto the grate!" Chris says. Everyone except Mooki scooches together trying to fit on the tiny metal square. Mooki's frozen in place, her antennae vibrating with alarm.

"Mr. Heller?" Everyone turns to Mooki. They are turning into a giant crustacean.

"CHITTER CHITTER CHITTER CHIT CHIT CHITTY!?"

"CHITTER CHITTER CHITTER CHIT," Heller holds up a claw, "CHIT."

"CHITTER CHITTER CHITTER?" Chris panics.

"CHITTER CHITTER CHITTER CHIT CHIT CHITTY CHITTER CHITTER CHITTER CHIT CHIT CHITTY CHITTER CHITTER CHITTER CHIT CHIT CHITTY CHITTER CHITTER CHITTER CHIT CHIT CHITTY CHITTER CHITTER CHITTER CHIT CHIT CHITTY CHIT.

"CHIT CHITTY CHITTER CHITTER CHITTER?" Sidd growls.

"CHITTY CHITTER CHITTER! CHITTY CHITTER CHITTER!"

"CHITTY CHITTER CHITTER, CHITTY," Octavia says.

"CHITTY CHITTER CHITTER CHITTY CHITTER CHITTER CHITTY CHITTER CHITTER CHIT CHIT CHITTY CHIT CHITTER CHITTER CHITTY CHITTER CHITTER CHITTY CHITTER CHITTER CHIT-"

"CHIT."

—CHITTY CHITTER CHITTER CHITTY CHITTER CHITTER CHIT."

"CHITTY CHITTER CHITTER," Sidd says.

"CHIT. CHIT. CHIT. CHIT. CHIT!?" Chris enunciates, his antennae wavering.

"CHITTY CHITTER CHITTER CHITTY CHITTER," Octavia says.

"CHITTER CHIT—" Said Christopher Adler Serve with Drawn Butter Montrose. "CHITTY CHITTER CHITTER CHITTY CHITTER!"

"CHITTY CHITTER CHITTER!" Heller yells.

"CHITTER CHIT!?" Chris disbelieves.

"CHITTY CHITTER CHITTER CHIT!"

"CHIT CHIT CHITTY CHIT CHIT!" The foursome of crustaceans turn to look at Mooki who has their claws up on either side of their carapace in the universal sign of I may have this figured out so would you please shut up for a minute? "Chitter chit"

"CHITTER, CHITTY," Octavia skitters closer to Mooki. "CHITTER CHITTER CHITTY CHITTER CHITTER CHITTY CHITTER CHITTER CHIT CHIT CHITTY CHIT CHITTER CHITTER CHITTY CHITTER CHITTER CHITTY CHITTER CHITTER CHIT CHITTER CHITTER CHITTY CHITTER CHITTER CHITTY CHITTER CHITTER CHIT CHIT CHITTY CHIT CHITTER CHITTER CHITTY CHITTER CHITTER CHITTY CHITTER CHITTER CHIT—"

"CHITTER CHITTER."

"—CHITTER CHITTER CHITTY CHITTER CHITTER CHITTY CHITTER CHITTER CHIT CHIT CHITTY CHIT CHITTER CHITTER CHITTY CHITTER CHITTER CHITTY CHITTER CHITTER CHIT CHIT CHITTER."

"CHITTER CHITTER CHIT. CHIT CHIT CHITTER. CHIT CHITTY CHIT CHITTER CHITTER CHITTY CHITTER CHITTER CHITTY CHITTER CHITTER."

"CHIT, CHITTY CHIT," says Ocvtavia, unimpressedly.

"CHITTY CHITTER?" Chris says.

"CHIT CHITTY CHIT CHITTER," Sidd adds. "CHIT CHITTY CHIT CHITTER CHITTER CHITTY CHITTER CHITTER CHITTY CHITTER CHITTER CHIT CHI." He looks at Mooki. "CHIT CHITTY CHIT CHITTER CHITTER CHITTY CHITTER CHITTER CHITTY CHITTER CHITTER CHIT CHI. CHITTY. CHIT . . . CHIT."

Mooki feels the sudden regard of patriarchal priviledge looming at them like a beam in the dark and they reject it. "CHIT CHITTY CHIT CHITTER CHITTER CHITTY?"

"CHIT CHIT?" Octavia whips around. "CHIT CHITTY CHIT CHITTER CHITTER?"

"CHITTER?" Chris raises a claw.

"CHIT CHIT, CHIT." Heller tries to take a matchstick out of his shirt pocket, but his giant claw doesn't get anywhere near it.

"CHIT CHITTN'T—" Sidd flounders.

"CHIT. CHIT CHITN'T," Mooki says. Disappointed. Dry eyed. "CHIT CHITTY CHIT CHITTER CHITTER CHITTY CHITTER CHITTER CHITTY CHITTER CHITTER CHIT CHITTY CHIT."

"CHIT CHITTED CHIT CHIT CHIT."

"CHITLY, CHIT."

"CHIT CHIT CHIT, CHIT CHIT CHITTER CHIT CHIT"

"CHIT, CHITTER, I think I—" Chris says.

"CHIT! CHITTER!"

"CHIT CHITTY CHIT CHITTER CHITTER CHITTY CHITTER CHITTER CHITTY CHITTER CHITTER CHIT CHITTY CHIT."

"CHITTY CHIT," Sidd gulps.

"CHIT, CHIT." Octavia snaps.

"CHIT CHIT CHIT CH—"

"CHIT, CHITTER CHITTY CHITT. CHITS."

"CHIT CHITTY CHIT CHITTER CHITTER CHITTY CHITTER CHITTER CHITTY CHITTER CHITTER CHIT—"

"CHITTER!"

"CHIT CHITTY CHIT CHITTER CHITTER CHITTY CHITTER," Octavia says. She tries to throw a claw around Mooki, but it won't work. "CHITTER. CHITTER CHITT CHIT?"

"CHIT CHITTY CHIT CHITTER CHITTER CHITTY CHITTER CHITTER CHITTY CHITTER CHITTER CHIT CHI—"

"CHIT CHITTY CHIT CHIT CHI!" Chris yells.

Everyone skitters around.

"CHIT, CHIT. CHIT. CHIT CHIT CHIT CHIT."

"CHIT CHIT CHIT CHITTER CHIT?!"

"CHITTER, CHITTER."

Heller tries again to reach into his pocket, stretched tight over his chitin.

"CHIT CHIT CHIT CHIT!"

Octavia skitters over and tries.

"CHITTER CHITS! CHIT CHIT CHIT CHIT CHITTER!"

"CHIT CHITS CHIT!" Chris yells.

"CHITTER CHITTER CHITTER—" Heller complains.

"CHIT!" Sidd warns too late.

Chris slices open Heller's pocket with his foreclaw. The spare watch and a box of Ohio Blue Tips tumbles out onto the ground. The box falls right through the gate. The watch bounces once then stops at the edge, like a golf ball teetering on the brink of a hole in one.

"CHIT CHIT CHITTY!"

Everyone dives for the watch, but they can't pick it up because of their claws.

"CHIT CHIT CHIT CHIT CHITS!" Chris yells.

Octavia skitters around and gets one of her legs behind the watch and flicks it out onto the sidewalk. Everyone dives again. Carapaces crunch. There is a tangle of Chitin. The watch skids across the pavement.

"CHITTER CHIT CHIT CHIT!" Mooki, though chitinous and lobster-like, glowers with the light of authority. Everyone stops.

"CHIT CHITTY CHIT CHITTER CHITTER CHITTY CHITTER CHITTER CHITTY CHITTER CHITTER CHIT CHICHIT CHITTY CHIT CHITTER CHITTER CHITTY CHITTER CHITTER CHITTY CHITTER CHITTER CHIT CHI CHIT CHITTY CHIT CHITTER CHITTER CHITTY CHITTER CHITTER CHITTY CHITTER CHITTER CHIT CHI!⁶"

He slips. He slips again. They almost drop it. But finally, it works. Reality roils.

---

6 "I CAN'T GET IT!"
Octavia skitters over and tries.
"[COLUMBIAN] FUCKING CLAWS! I CAN'T GET IT EITHER!"
"RIP HIS SHIRT!" Chris yells.
"It's a fucking Guayabera—" Heller complains.
"WAIT!" Sidd warns too late.
Chris slices open Heller's pocket with his foreclaw. The watch and a box of Ohio Blue Tips tumbles out onto the ground. The box falls right through the gate. The watch bounces once then stops at the edge, like a golf ball teetering on the brink of a hole in one.
"FUCK CHOKE MOUNTAIN!"
Everyone dives or the watch, but they can't pick it up because of their claws.
"USE YOUR LEGS!" Chris yells.
Octavia skitters around and gets one of her legs behind the watch and flicks it out onto the sidewalk. Everyone dives again. Carapaces crunch. There is a tangle of Chitin. The watch skids across the pavement. "EVERYBODY BE COOL!" Mooki, though chitinous and lobster like, glowers with the light of authority. Everyone stops.
"Heller lie down and put one leg on the watchband. Sidd, do the other one. Push them together!" The watch bands scrunch up raising the watch off the pavement. "Octavia, slip the tip of your foreclaw under it. Everyone hold tight and stand up slowly. Yeah, like that. Now move apart just a little to stretch it tight. Yeah. Now, Chris, use just the tippiest tips of your claw and spin that fucking dial!

Chapter 45

"Ariadne was the daughter of Minos. She volunteered to accompany the youths sacrificed to the Minotaur and brought a roll of red thread with her. She tied it off at the beginning then after Theseus killed the minotaur, the youths followed her thread to get out of the maze. It's a metaphor for logical problem solving by exhausting every possible solution and keeping track of your efforts."

"I JUST WANT MY RETIREMENT PACKAGE!" Heller, ordinarily a column of calm, has had it. He hates being a crab and he hates putting people in actual danger and he hates not knowing what's going to happen, even though he navigates random timeline jumps for a living, and most of all he hates looking like a jackass in front of Octavia, which has happened far too many times for his comfort. And is happening again. Which makes it worse.

"Oh, you want your retirement package? You want the Platinum Package, abuela? That's what we're doing here? Cause I thought we were trying to get everybody back to base. I want to get home to my dog and maybe watch a little Telemundo then go to bed. I am personally exhausted from managing this fucking tragedy and trying to save these—look at them, they didn't ask for this. We're fucking their life all the way up, we turned them into seafoodand almost left them there, and now we're lost in a goddam throw rug of alternate reality threads— there's no guarantee we're gonna find our way home, you know—"

"What?"

"—but whatever, that's not important, what matters here is you might—and I would like to stress the maximum goddam level of uncertainty there—might not get your fucking retirement gift?"

"What do you mean we might not find our way home?" Sidd asks.

"We have my watch," Chris points out.

Heller stands like a rickety old man with his hands on his hips trying to work out an apology, but it won't come. The truth is in its way.

"It's uncalibrated."

"So?"

"It doesn't know where to go. If I spin that thing again, we could end up anywhere. Frankly, I don't know how we managed to drop into a timeline that's so normal."

One of the buildings arches it's back and sneezes.

"See what I mean?" Heller says.

"Isn't it always random?" Chris asks.

"Not for us. We're given a watch calibrated to the client's temporal footprint. So, yeah, it's random, but it's limited random."

"Limited—" Sidd is beside himself with indignant disbelief. "Limited random? What kind of low ganja bullshit is this?"

"There is a finite number of possible timelines—"

"Finite infinity? You're fucking with my cosmology, Mr. Heller. You're telling me we're in a determinate indeterminate universe?"

"I'm telling you that the infinite universe is complex enough to contain models of itself which are determinate."

"Which are . . . What?" Sidd says.

"Fixed. Restricted. Circumscribed."

Octavia snorts. "Why were you gonna give him a watch? We didn't even hire him yet, he's an intern." She snatches the watch out of his hand. "Where did you get this thing?"

"Ganked it off Rose's desk when she wasn't looking."

"Heller." Octavia slips the watch onto her wrist. She punches Heller hard in his shoulder. "You dumb fuck, this is Rose's watch—The Manager's Special Device from the handbook. It's like a janitor's key. It goes to all the timelines."

"Oh hell," Heller smiles.

"We're saved!"

"Are we?" Sidd says flatly. Mooki realizes he's using the voice he uses when he's raced ahead of class and solved the problem and everyone else is doing it wrong and he's disgusted by their stupidity. "We're right back where we were two seconds ago."

"You want to mansplain that for me, skinny jeans?" Octavia is having none of his shit. Mooki grins.

"Being able to go anywhere is merely agency. We still have to know how to get home. Where to go. If her watch is calibrated for every timeline—"

"It's not calibrated for any timeline," Heller says.

"We have all the keys," Chris says.

"But we don't know which door they're for," Octavia finishes.

"We can figure that out." Mooki says. "That's exactly what Ariadne's thread is for. We're not lost in a bundle of timelines, we're in a maze."

Octavia curses quietly to herself in colorful Columbian. She sits down on a bench which thanks her. She jumps up.

"Fuck!" She holds out the watch like she's never used one before. "I never used one of these things," she says. "Everybody get over here. I need a place to sit down that won't talk to me." They gather around her. "Here's what I know from training: spin it this way," Octavia whirls her fingers clockwise," and you can go to any timeline. This way," she waggles her fingertip counter-clockwise, "This way resets the whole world." Octavia looks at everyone looking down at her. She spins the dial.

Chapter 46

The world whirls and they're in the 1970s Chicago again.

Mooki throws her hands out to their sides, palms out.

"We need stationery!"

"We need what?" Chris says. Sidd runs into traffic.

"Sidd!" Heller yells. Mooki looks past him to an office supply store across Michigan avenue. They break into a run after Sidd. As they run across the street, the Magnificent Mile fractures around them, the long flared fenders of the 70s cars at the red-light crackling into the high arched fender wells of gaslight carriages, then the carriages stutter into palanquins held aloft by bewigged sweaty footmen, who morph into giant, fat balloon tires in a cartoon, which pops into a wide dirt road peppered with Ben Franklinesque Chicagoans. They burst through the quaint door into a quaint shoppe stuffed to its quaint ass eaves with quaint. Chris skids to a stop at an open box of quill pens. Sidd is stuffing parchment folios into a sack.

"Quills!? QUILLS!"

"Wait!" Sidd says, everyone looks at him as he stands frozen in his knickers and his felt hat. The store sags and resets into black and white. Bebop jazz floats out of the speakers. Mooki's holding a fist full of ballpoint pens. Sidd has two mini legal pads in his hands. Heller pushes them out the door as he pops a business card on the counter.

"Send the bill to my office."

The world shifts through three crustaceous timelines.

"Fucknificent," Heller says wearily. "New problem. The cycle is narrowing down. Lot of crabs. If we don't get out of this thing quick, we're gonna end up with the frozen shrimp."

They hunch together on the sidewalk outside the store. Mooki snatches a legal pad from Sidd, slams it down onto the top of a metal newspaper box with a loud boom. They click their pen then draw a logic array like a giant chess board. They slam the other pad down and draw a target like a dart board. In the bullseye, they draw an X.

"Octavia, this is our target timeline. You and Heller use your experience to make a map. Sidd," Sidd's already next to Mooki. They look at each other. Mooki barely suppresses a grin.

Sidd says. "We follow the string."

"We follow the string." Mooki looks at Heller. "You ready?"

Heller spins. They land in a world that's all fire. The notebooks incinerate.

"Fuckalicious." Heller spins again. The notebooks are back. They're naked. They instantly turn their backs. Sidd was looking at Octavia when they landed and he turned toward Christopher Aldous My God, Seriously? Really? Montgomery as they tried to hide from each other so even now, even in this remarkable moment he doesn't know Mooki's secret. Ah but he wants to know. He could just whip around and look. They're right there next to him smoldering in their embarrassment, a thousand degrees of heat radiating off their body. But he won't. He doesn't.

Heller and Octavia are the only ones who didn't turn around. They're both looking right at each other. Heller is embarrassed as hell. Octavia almost grins.

"What, School—you never seen a naked woman before?"

Heller rattles a match around an impish grin.

"I thought I had."

Octavia blushes.

"Fucking spin the fucking watch already Heller" Octavia smiles.

The world flips. They're reclothed.

As Heller dials them in and out of timelines, and as the camera of the story whirls around them, and as the background reality melts and shimmers and shunts through its infinite iterations, Sidd and Mooki fill in the boxes of the chart. Heller and Octavia write single word titles for each one–pigs, RED, angles, horses, bubbles. As the pages fill up with scribbles, the words on Octavia's pad get closer and closer to the middle.

"Heller!" She holds up the pad. They are one ring away from the bulls eye.

"Mr. Heller," Sidd is staring down into their logic array. "Are the iterations contiguous?"

"Like trees in a park, Sidd."

"Why not just go tree to tree?"

"If the tech department sets it up like that, sure. But unless they drop a map into your watch, it's a crap shoot. Like lighting fireworks in midair. You have no idea where they're going to go."

"But, if we see patterns here, then those realities are like—"

"—the same species of trees—" Mooki finishes.

"—so if we can follow the line to the middle—"

"We get home." Mooki says.

Everyone looks down at the map. Octavia jabs a perfectly manicured nail onto the word RED on the outer circle.

"Red," then she traces it to the next circle, almost all the way around to the word PINK. "Pink."

Heller touches the word ORANGE in the next circle with the dry blue tip of a new match.

"Orange," he says.

Sidd points to the next inner circle at the word FUSCIA. "Extra pink," he says. Then they all follow Mooki's pen as Mooki draws a line from Fuscia to a word on the edge of the most inner circle.

"Rose," they whisper.

"Ok, but how do we . . . How can we . . ." Octavia erupts into lurid Colombian. "I'm still mad at you, School!"

"We do make a great team."

"We ain't home yet, Junkyard." Octavia looks at Mooks.

"What do we do?"

"We compute the nodes—" Mooki says to herself.

"—divide by the total number of iterations—" Sidd says to himself.

"—plot the frequency scatter of red timelines—"

"—and where they were on the dial—"

"—then we just . . ." Mooki looks up at Sidd.

"Count." He says. They high five. Miss by a mile. Try to recover and accidentally hold hands for a nano-second.

"It's eleven." Heller says. Everyone looks at him. "What? I'm a fucking professional."

They all crowd around Heller as the world around them becomes a blur of antennae and claws. Heller puts his fingers on the dial. Octavia shifts to bump her hip up against Heller's. Mooki gently folds their fingers into Sidd's. Heller turns the dial and counts under his breath.

"... Nine, ten, eleven." He looks up at everyone, releases the bezel, and the world disappears.

Chapter 47

CREDITS: PRESS JUNKET—"THREADBARE—THE MAKING OF THE PLATINUM-LEVEL TRANSLUMINAL VACATION PACKAGE OF YOUR DREAMS"
HOST:

I'm here with the Whitfield twins, Morgan and Marin, who play the break-out character Mooki in *The Platinum-Level Transluminal Vacation Package of Your Dreams*. Morgan, what was it like playing a non-binary character?

MARIN

I'm Marin.

HOST

Mea culpa.

Turns to Morgan

HOST

Morgan?

MORGAN

That's your first question?

HOST

Sorry?

MORGAN

There's so much about this story that's vital–

MARIN

Vital.

MORGAN

–To the general public. We have billionaires paying billions–

MARIN

Billions.

MORGAN

–And reality hacking from timeline to timeline looking for the one where they make bank. It affects everyone.

MARIN

When they jump we all jump.

MORGAN

And you're first question is about being non-binary?

HOST

You are fraternal twins, correct?

MARIN

Here we go.

MORGAN

Billions.

HOST

Which one of you is male?

Marin detaches their microphone. Walks off the set grumbling.

HOST

We submitted these questions to your PR team. No surprises here. People are curious.

MORGAN

That's just it though. People are curious. The whole point of being non-binary is to reject that very curiosity. It's nobody's business.

HOST

Your voice is kind of husky. Are you a man?

MARIN

(off stage)

Are you!?

MORGAN

(sighing)

The important takeaway from *Transluminal* is that there is technology allowing anyone to visit adjacent timelines. There are valuable implications for, well, everyone. We could collect best practices from a nearly infinite bundle of horological threads until we—

HOST

It says in your one-sheet the reason producers cast you both is specifically because you are fraternal, and they wanted to keep the audience guessing. Is it

true the make out scenes had the male paired with
D.J. Avalanche who plays Christopher Aldous Hot
Shit Montgomery?

MORGAN

—So, we can apply them here to solve seemingly
unsolvable problems. But we can't because the tech
is privately owned and the company charges literally
eight billion dollars annually for each–

HOST

You have a very strong jaw. Come on, it's you,
isn't it?

A thin Filipino man dressed in black skinny jeans and a matching
shirt appears nearby. There is some commotion as the crew scrambles to
react. They try to frame the guy in the shot.

SIDD

Mooks?

MORGAN

Sidd!

HOST

The love interest. Mr. Ough, you played yourself
in *The Platinum-Level Transluminal Vacation Package
of Your Dreams*. Does it bother you that in your make-
out scenes with Morgan, you were kissing a man?

SIDD

Make out scenes?

Sidd looks around at the lighting rigs, the cameras, the crew.

SIDD

Where are we?

                    MORGAN

I don't know, baby. I don't know. I was with
Lakshmi in the gardens and Kama was hitting on me
then we were crabs–

                     SIDD

Lakshmi?

                    MORGAN

Right? She's a legit goddess. Sidd. So much—. I
thought I lost you.

                     SIDD

I was in hell?

                    MORGAN

I was in heaven?

                     HOST

Mr. Ough, can you just tell us–

                     SIDD

This is a press junket.

                    MORGAN

I just kind of showed up.

                    MARIN

(offstage)

He's cute!

                     SIDD

(noticing Marin)

Holy shit.

                    MORGAN

Apparently, I'm twins.

                      251

                    SIDD

No, you're not. It's some kind of transluminal
ground hogging trick. This guy's probably a lesser
deity or something.

                    HOST

I'm in SAG...

                   MORGAN

Lakshmi thinks you're cute too.

                    SIDD

I never . . . I don't . . .

                   MARIN

(offstsage)

Kiss him already!

                   MORGAN

Shut up!

                    SIDD

How do we get out?

                   MORGAN

No idea.

                    HOST

Mr. Ough, we have three minutes left in the
interview. Can you describe the scene from the movie
where you, Morgan, and D.J. Avalanche disappear–

                    SIDD

You disappeared?

                   MORGAN

I ran after you.

                              SIDD

Mooks.

                            MORGAN

Couldn't help it.

                              SIDD

Are we dead?

Sidd looks around the studio and sees HELLER and OCTAVIA
offstage drinking takeout coffee.

                              SIDD

Hat!

                            HELLER

(in a thick English accent)

Right, he's meshuggenah.

                            OCTAVIA

(Same Columbian accent)

Are we still doing the press thing because this
looks a lot like a shit show. Angela!

Octavia drops her coffee into a can and confers with her agent.

HELLER

(thick English accent)

Oi. That's kidney punch, that is.

Octavia looks out at MORGAN and SIDD

                            OCTAVIA

Morgs! Sidd! We're out.

They tear off their mikes. Walk out a side door.

Chapter 48

George had to push the lodge door open with his shoulder. The bottom edge scraped along the frozen floor.

The first level was floor-to-ceiling snow drifts. Ice hung from the low-slung roof beams. He wrenched open the door to the stairs, made his way to the lodge room proper on the second floor, and there, between two glistening banks of snow sat Frank.

"Brother Frank?"

"Password."

"Frank, it's been the end of the world for like three years. Have you been here the whole time?"

"I am the door keeper. I keep the door." Frank's voice was dry as an arctic wind.

"Frank, half the Brothers are dead. The other half are lost out in the wilds. The Uppy Downies rode through town on giant copepods. Part of this building is missing—they just swallowed it whole, Frank. Go home."

Frank turned bleary eyespots toward George. His lower arms hung limp. One middle arm still gripped a rusty sword. He wore his formal Door Keeper's uniform with its breastplate and its mail. His papillae drooped on either side of his muzzle, gray and nearly transparent with age. He looked like an ancient knight.

"Let me show you what it is that we protect, neophyte."

Frank trudged through the doors into the open lodge room between sloping hills of silver snowdrifts, past the rows of seats, onto the dais, stopping behind the Big Chair in the Front. He sheathed his rusty sword then put his bony shoulder plates to the Big Chair and shoved. It moved an inch, but it moved enough for George to see that beneath the chair, instead of a floor, was a dark open space. He kicked the big chair with two legs and it fell over. The dark open space had steps. He looked at Frank.

"Too many for me, neophyte—"

"I am a Fifteenth Magnitude—"

"You are a neophyte. A zygote. Larval," Frank glared. "But at the bottom of those steps lies the Chamber of the Mystic Toggle."

"That's just mumbo jumbo for the new guys—"

"NO! *It's real!* It is the final task which befalls the Guy in the Big Chair in Front before he transitions from a Neophyte to a true Master of the Sash."

"Yeah, ok, well let's take a look." George steps down one step. Frank grabs his arm.

"Many have gone before you. Not all have returned."

"Honestly, you old guys and your mystic degrees. Just wait here, Franky old Boy. George will sort it out."

He descended. Step by step he dropped deeper and deeper into the dark. The stairwell turned and twisted until he didn't know which way he was going. Soon, a faint blue glow showed far at the bottom and as he decended it became the outline of an arched door, ancient and worn, with runes carved above in the secret code of the Most Supreme Chancellery of Exalted Brethren of the A.C.O.T.A.S. It said:

BEWARE THE BIG BUTTON ON THE WALL!

The faint light came from millions of luminescent florae who flashed bright purple in his wake as George drifted across the room to discover a massive toggle. It was bigger than he was! Carved, legend told him, from a single lobe of ancient turquoise gravel. It jutted from an ornate escutcheon bearing the word *proelium* above and beneath it, *libero*. George's ancient Mosspiglatin was pretty bad, but that didn't matter because his high school history teacher–who always wore the ring of the Supreme Chancellery, now that George thought about it— had those words written around the light switch in their classroom. Activate and Disengage. On. Off.

Chapter 49

The crew gathers on a sidewalk in downtown Chicago outside the studio. Heller pops a Blue Tip into his mouth. "Something feels weird."

Christopher Aldous Almost Beheaded Montgomery skids to a stop right next to them.

"Jesus, Heller, is this part of my training?" The kid dusts himself off. Smiles at Mookie.

Octavia flares into fury. "Jesucristo, la maldita desorganización en este maldito lugar. Estoy perdiendo la mente. ¿Qué diablos somos? ¿Qué es esto, viajes en el tiempo? Estoy viviendo en una puta novela de ciencia ficción. ¡Maldita sea!"

"Is she ok?" Chris asks.

"We're all due for some stress cursing right about now," Heller says.

"It's not happening." Sidd says.

"What's not happening?" Heller asks.

"Ground-hogging. Everything is normal."

Heller looks around. Everything is normal. "Crane froze the lab."

"Oh My God, yay?" Mooki says. They throw their arms around

Sidd. Sidd falls into their eyes then he leans forward. Their first kiss is tentative. Cautious. Mooki looks at him again. They survey the landscape of his eyes, the epicanthic folds, the single errant eyebrow hair alone, way off to the side, midnight black against his burnt mango skin, then back to his deep brown, almost black eyes. Checking. Asking. Then they kiss him again and it is volcanic.

"Finally," Octavia says.

Christopher Aldous Jealous Fucktard Montgomery's crest falls. His begone woes. His choly melons. His heart fractures. He turns away, every part of him rejecting his lust for Mooki. Every cell in him checking off a box. Closing a book. Giving up. He just wants to go home so he steps blindly off the Lake Street curb into the path of a six-ton Lobster King delivery truck.

"Chris!" Mooki lunges after him, snatches the hem of his shirt, falls backward and sideways and whirls Christopher Aldous I Guess He'll Probably Live Montgomery out of the way ninja-style, swapping places so now he is teetering on the curb staring at Mooki who instantly stands erect, a peaceful, accepting, resigned look on their face, their eyes closing and their head tilting back slightly as The Lobster King Delivery truck plows through them without even slowing down.

Chapter 50

"Ugh, look at this profile picture," Kama holds his phone up to Rati who steadfastly ignores it. They're at a long table in a conference room. Rati is watching *Amish Fight Club* on a wall monitor. Vishnu walks in.

"Dad!" Kama stands up, but Vishnu ignores him. Grabs the remote off the table, points it at the T.V.

"I'm watching that," Rati says.

"It's a terrible show." Vishnu falls into a tall-backed executive desk chair. "They think Dr. Phibbs is beer. They're idiots."

"They are innocents," Rati says.

"They're actors," Kama swipes furiously at his phone.

"They are not actors, you Y-chromosome-soaked meat puppet."

"Ok, so, like they start out that way. They're just a couple of Amish guys harvesting corn or something when some T.V. company approaches them and says hey can we follow you around and film you being all Amish?"

"That's what a documentary is," Rati says.

Lakshmi sweeps into the room, followed by Jesus, the other one, and Ksitigharba.

"That's not a documentary," says Ksitigharba.

"You too?" Rati says.

"It's called a non-scripted docu-drama," Jesus says, grabbing the remote. "The crew constantly leads them into confrontational situations and pits them against each other behind their backs."

"Sounds biblical...." Rati sneers.

"They are definitely going to hell," Jesus glances across the table at Vishnu who nods. Jesus changes the channel to *Monk and Master*. "Now this one, this is a real documentary. They don't even know the cameras are there."

"Isn't that illegal?" Lord Yama scoots his oversized chair over to make room for Ksitigharba who rolls a chair up to the table and sits down. Crane slides into the room like a dead lizard on a cold rock. He sits at the far end, across from Vishnu.

"Define illegal," Crane says. Rati looks over at him and frowns.

"Like pretty much everything you do?" She says.

"We are Gods." Crane leans back into his chair but the chair hardly registers him as he is light as a feather and thin as a reed. Ksitigharba tabs the remote again. The screen shows Mooki, Heller, Sidd and the crew staring at the lab while vibrating luminescent time lines quiver and pulse.

"This looks good," Vishnu says.

"Hey, wait, I know that guy," Lord Yama says. "That's the little fucker who organized hell!"

"Gross," Kama says.

"Mooki?" Lakshmi and Rama say.

"What the hell is this show?" Vishnu growls. Everyone turns to Crane.

"Lord Thoth," Lakshmi says coldly. "Are those timelines that are flashing through that laboratory?"

Crane, who, in case you missed that jump up above, is actually Thoth, the Egyptian God of Writing except he was old as dirt when Egypt grew up around him and he's actually the god of Plotlines and story and the endless click track of sequential order from which all halfway decent storytelling arises but also the one-two-threeishness of ordinary reality and, like the other gods in the room, is supposed to abide by the scarce rules printed in a thin binder of divine legislation that keeps him in his lane and prevents him from engaging in excessive cruelty, a rule he flagrantly ignores.

"Goddammit Thoth," Vishnu stands, an imperial blue index finger pointed down the table at Thoth "I've been pretty specific about fucking around with the timeline. I swear on me—"

Crane snaps his finger. Everyone freezes. Crane stands up, walks through the door of the conference room out into a hot, moist, Jurassic jungle. Massive beasts slither and stomp through gigantic leathery leaves as Crane carefully picks his way a few yards into the tangle of vines until he sees a massive azure butterfly drinking from the upturned skull of a dead Archaeopteryx. Diligently, with excessive accuracy and precision, he traps it under his heel, driving it and the skull into the mud floor of the jungle, grinding its foot-wide wings beneath his tiny boot, splattering its guts all over his stovepipe pants legs. Then he stomps its shattered carcass a few more times until it's just a vague cerulean smear. He turns back, makes his way carefully toward the conference room door just hanging there in the middle of a million years ago. He dips his boot into a handy pool then scrapes mud off on a branch. Walks into the conference room, shuts the door. Sits down and snaps his fingers again.

"—Krishna's tits if you've done something hinky, I'll pluck you over a goddam fire." Vishnu sits back down, his new five-inch-long warty nose jiggling angrily.

Crane smiles. "I'm just trying to entertain myself."

They watch Sidd disappear, then Mooki, then Chris. Then Crane shows up with Herbert. They freeze the lab. Time readjusts to normal. Cut to the T.V. studio.

"Well, that's just gratuitous," Rati says.

"Shhh!" Vishnu slides onto the edge of his seat. Mooki tears off the mike. They convene on the sidewalk. Cut to the P.O.V. of the lobster truck screaming down on them as Chris steps off the curb.

"Whoa!" Lord Yama says.

Then Mooki, perfectly calm, perfectly in control, swings Chris back onto the curb, then turns to face the oncoming truck, their determined features filling the screen as it plows into them, smashing them into a well-dressed bag of shattered bones, ruptured organs, splattered blood, and death. Vishnu pauses the show. The entire group looks down the table at Crane. Vishnu erupts.

"You sorry sack of monkey nuts, that creature was Sidd's true love and you just killed—"

"I did no such thing, Lord Vishnu, I merely rearranged a few timelines to see what would happen. It's no different than changing channels," Crane wiggles a finger at the TV which changes to *Monk and Master* (just the Master sitting on the couch watching *Amish Fight Club*) then *Amish Fight Club* (Aaron and Eli watching *Master and Monk*) then a static security cam of all of them sitting in this room at this table. "It's all just a show we put together to amuse ourselves through the endless boredom of eternity."

"You're bored?!" Kama is genuinely curious.

"Well, not now." Crane says, flicking the channel back to the crew on the sidewalk. Heller is hysterical. E.M.T.s are pouring Mooki's corpse into an ambulance. Sidd is perfectly still, tears streaming down his cheeks.

Chapter 51

Sidd hasn't moved. Heller tried to talk to him, tried to get him to come back to the offices, get processed. Remove this horror. But Sidd was a rock. Solid granite. Everyone had gone.

Now the city sanitation truck had come alongside the curb in its great hulking blueness, sweeping broken glass and shattered plastic and what was surely Mooki's remains into its tanks.

Sidd had no model for this tragedy. He dug down inside himself to find instruction, to mitigate the enormous sorrow. *I could go to the temple,* he thought. *But the Master is just going to yell at me.*

The street sweeper lumbered away and in the pool of mango colored light from the street lamp the asphalt was perfectly clean. Sterile. As if Mooks had never existed.

The lab. Sidd ran back to the university. The lab was open. Inside, Ovales was crouched over his bench, insectoid goggles fastened tight, working. He looks up just as Sidd grabs a moop and swipes the long wooden handle through every glass tube on the shelf, including the normally unbroken vacuum hydrolysis tube wherein lolled the newly contented tardigara in their newly mollified and much preferred stasis.

As the pond water and shards of glass burst into the air, Ovales flips his goggles up, calmly reaches for his backpack and his keys and says to no one in particular, certainly not to Sidd Hearth Ough, snarling and wanging the mop handle through every fragile piece of equipment in view, and certainly not to his wards, the microscopic river pigs whose placid lives he so diligently curates, not to them, not to anyone, he says: *Jesus Fuck Everything Christ.*

***

In the subterranean grotto of the lodge, George faces The Switch.

I don't have to do this. I can ride it out. Eventually the weather will clear, and the water will thaw, and the paramecium herds will return. We'll make it. Most of us will make it. It's not like an emergency emergency. It's more like a slow freeze disaster. I don't have to flip this switch. Cause if I do, if I move this massive knob, we all jump. We'll probably be safe. We'll probably be ok. It won't be like the last time, it won't be the fluttering flash of new realities. It'll be . . . Further. We'll sail over adjacent timelines and timelines adjacent to those timelines until we fly into unknown braids of reality's vermin riddled wig, landing in who knows what quagmire of the here-and-now (only it'll be the there-and-when).

Perhaps it was not his burden. Perhaps this was the test, the final degree; not the act of engaging the switch but, instead, the act of not engaging the switch.

Oh, ok Here we go, then, thought George. *Here's a way out. Here's the logic I take with me back up the stairs. Here's—holy crap am I having an epiphany? Is this what an epiphany feels like?! OH, ANCIENT TARDIGRADE, I'M ON TOP OF THE WORLD!*

But up in the lodge, in the perfect stillness of the fluid atmosphere of pond water, a massive invisible wave washed through the debris. It swept up Frank and circulated him through the temple, swirling him around the big chair in front before flushing him down the hole, his eight feet paddling furiously against the current. He flowed into George who flipped and whirled around as Frank crashed against the far wall.

"What the hell, Frank?"

"It's the end of the Whirl!"

"WHAT?!"

"The water–it's swishing in all directions. Up and down, back and forth. We're doomed!"

Frank's eyes tracked past George, paddling furiously to remain in place, to the great switch. George turned down the length of that gaze as the currents battered him in a cyclonic whorl. George was driven into the switch. He braced himself against it, taking in the darkening waters of the grotto as the currents picked up debris. It was indeed the end of the Whirl. There was nothing to recommend. No course save one. For his mate. For his son.

He wedged his pudgy carcass under the toggle. He bent his back beneath the massive stone nubbin, rising gently until his mantle pressed against the ancient stone, then he gripped it with four hands and pushed with all his might.

Chapter 52

Crane's AIDE DE CAMP, Herbert, ahems in a manner that explains—carefully because the boss is a little touchy right now; and tactfully, because the boss is always on edge when he's hanging out with his peers, as if he's being judged (which he is)–yet in a thorough, succinct, concise manner, that there is a video which is being captured live on CCTV of Sidd smashing lab equipment–including the No. 12 Hydrolysis Tube wherein Crane had sequestered his vicious little hack, the time traveling tardigara, the very thought of which occasionally caused Crane to squawk with unprecedented mirth; this is an ahem with a modicum of urgency as Herbert–hired for his uncanny attunement to the material world–feels as if certain vital seams of reality are unraveling; quickly.

"Well show it to me," Crane said impatiently. Crane's assistant–

Aide de camp, Herbert sotto vocced.

–AIDE DE FREAKING CAMP held his phone sideways and tabbed its glassine surface opening a live feed to the lab. Sidd, looking wild, looking haggard, his face slick with furious tears, mouth breathing in the middle of a mound of macerated debris.

Crane reaches out to move the camera for a better shot. Sidd rolls his eyes up toward the tiny whining slowly sliding lipstick tube, snarls, and whips the broom handle–

Crane snaps his fingers.

"What about lunch? What do you think? I'm thinking something rustic and daring. What about Thai food?"

Herbert pockets his phone. He glances meaningfully at Crane, then gathers Crane's papers. The other gods have already winked out of existence into their various hallowed halls to process the gruesome vignette outside the television studios. Crane was alone.

Ahem, Herbert ahemmed.

EXCEPT FOR HIS AIDE DE CAMP who clapped the buttons on Crane's ancient attaché and aimed himself doorwise. Crane cocked a nostril and disappeared.

Herbert stared at the vaguely avian shaped empty space then sniffed quietly and walked out.

***

Sidd landed in the dust outside Lord Yama's tent. Horseface and Oxhead jabbed their spearpoints mere millimeters from his nose then realized it was him and relaxed.

"NEIGH."

"SNORT."

"I had nothing to do with it," Lord Yama yelled from his tent, his face a faint azure from the glow of his off-brand tablet. Sidd stalked between the guards, leaned across the knickknacks on Lord Yama's desk and growled.

"Where's Mooki?"

"How would I know?"

"She's dead."

"Well there's your answ–"

Sidd snatched the tablet, swiped upward. He typed "Mooki" into the search bar but all he got was two girls from Arizona and a dead hamster. Sidd sneered. Of course he got nothing. Of course he didn't. Mooki is a nickname. He didn't know their real name. Could be Alouicious for all he knew. Sidd snarled, tapped a command, then tossed it back at the ancient Guardian of death who looked at it and saw nothing amiss.

"Look, I know you're pissed, Sidd, but . . ."

There was a low rumbling. The ground shook. Oxhead snorted and Horseface neighed. They slammed the butts of their spear handles into the ground. A luminous veil sprang up between them, wrapping itself around the camp and glowing with a venomous hum as thousands of dead souls rushed the tent.

"What did you do!?" Lord Yama howled, rising. Lord Ksitigharba popped into existence.

"Oh hello, Sidd. Shit, are you for real dead?"

"He's mad and he did something with the files!"

"Well, that's why I'm here. Are you experiencing–" Lord Ksitigharba followed Yama's gaze out at the thousands of souls pressed against the luminous wall, which was sizzling and crackling from the supernatural efforts of Horseface and Oxhead to keep it going.

"Jesus."

"Yes?" Lord Jesus was standing there all of a sudden. "Oh, hello Sidd–why is he so angry? Sidd, hast thy father forsaken thee?"

"Really?" Yama whispered.

"It's not a competition," said Lord Ksitigharba.

A dusty Indian man flickered in front of them like a ghost. He seemed to be mouthing *what the unliving hell is going on?* Then Vishnu showed up.

"Krishna's kneecaps," Yama whispered before adding "Lord Vishnu."

"WHAT THE HELL, YAMA?!"

Yama held his six hands out toward Sidd who stood resolutely cementish.

"You will repair this issue instantly!"

Sidd didn't move.

"I am a GOD, kiddo!"

Sidd didn't move.

"He can hear me, right?" Vishnu waved a couple of hands in front of Sidd's face.

"He's pissed," Lord Ksitigharba explained. "Thoth killed his girlfriend."

"Well, what of it? We're gods, that's our job!"

"SNORT!" explained Oxhead.

"NEIGH!" pleaded Horseface.

The barrier between their rods was cracking under the strain of the dead. Long yellow and purple fissures zig zagged across the surface of the veil.

"I COMMAND YOU TO DO SOMETHING!" Vishnu roared, his voice a comet, the heavens dimming in its wake, the gathered deities crouching in fear, the pressing dead halting, briefly, their morbid press.

Sidd moved, but only in the sense that no he didn't.

"The moons on this guy," Vishnu chuckled, not believing his deific roar hadn't inspired the lay priest to jump. But Sidd was angry and the kind of angry he was had no endgame. It was a fuck it all level of fury where the Angerer had less than nothing to lose. Had already lost everything then found themselves auspiciously still alive (technically) and fortuitously deep behind enemy lines with a sharp thing in their white knuckled fist. Only the thing Sidd had that was dangerously sharp was his mind and the dexterity (and severity) of his database hacking chops.

"Lord Vishnu," Sidd said quietly, bowing the teensiest bow. Somehow, this tiny genuflection carried far more weight than the deep 30-degree hinge reserved for dignitaries and kings. It was a bow of Sidd's bone deep respect for Vishnu and, indeed, all the deities stacked on top of one another like turtles. "It is with sadness and regret that I must inform you that as a consequence for Mooki's death, I have cleared the traditional boundaries and hurdles from a soul's demise to their judgement here before Lord Yama. No soul will return to its life. No soul will find the least bit of hinderance in its journey to your gate. Usually, a million people a day pass into this realm but they are channeled and herded to give you time to do your job," Sidd sighed. "No more."

Sidd glanced up at Vishnu from the shallow ledge of his brow, then, like a bored British aristocrat, his delicate hands nested behind his back, walked away into hell.

Vishnu watched Sidd's disappearing form. He waved his hand imperiously and Sidd was suddenly walking into a soybean field just outside Arthur, Illinois. Not that Sidd even noticed. He just kept going with a kind of dogged purpose any half-witted dork could see would carry him three quarters of the way across the arctic circle before he even looked up and noticed the snow.

On the porch of his homestead cabin, Lamar Sherrell saw Sidd appear way out in the middle of his bean field. Lamar'd been carving a spoon from a hickory limb and his fingers froze over the fragrant wood. Sidd walked across the field passing perpendicular to the road in front of the cabin and, the big elm he'd grown up with having been tore out by a twister two summers back, Lamar had a good long look at this thoughtful, dark-suited apparition.

At first, he thought it was one of his Mennonite neighbors–good people, all of 'em–but the guy had no beard and had kind of a fruity collar and so Lamar figured he was a college kid out picking shrooms, but the guy never bent down, never looked right ner left. Just kept plowing along, which was funny cause that's what Lamar normally did except with an actual plow and he was about to grin over that one when a light come out of the sky solid as a pipe right on the guy. The light was bright as the noontime sun and lit the man up clear as day and followed him as he walked. Lamar leaned forward over the railing of his porch, one hand automatically reaching for his thirty-ought which he kept leaned up against the rail in case a damned liberal come by to get him to vote, and he looked up to see where the beam was coming from but just like that, it was gone.

So was Sidd.

Chapter 53

Hank and [sPlat!] are in stationary orbit over Chicago on Hank's 11,924th mission to Earth. Hank is a scientist from a small collection of networked Cironovillial orbital stations around a planet just to the left of the Crab Nebula's elbow. [SPlat!] is a fourth dimensional trust-fund legacy student from [plRp?] currently located in the gas giant [glmGj:] and has manifested as a tiny infant star, meaning he is in his gas plasma stage, currently, and is Hank's intern for the summer.

"Ok, ok. Ok," [sPlat!] pulses in frustration. "What you're telling me, Hankster, is you're willing to load these things into the lab and stick 'em full of probes but you won't sit down and have a conversation with them?"

"It's called analytical detachment, [sPlat!]" Hank says, not looking up from his scope. "You should give it a once around."

[SPlat!] looks into the lab section of their Unilateral Flowjection Omosphere 2000 at the pinkish being slumped naked and unconscious on the slab with its ass in the air, drool running off the table. It reminds him of Specimen—144000:M (a sea urchin). It shudders. Hank unfolds from over his scope and glides over to the being. He flips a switch and high voltage gas jets dance across the tips of the many, many painful implants jammed painfully into its naked back. It screams. A tiny grin plays around Hank's beak.

"How long have you been out here, Hank?" [SPlat!]'s been on the U.F.O. for about three days, earth time, and he's beginning to suspect his mentor's internal files are scrambled.

"I don't know, like, a solid four thousand cycles? I'm pretty close to a conclusion."

[SPlat!]'s stratosphere flashes from blue to pink and his core twinkles. "Really, like what?"

Hank turns to [sPlat!] with a weird grin on his face. [SPlat!] gets a queasy feeling. His course admin warned him about Hank but [sPlat!] needed the credits so he could molt and move on to the senior level and maybe encorpulate and Hank's 'Mebraneous Outlying Planetary Catalog–Temp' posting was the only job that fit his schedule. Whenever [sPlat!] thought about having a morphic form, his stratosphere pimpled. Whatever. He only had a few weeks. So, he has to spend them with an evil Cironovillialian Exoethno Data Cataloger. He can hack it.

Hank shuts down the gas jets. The pink thing sags, panting, still unconscious. Hank slithers out into the main area and peers into [sPlat!]'s core.

"They've got gods."

"Shit," [sPlat!] barks. He spins around looking at the sealed hatches and tightened cargo sphincters. "Are we ok? Do I need to get a shot? I'm kind of itchy. OH, SHIT DO I HAVE GODS TOO?!"

"Relax, we're ok. They're all down there," Hank cocks his carapace earthward. "But" he grins at [sPlat!]. "I'm telling you." He waggles his gas jets like an old man waggling his eyebrows. "Gods!"

"Shut the dwarf star up, Hankster. That's dark matter talk."

"I know. I can't put it in the reports, but believe me, they're riddled with them. Look at this."

Hank waggles a tentacle toward the bulkhead of the U.F.O. where a flatscreen T.V. is glued to the vertice. It flares to life, showing a video of a revivalist preacher under a hot tent in south Mississippi yelling at his congregation. The video switches to an Imam in Utah under a hot tent yelling at his congregation. Then an atheist standing in front of a seminar yelling at atheists. They're all the same. "See the similarity of contortions and rictus? I'm telling you, they've all got it–and it's spreading." The video continued suddenly with just a close up of a man's hands washing a very soapy dish in slow motion to some gadunkedunk funk. Hank slapped a blushing tentacle at the off switch and the screen went blank.

"Is that why we can't go down there?"

"Well," Frank hemmed. "Not officially. I've catalogued a hundred thousand virulent corpuscles, each of which would wipe us out in a split second if we so much as smelled them. So that's the official reason we don't decamp. But, you know, if we really wanted to, we could suit up and land. Others do it. Our directive is certainly not universal. I mean, look at the Venusians."

[SPlat!] shuddered.

"They've co-opted the terran music industry and nobody can even tell. You think those singers look like that because they're just naturally hot? Hell no. Venusians. Goddam arrogant—"

"What if they saw us?"

"Oh, shit, kid, no. They'd try to contact us—and believe me, they'd succeed—and then, boom! We've got gods!"

"I don't know, man. I've seen some shows about this, but they all seem to kind of be joking around."

"I know. I'd be laughed out of the Universesity. This is just . . . It's a theory."

[SPlat!] rotated along his equatorial line thoughtfully. "You believe it."

"Well, yeah. But I can't tell anybody."

"Have you seen them?"

"Good lord, no. But weird shit's been happening over the last 80 close-star-orbits and I'm convinced."

"If you could document them, that would be something."

"Please. I'd have to go into polar orbit. I'd have to do it in the early morning when no one is sky-curious," Hank chuckled darkly. "I'd have to uncloak."

[SPlat!] orbited over to the bulkhead.

"Hey, be careful over there. You haven't been trained."

"I've done the simulations," [sPlat!] said. A blobulous appendage grew from his pulsating stratosphere and wrapped itself around a lever. Hank got very serious, very fast.

"Take your vaporous blob off the cloaking device."

"If they can't see us, we can't see them. It's science."

"Kid you don't know what–" but it was too late. [SPlat!] pulled the lever. The U.F.O. shimmered and a sparkling gigantic, winged creature appeared just kind of hanging out in space right in front of their main viewscreen. It snapped its hideous head around in surprise, then was suddenly pushing itself through the formerly impenetrable wall of the U.F.O.

"OH SHIT OH SHIT OH SHIT!" [sPlat!] spun wildly, flashing spectrums before sealing himself off and falling to the deck with a thump. The creature stood up, bending slightly because the ceiling was only seven feet high. It was brilliantly red, with a kind of deep purple sheen. Its eyes were yellow. Its hair was a color Hank could only smell.

Hank withdrew his tentacles in fear, flashing warning patterns across his mantle. The creature knelt and poked Hank curiously with an enormous bright red finger.

"Blobbish thing, you are far from home."

"YOU SPEAK CIROVILLIAN?"

"Of course not. I speak Enochian with a distinct Nephilimaen brogue. But you hear what you hear, snotty arthropod." The winged being noticed the multiply stabbed human on the slab. "Well now, who's been a naughty little alien?"

"WHAT ARE YOU?"

"Name's Baraqijal."

"ARE YOU A GOD?"

"Negative, my eight-legged friend. And who the fnord are you?"

"HANK! I'M . . . I'm a research scientist from," Hank thought better on naming his home orbitals. He waved a leg vaguely at the stars.

"Hmm. Been meaning to fly out there, check it out. So, you're a watcher?"

"You could say that."

"Ha! I'm a watcher! We've got that, right buddy?" Baraqijal reached out to fist bump Hank. Hank grew a tentative tentacle toward the huge fist.

"Boop," Baraqijal said quietly.

"I think they have gods," Hank said, nodding toward Earth.

"Oh, yeah, shit tons of 'em. Swarms! I gotta say, I was really happy to see you pop into existence." Baraqijal looked for a friendly reaction but Hank's cephalopodial face showed pure alien dread. Baraqijal looked out the big bay window at the planet and sighed. "Watching."

Hank slithered slightly backward. Baraqijal snapped his golden wings open and shut. A feather fluttered out and landed on the pin cushioned human. The creature glanced over at it and remembered.

"I should report this."

"Please–"

The creature reared back his head and gargled a long collection of distinctly gargled garglings.

"WHAT WAS THAT!?" Hank squirted.

"Enochian call. I observe the Northwest quadrant. Gotta follow protocol, right?" Baraqijal reached out for another fist bump. "Buddy?"

"WHO DID YOU CALL?"

"Aw, come on, man. I'm just doing my job. Now you got to go and get all—do you know how lonely I get out here? It's cold, creature. And dark. And quiet," Baraqijal shivered. "Jesus."

A being burst through the hull of the ship as if it didn't even exist. [SPlat!], sealed like a crusty ball bearing, wanged off the being's protruding pedipode and lodged himself under the lab table where the human was still enstabulated. The creature was a small God, shaped vaguely and enormously snailish, and roiling in furious righteousness.

WHO DARES INTERRUPT MY–BARAQ! B DOG! NORTHWEST SIDE REPRESENT! IT'S BEEN A MINUTE.

"Lord, forgive me. This pliable being has been molesting the locals."

WHAT DOTH THOU a thousand rolling eyes shifted across the morpheal surface of the God toward the needle bewigged human OH. WOW. YOU DID THIS? THIS IS EXCELLENT WORK. LOOK AT HOW MUCH PAIN IT IS IN. THIS IS EXQUISITE!

"ARE YOU A GOD?"

OF COURSE I'M A GOD. WHY ARE YOU STABBING MY CONSITUTENT? WHAT PUNISHMENT IS THIS?

Suddenly, Lord Yama winks into existence.

"Oh, come on, now." He crosses multiple arms. Horseface and Oxhead wink in next to him, spears aimed at the mucilaginous deity. "Ya'll can't just probe anyone you want. Where the fuck are we?"

"This oozy animal's flying saucer," Baraqijal said. "I'm just doing my job."

Yama glared at the small God.

"What the hell do you think you're doing manifesting out here off schedule?

I WAS SUMMONED BY THE NEPHIL-

"Do you have any idea of the kind of racquet you're making? We're trying to run a nice quiet little planet down there, harvesting some souls, eking out a little corporeal punishment–fairly, mind you. And you're up here perving out and probing people?"

"For Science," Hank argued, backing as far away from Yama as he could.

THE OBLATE ONE HAS PRICKED YOUR CHILD, DEITY. I HAVE ONLY ARRIVED TO-

"Krishna's side saddling sister, can you dial it down a little grandpa?"

"I AM SOR-I'm Sorry," the Small God dialed it back a little. "I am a god, after all."

"Shit, shit, shit," Hank whispered.

"So am I," Yama said.

"SNORT!"

"Well, a Lord. It's like a God. Close enough."

"NEIGH."

Lord Ksitigharba winked into existence next to Yama.

"Did you find out where–holy shit!"

"Right," Yama grinned. "Fucking aliens!"

"And this deity here," Lord Ksitigharba said, more or less respectfully.

I AM HE WHO

"Dude!" Yama winced.

"I am he who lives. I govern the Western lands and was summoned by Baraqujial because this interloping shellfish is torturing humans."

"For, and I can't stress this enough–science," Hank said, fiddling in a drawer for a can of pesticide which he sprayed at the assembled deities who waved it off, coughing quietly.

"Being," a thin, long-haired man stepped into their reality. "Have you heard the news?"

"Every fucking time," Yama stage whispered.

"Yama. Ksitigharba. You know, my father–hey, isn't that your boy over there?" They all looked at the stellated monkey on the slab who turned out to be Siddney Hearth Ough, Lay Priest, Database Hacker, and drooling abductee.

"NEIGH!"

"SNORT!"

"Like a bad penny," Yama said. Vishnu leaned over Yama's shoulder out of nowhere. Hank was putting on his suit and firing up the escape module and muttering *gods everywhere.*

"I think it's time," Vishnu said gravely.

"No, not now," Yama growled. "I have eight million unleashed souls to deal with down there!"

"No, he's right. Lakshmi should be here. Rati. The whole crew. It is time."

"Time for what," asked the mollusk god.

"Time for a meeting," Yama said.

"Neigh," Horseface added thoughtfully, pulling probes out of Sidd.

"Snort," Oxhead said, with feeling, while shoving probes into Hank.

Chapter 54

Wagner's "Ride of the Valkyries" plays nowhere and everywhere, trilling its exhilarating opening strings, as into the starry darkness, Crane (Thoth, Horus, Hermes Trismegistus) rockets skyward, flaming wings extended into burning golden deltas, leaving a radiant contrail like a scarlet ice pick plunged into the center of the earth–except it plunges right through the laboratory like a needle through a desiccated butterfly in, like, a collection, maybe in a dusty old British museum like one in one of those wide shallow drawers some nerd always pulls out slowly in science documentaries when–

Crane reaches a kind of apogee and hangs there in space, his hands holding twin caducei, a complicated geometrical orb spinning over his head bearing mystical letters in a thousand dead languages: on one side the sun, on his other the moon, and beneath his winged feet, the glimmering earth. Crane's eyes glow as he gathers a wicked energy and flings his scepters toward Chicago. The earth, a million miles below, shimmers and shakes as a lurid golden jagged seam runs all the way around its middle. Earth shudders in its orbit then cracks in two with a thunderous pop.

Glowing temporal threads arc out of the planet's dissolving molten core illuminating hosts of angels racing toward Crane wearing their war faces. The six watchers shatter into being at the vertices of an invisible cube with Crane floating in its center, his eyes blazing righteous fire. Around him unfurl the *hmnyw,* the Eightfold, his spectral generals in vicious pairs charging the Watchers like sentient fanged flags.

Mahavishnu appears in a ring of his 80 forms all regarding Crane in the center of the invisible cube. The Mollusk Deity from earlier whooshes up.

IS THIS A BAD TIME?

"Squishable entity, I am at war," Crane says.

I'M JUST NOTICING I'VE NEVER SEEN YOU AROUND HERE AND YOU'RE KIND OF TAKING UP A LOT OF ANGELIC PROCESSING POWER AND, NOT JUDGING HERE, BUT I CAN'T HELP BUT NOTICE YOU'VE BLOWN UP THE WORLD.

"It's mostly dirt."

JUST SO I CAN FILL OUT THE RIGHT FORMS, WAS THIS OUT OF ANGER, OR . . .

"Just sick of dealing with them. Damned gods."

AGAIN, PURELY OF THE OFFICE, I BELIEVE YOU AND I ARE FULLY DEIFIC?

"We are eternal all-knowing and all-powerful manifestations of the endless divine. They are mere gods. Local," Crane sneers as his Eightfold fend off arrows and lightning bolts of the Watchers, "bumpkins."

The Slimy deity ahems. Crane glances over at its coiled squishiness because the ahem sounded alarmingly familiar.

***

Earlier Crane had been invited to a nice lunch by Lord Ksitigharba. He'd opened a door in a hallway at the Blackstone on Michigan avenue expecting a white linen-covered table piled with delicacies and fine wine but instead he stepped into a private lounge where his peers were all seated on low couches lining the walls, slips of paper in hand, their faces contorted with sympathy and concern.

"What the–" Crane's eyes narrowed when they fell onto Herbert, his aide de camp, whose eyebrows raised ever so slightly at reading his title properly typed for the first time ever. "Herbert, what's going on?"

"Lord Thoth," Herbert guided Crane to a seat between Yama and Jesus. "Everyone here cares for you a great deal."

"We really do," said Lakshmi.

"What is this?" Crane asked.

"It's a divine intervention," Herbert said. He nodded to Rati who cleared her throat and read from her tear-stained page.

"Lord Thoth, your actions have harmed me in the following ways–"

"I think perhaps, not." Crane stood up. Herbert slipped in front of the door. "Herbert? Did you do this?"

"Boss, I believe your agenda has gone sideways and, well, I've been ahemming an awful lot lately and, well, I don't like the way you smote the floppy human–"

"Mooki," Rati said.

"Morgan," Lakshmi corrected.

"They're really quite heroic," Kama added, twiddling his bow. "Thinking of nominating them to level up." Rati snuck a glance at her brother, thinking maybe he wasn't such a bubbling cyst after all.

Crane fell back into his seat. Jesus rubbed his shoulder. "In his book, my Father said–"

"He's next," said Lord Ksitigharba.

"Every. Single. Time," Yama whispered.

"–my house has many mansions. Now, we all know what that

means," Jesus glanced at Mahavishnu who was wearing a necklace of cherished universes. "And it's ok for us to sometimes dart between them, to visit a different mansion–"

"Mansion hopping," Kama chuckled.

"Privileged son of a–" Yama elbowed Lord Ksitigharba in his ribs. Jesus went on.

"But we all agreed many millennia ago to interfere rarely and with great care in the affairs of men."

"And women," Lakshmi and Rati high-fived silently.

Horseface leaned forward, "Neigh neigh neigh neigh neigh neigh," he wiped a delicate tear out of his enormous eye. "Neigh neigh neigh."

"May I remind you," Crane stood, shooting his cuffs and adjusting his lapels, a vision of understated indignation. "May I remind you I am the only natural God in the room? The rest of you are extrapolations. You're made up."

The group glared at Crane. Herbert shuffled his papers.

"And you," Crane looked at his aide de camp. "How easily you betray me. You're fired." Crane snapped his fingers, expecting Herbert to disappear–as did the other gods who shielded their faces in case it was a disappearance of the explosive kind. But Herbert remained right where he stood. He bent down, slid his papers into his open attaché. Then Herbert left. Through the door. Like a person.

"Well, I think I've had just about enough. It's been a real party." Crane went to snap his fingers but Oxhead laid the shaft of his spear into Cranes hand.

"Snort."

"Oh great, now the sidekicks are in on it? This is really too much–"

"Thoth! I swear to us, if you don't put everything back the way it was, I will smite the crap out of you."

"Ok, boomer. Smite me. Go ahead. SMITE ME! SMIIIIIITE MEEEEEEEE!"

Everyone dives behind furniture.

"It would make such a mess," Vishnu said. "We had to put down a significant deposit on this room."

"Amateurs!"

"Thoth," Lakshmi rose, glowering like an emergent storm. "If you do not relieve the afflictions you've visited on these people, it won't just be my husband smiting you. It will be all of us, and all our associates, and all the gods, no matter how contrived they are from the imaginations of our mortal hosts. How do you think you got here? A natural god? What dearth of imagination you possess. What a miserly and miserable mythos. Fine, eject, remove; poof and powder if you so desire. We can do this without you. Your powers are not unique. We'll put your little woodshed project back in order toote," Lakshmi zigged her finger through the air in a righteous swirl and jammed it into nothing like a cosmic punctuation mark, "suite!"

Crane looked at Lakshmi and the assembled crew peering nervously over the backs of the furniture and said:

"Fix this."

***

Even *earlier,* Heller and Octavia sat on either side of Christopher Aldous What Have I Done Montgomery rubbing his back and trying to console him, but it was no use.

"It's my fault. I killed her. What was I thinking?"

"Kid," Heller took a blue tip out of his mouth and flicked it into a trash can. They were back at Grant Park on a bench looking across Michigan Ave which was aswarm with vehicles and people in constant flux. Crabs giraffes, great arachnids, naked septuagenarians, glassine orbs, and medieval carts lumbered and floated and slunk back and forth as everyone ran around with their claws in their antennae screaming in fear. It was mayhem and horror as adjacent timelines merged before their very eyes. But Chris didn't care.

Heller looked across him at Octavia. She leaned back against the bench and popped a smoke into her mouth, leaned across Chris's back.

"Light me," she says to Heller, who's already struck a match. He cups the flame under her cigarette and glances into her eyes, reflecting fire. She holds his gaze, takes a steady drag off the Halliwell Light, then gets up, walks around and sits down on the other side of him. She snakes her arm through his and weaves her fingers into his warm, rough hand and leans against him, smoking and watching the chaos.

"I remember every time you jumped."

"Well, you're the coordinator," Heller stammered, trying desperately to understand how to not fuck up this moment.

"No, I mean, when you dialed up the Librarian."

"When I–"

"When you jumped to the timeline where I liked you?"

"I didn't know–"

"I knew. Every single time. OK, not the first time," Octavia gently nudged a curious spider hound away with her foot, slipped off her shoes and tucked her legs up under herself, leaning her weight into Heller's side. She radiated heat. "But once I figured it out, I put a marker on the moment and when you jumped, I jumped." Heller stared forward, eyes wide, worried. "I was like, what's this motherfucker think he's doing? I figured you were diddling my doppelganger and I was prepared to fuck your shit, as they say, all the way up. And I was like, dismissing my feelings in that timeline and everything but you never, ever, not even once, took advantage." She blew a cloud of smoke at a naked accountant who frowned at her. "You could've, you know. The librarian would've been into it." She snuggled closer. "I would. Have." Heller sagged.

"Wouldn't have been proper."

"You're such a nerd," she smiled.

She turned her face toward his. She was only an inch away, her eyes like twin planets.

"I'm gonna fuck this up," Heller stared into her eyes, a kiss welling up between them.

"Definitely," She said. "But you fuck up all the time and I've loved you since the day we met. I'm sorry for all the–I had to be sure, Old School, you know?"

"Sure of what?"

"Sure you could hack it. Sure you were strong enough for a girl like me."

"Am I?"

She leaned forward, their lips almost brushing, when Horsehead and Oxface walked out of the hotel across the street dragging Sidd between them, unconscious and naked, his body pierced like a pincushion, drooling.

"Neigh!"

"Snort!"

Octavia and Heller grabbed Sidd as the two lesser deities disappeared with urgent kapows.

"What the hell happened?" Heller and Octavia lay Sidd on the bench. "Did he do this to himself? Who were those guys?"

"Something's up, School." Octavia says. "We need to brace for maximum weirdness."

"Godammit, I've been waiting to kiss you for a solid fucknacular year, and I swear to God if–" But he couldn't talk through Octavia's searing silken lips which were suddenly pressing pretty hard against his. Heller put his arms around her waist and a golden searing seam opened up in the earth between them, and the world shattered, and with a deafening CRACK sheared through its center, Heller on one hemisphere, Octavia on the other, hurtling away from each other into space, Octavia cursing in fluid Columbian as Heller growled deep in his throat, popped a Blue Tip into his tingling teeth, and looked down at his watch.

Chapter 55

Gravity snapped. Gravity popped like a soap bubble. Gravity stopped working and as it fled, whipping out into local space like great invisible bedsheets hung out to dry then lifted by a storm to sail away over the neighborhood, snapping and popping as they go; as gravity did that, it took the atmospheres with it. And most of the oceans. And all the boats in all the harbors. And New Jersey.

Heller lifted into the Chicago sky with Christopher Aldous We're Not in Kansas Anymore Montgomery hanging desperately to one leg and Siddney Hearth Ough dangling upside down limply from one skinny ankle in Heller's vice-like grip and nearly all of Chicago went with him.

"Grab Sidd!" Heller yelled down to his terrified apprentice.

"Rancid?"

"GRAB SIDD!" Heller pointed statuesquely at the unconscious lay priest.

Chris reached over and grabbed Sidd's wrist and Heller let go and with a matchstick grimace grabbed the bezel of Rose's watch.

"I can't hold him!" Chris yelled. Sidd was flopping like a rag doll as the trio arced out over Lake Michigan which was rising up into some kind of snowstorm as space's endless chill took hold over everything not protected by a greenhouse effect which was, pretty much, everything. "My hands!"

Heller would have glanced at Christopher Aldous Fuck, I'm Freezing Solid Montgomery but his face was icing over, little white crystals forming on his eyelashes, his gaze locked onto the watch. Chris's face turned a dull periwinkle and Heller felt his entire body fart. Air leaked out of every orifice, he farted from his regular farting place, he farted from his nostrils, he farted around his eyeballs, he farted out of his ears as the vacuum of space slowly deflated him. His last fleeting thought was a weird childlike cartoon of himself turning the Manager's Special Device watch, him turning into a Hellercicle, and him folding up like a worn-out lunch sack then, as his frosted fingers turned the dial, everything went black.

Octavia felt her feet rise up off the sidewalk as she watched Heller rise and fly away and she flung her arms in wide circles and screamed and lost a shoe and grabbed some old lady and screamed into her face as she held on like she was drowning while the old woman stared at her as if she was trying to do algebra. She was very, very old. Her name was Adelaide Whitfield Duffy, and she was a professor emeritus of analytical physics at Columbia who spent many of her days at the cigar shop on Howard in a deep leather chair smoking a pipe full of English Witch while transcribing rare folios from 4th century mathematicians of the Ottoman Empire and though she had a pretty good general take on what had just happened, re: the planet calving, she was still pretty freaked out by the whole rising into the air thing. It had a quality of irrevocability that prayed on her faith. Octavia didn't help any, as she was screaming in Columbian and though Dr. Duffy spoke fluent Latin, she spoke it quietly and therefore couldn't understand a Goddam thing Octavia was screaming but it was clear the woman was in love.

Tears streamed back away from Octavia's face as Dr. Duffy reached up with a gnarled, arthritic, ink and tobacco-stained index finger under her chin and closed her mouth. Dr. Duffy stroked Octavia's hair and looked into her eyes and smiled the gentle and warm and healing smile only the ancient and wise can smile then farted, long and slow, from every orifice on her body as she laid Octavia's head on her shoulder and stroked her hair, they both farted some more and froze silently, two total strangers totally getting each other as they died in each other's arms. Farting.

Octavia's last fleeting thought was of Heller's leathery face, every argent bristle burning with a white fire, as he slowly shifted a blue tip match around a shit eating grin.

Dr. Duffy thought, *this woman smells amazing.*

Ovale Calvarium was dropping his book bag in the back of house closet behind the dishwashers' station when there was a crash in the kitchen, which Ovales didn't even register since there are always crashes in the kitchen. Working a second job as a barback gave him a worm's eye view into the wild machinations of a busy downtown restaurant and it paid more than his career as a hydraulic engineer in the lab. Then he heard another crash, then it sounded like everything crashed and his feet left the floor and he thought, *goddammit, the busboys slipped acid into the coffee again* as he pressed against the ceiling and the building came apart around him and he thought not of the poor wait staff nor the screaming managers nor the early bird patrons nor anyone in the demolishing restaurant, but of the tardigrades, those placid creatures he curated, those timeline jumping pudgy little river pigs. As Ovale froze, his last fleeting thought was *those motherfuckers.*

***

High above the disassembling world, Crane floated in livid fury dead center of the invisible cube arranged by the Watchers glaring at him from each vertice. His fanged flags were in tatters and Mahavishnu's circle of selves was tightening. He flung searing arcs of nova hot light at every target, but they managed to dodge, to parry, to handle it and send it back.

But none of that interested Crane. He'd been in a war with gods before. NBD. You just keep it up for a while until they run out of lightning bolts or some prophecy clocks in. It's a waiting game, really. The creature beside him, however, fascinating in its snailish architecture, was morphing as he watched and the resolving shape was surprisingly alarming as it was Herbert, his aide de camp. Herbert ahemmed. It didn't mean anything, he just needed to clear his throat after being a mollusk deity, however briefly.

"Which name would you prefer?" Herbert asked.

"Still Crane," Crane said, folding his arms as long tongues of the Watchers' sizzling fusion arcs tore through him with no effect.

"This is a bit of a mess," Herbert said, nodding toward the rubble of Terra.

"Are you actually Herbert?"

"Always have been."

"Strange occupation for a deity."

"Look who's talking."

"I wished to amuse myself."

"Isn't it like that for all of us? We manifest in the material world to learn new things, to feel new stuff. I once obtained because I had a hankering for a deep fried pimento cheese sandwich. Ever had one of those?"

"What are we doing?"

"These creatures are the best batch yet," Herbert said, his rich melliflous voice washing across the void like warm molasses. "Wildly inventive. A little rough. Messy. But still. Fried pimento cheese sandwiches. That's worth manifesting for."

"I have enjoyed the coffee," Crane said.

"And yet–" They both looked at the ruins of the planet.

"I regret nothing. What is a million years of evolution to us? We're immortal. We can go chill and wait a tick and boom, new mortals chanting our name. Or whatever name they name us. Same very old song and dance."

"Crane, are you really that cynical?"

"Asks Thou who knoweth my downsitting and my upstanding," he folded his arms. "Why are we even bothering with speech? Do your mind meld thing. Read me. I'm kind of busy."

Herbert held a hand up to the Watchers who, along with Vishnu and all the other warring deities, took a breather. Crane looked around.

"Who are you *really?* You said you were the Supreme Leader of the Northwest quadrant but this," Crane waggles his hand around. "This seems like you're punching out of your weight class."

"I am—" Herbert was just about to reveal his true self when there was a planet sized whoomph and everyone whirled around to see earth's two halves screw themselves back together.

Chapter 56

Inside Heller's watch, bucolic tanarctus chronochalarapoutinka wafted gently through fields of microscopic flora munching contentedly and chewing happily as the world outside their encapsulated universe split. They went on paddling, their eyespots slowly dilating then undilating not realizing their host was turning into a frozen tabletop wedding sculpture. But then Heller's frigid digits spun the bezel which swirled their waters and annoyed them horridly and they raised their knobby heads on their stubby necks and blinked themselves into a parallel thread. As the waters stilled, they returned to their munching and chewing and blinking like nothing had happened.

BUT STUFF HAD HAPPENED!

They had jumped into a timeline where the world had not yet deplanetized and Heller and Octavia were still mashed together lipishly. Heller drew back, his grip on Octavia tightening.

"Hey," she whispered.

"Hold on, Eights, something is about to happen."

"Well, it *was* a pretty good kiss—"

"Serious," he wrapped his arms around her and crushed her face into his neck as the seam of the world unzipped itself and gravity whipped its arms out for balance, grabbed Octavia by the ankle, and wrenched her from Heller's embrace. Her half of the world carried her away. His half of the world carried him away. Dr. Duffy looked down at her sensible shoes as they rose off the pavement. Heller snarled *fucksolutely not,* grabbed his watch, and spun the dial.

Inside Heller's watch, pacific tanarctus chronosfichtosvarelli drifted placidly among heaps of microflora munching contentedly and chewing happily as the world outside their encapsulated universe exploded into madness. They paddled on, blinking stupidly, not realizing their host was freezing solid. However, Heller's hyperchilled hand hooks turned the bezel which swished them menacingly until they raised their knobby heads on their stubby necks and blinked themselves sideways, time wise. As their waters stilled, they returned to their munching and chewing and blinking like nothing had happened.

BUT HAPPENED STUFF HAD!

Heller and Octavia and then kissing and oh shit and Dr. Duffy and so cold and then swack!

Inside Heller's watch, a lone tanarctus chronochalarapoutinka wafted gently as it chewed through a tangle of chlamydomonous. This was by far the most delicious flagellate she'd ever slurped, and her stylets practically vibrated with pleasure. Then some idiot jumped and suddenly her mouth was full of hellomonadidae which taste terrible and are gross. She paddled peacefully staring at the horrible dinner before her wondering what to do. She almost jumped but then wondered. Why is it always sideways? Why do we jump laterally? Is there another direction? Can we jump dorsally? Frontwise? Down? She ran calculations and pictured diagrams and crunched numbers until she realized it was just a matter of mindful orientation, took a deep breath, visualized jumping backward, then jumped backward. She opened her eyes and found herself in a lush field of vibrant chlamydomonous. She took a bite, closed her eyeholes, and chewed.

Heller was in the lab with Octavia with his finger in Crane's beak.

"We had impossible for lunch," Octavia said. "Try harder." Only when she said try harder, Heller whispered it under his breath.

"What?" Octavia confused.

Heller looked down at Ovale.

"Now he tells us we can put a marker on Mooks and Sidd."

"Weh ewe gan," Ovale agrees.

"Then you say–"

Octavia glares at Ovales, as Heller whispers along with her she yells, "But they're already gone!"

"Now he says go back."

"Doe? Go bag-oh, wade, ah din day dad"

"Then I say go back where and you say,"

Together, Octavia and Heller say, "Or when?"

"Then," Heller looks at Herbert. "Then you clear your throat." Herbert is already ahemming.

"What's happening?" Octavia asks. Heller answers her by strangling Crane who reacts to Heller's beefy hands suddenly crushing his throat with suspiciously calm interest. Herbert says to the both of them, "No," and Heller lets go.

"I don't know what the fuckwardian maleficence is going on, but I seem to remember the world blowing up a few minutes ago," Heller thinks about it. "From now, and I'm pretty sure you two have more than a little to do with it. Last time we were here you snapped—" Heller sees Crane's hand rising with his middle finger and his thumb coming together for a snap and he flicks Crane's hand like an errant bug. There is a crunching sound like a chef twisting a fistful of rhubarb and Crane whelps like a puppy. Heller looks down and sees Herbert's feet are planted on the ground in a V shape, while Crane's feet are pointing away from him in an H configuration and Herbert's right foot shifts slightly toward Heller, so Heller grabs a shattered hydrolysis tube like a knife, snatches Crane to his chest like a startled heron, and presses the jagged edge of the glass tube against Crane's spaghetti noodle neck.

For a moment, everyone's eyes are wide, everyone is silent, everyone is holding their breath, everyone is watching the sharp shards of the shattered hydrolysis tube intently. Then Herbert, calm, together, serene, looks at Heller and Heller says:

"Fill us in."

Herbert ahems. It's a long-ragged harrumph that carries grave truths and is the prelude to a terse explanation of Post-Modern Deity Management, time travel pranks, and humanity en toto.

"Well, he's a god."

"Fuckidently."

"And this," Herbert looks around at the mayhem of the lab. "Is him just, as they say in the vernacular, 'fucking around.'"

"What's that make you?"

"His aide de camp."

"Try again."

Herbert looked into Heller's steely eyes, eyes that had witnessed the world blown up–twice; eyes that had watched his true love float away into death–twice; eyes that had seen the myriad zoologically distinct alternate realities hundreds of times. Heller was no mere mortal. Heller had crossed the threshold into the unknown. And he was cool with it. His nerves were carved from granite slabs.

He was a salesman.

And his heart, Herbert saw, rolled in a cradle of love so strong it could hipcheck a continent. He was a man who deserved respect. So Herbert gave him some.

"Also a God. Well, *the* God, to be precise."

Heller took Herbert's measure and snorted.

"Fucktacular." He shoved Crane away. "Everyone out." Heller guided Octavia and Ovales toward the door, then glared Herbert and Crane along behind them. When they were out, he grabbed a canister of liquid butane, opened the cap, set it on its side on the lab table, walked into the vestibule and looked out at his crew. He took his tin of Blue Tip matches from his pocket and popped one into his mouth, then, the tips of his teeth crimping the corners of the wood, he took another, struck it on the scratchy strip, tossed it over his shoulder into the lab, and kicked the door closed.

As he took a step toward the group, the butane lit, filling the lab with blue fire. He gathered Octavia under his arm and together they walked away as the lab's roof blew off and white-hot Halloween flames rocketed into the night like a backdrop in an 80s movie.

Chapter 57

Heller and Octavia stroll into Transluminal and Rose yells at them from across the room.

"Heller! My office!"

"Yeah, well, this had to be the way it ends, Eights." Heller glanced down at Octavia and winked. "I gave it my best shot."

"What do you mean, School?"

"The Platinum Package. I didn't close."

Octavia reached out and squeezed his elbow (cause she's a professional and a public display of affection is not cool). "You don't look too upset."

Heller blushed. Looked down at the carpet. "Well, I suppose I got a better deal." Then glanced at her with a look that radiated potential, a look that opened a vast gallery of snapshots of caresses, of looks, of smiles, of leaning against each other, of high fives, of smoldering kisses, and more. Octavia—for the first time in decades—blushed back.

They walked into Rose's office. Heller took off his watch and laid it on her desk.

"What the hell are you doing?" She asked.

"I'm turning in my badge. I'm gettin' too old for this sh–"

"What the holy hounds of hell are you talking about, Heller? You closed, you big dumb idiot! You closed!"

Heller stared at her for a minute like a big dumb idiot then a roar erupted from the office as they burst into applause. Rose handed Heller a dry erase marker and Heller, still in shock, crossed out the last box on his chart. Randall Jane, in a rare display of respect, played CCR over the speakers and everyone danced.

"But how," Heller asked. Rosie grinned. "Did the priest pony up?"

"Not the priest," said a voice dripping with privilege. Heller turned to see Christopher Aldous Knows a Good Thing When He Sees it Montgomery in a Hawaiian shirt and leis around his neck grinning around a fat cigar. "I couldn't pass it up. After you showed me my own fuck you money timeline, I just came in and signed up. Smugg went public. I'm rolling in it."

Heller grinned. "So I'm retired?"

Rose reached out her nubbin dwarfish paw, "Not until four, but yeah."

Heller curled an arm around Octavia's waist and went to pull her tight, but she beat him to it, grabbed him by the back of his neck, and planted a kiss so hot half the room turned away and the other half took up smoking.

Heller pulled away and looked at her with a question in his eyes.

"Oh, what?" she asked. "You want something, School?"

"I was wondering if you'd like to take a vacation?"

"Sorry, I'm booked."

Heller looked genuinely crestfallen. His crest, generally brave, waved goodbye to the cruel world and dove resolutely off his shoulder.

"But . . ."

"What, you think you're the only one with a Fuck You Money Timeline?"

"Oh," Heller said, loosening his grip. "Well–"

"Apparently, I end up married to a bajillionaire."

Heller's crest tried to dig a hole in the floor. Octavia pulled away and punched him in the shoulder. "It's you, pinchè abuelo idioto. You! I marry *you!* Jesu *Christo,* is it always gonna take you this long to catch on?"

Heller smiled wide enough to sever his own skull.

Rose took Heller's watch and stood between the two of them, dialed it to a specific node she felt beneath her fat microfingertips then handed it back to him.

"Octavia, be back by January. Heller," he looked down into her impish dried-apple face. "I will say this once and only once." She cleared her throat and crossed her arms. "You were the best salesmen who has ever worked here, hands down, no backsies, serious." She stuck out her hand. It disappeared into Heller's mitt.

They took a town car to the Ravenswood Episcopal Church, but the doorman didn't know anyone named Sidd and when Heller asked about Mooki the doorman kept asking him what 'her' name was again, and Heller just gave up.

Some weeks later on their yacht in Palau, Heller was standing on the aft deck with his binoculars jammed into his face looking for the taco boat when he saw a weird leisure craft fly out from behind one of the islands. He swung the binocs around and zoomed in to see a familiar floppy person sunning on the deck in a spectacular white outfit that revealed an awful lot of beautifully tanned skin without revealing anything that would evidence gender.

"Fuckstonishing," Heller whispered, then he yelled "Eights, get up here!" Octavia walked out from the lounge onto the deck beside him. He handed her the binoculars. "The sunbather."

"Oh, dios míos, ¿se Mooks en un bikini?!" Octavia jumped up and down waving and yelling "Mooki!" Heller opened up his phone and tabbed the airhorn app. It blasted across the waves, calling Mooki's yacht alongside. When it pulled up, Sidd was at the helm looking down at them with a big shit eating grin on his face. He was shirtless, wearing blinding white cargo shorts, and ray-bans as sharp as a knife. On the side of his boat, it read: Krishna's Tits.

They gathered on Heller's boat. Sidd nearly knocked Heller down. They hugged like long lost brothers. Mooks and Octavia disappeared below decks to look at her closet. Heller texted for a set up and in a moment, crewman Ovale Calvarium appeared with a tray of Mezcal shots and guacamole and a bucket of cheap ice-cold British War Widows. He set it all down with remarkable precision as Sidd watched him in near disbelief. *Well, kid probably needed a job,* he thought, *and Heller was a teddy bear, deep down. Makes sense.* Ovales smiled politely at Sidd, then looked pointedly at all the expensive crystal then nodded a nod that meant, *nice to see you, please don't shatter the glassware, again, sir.* Then he stowed his tray under his arm and disappeared into the galley to work on sandwiches. He cranked up the tunes while he worked, soft rock hits from the 70s were his jam. He smiled, despite his circumstances, as he danced a little and thought about the No. 12 Hydrolysis tube he had stored behind a secret plank in the narrow closet in his quarters.

"Sidd, what happened to being a Monk?"

"I got kicked out."

"Why?"

"My master said I was an idiot when I told him about TVI. He was like, we need a goddam air conditioner, Sidd. Go get that money! Then he slapped me."

"So, is it your string of sandwich shops?"

"It was, but I sold them and started a data management company."

"Holy shit. Who're your clients?"

"Oh, you know how it is, Heller, NDAs et cetera, et cetera. How about you?"

"Barbecue sauce king of the world."

"Fucknacular," Sidd grinned.

"Fucknacular indeed," Heller agreed.

They clinked their bottles together and sank back into luxurious deck chairs to watch the bright blue world and fuck around.

Ovales turned up the music.

Yachting your way on the Southern Seas

Light in your head and you're ready to eat

Well, it's another crazy day

You'll anchor in a bay

And forget about everything . . .

Epilogues

Amish Fight Club's Final Season

Back in the temple, the Master is yelling at an HVAC tech who's finishing up the new install. It's already running, he's just tweaking levels and cleaning up and trying his damndest to refrain from priesticide. The temple is still hot and humid as a jungle. The master is screaming in a rare fury. He couldn't be happier.

"Aaron, look at him." Says Eli, sitting in the only barbershop in Arthur, Illinois, looking up at their ridiculous tiny television as Eli gets his eyebrows threaded.

"I fear the show has come to its conclusion, Aaron."

"Where do you think the Monk got off to?"

"That old English sent him on an impossible quest."

"He did not, Eli. He dismissed him. He was ejected, just as you may eject one of your mother's salt pork nuggets which surely hath not digested–" Aaron didn't finish because Eli smacked him in the mouth with a rolled-up copy of *Feed & Supply Monthly,* which is a pretty thick magazine.

Back at the temple, the Master slammed the door shut behind the departing HVAC tech then fell back into his plush chair, tabbed the remote at the tiny T.V. which played *Amish Fight Club's* final season, and there was Aaron and Eli duking it out in the only barbershop in Arthur Illinois.

"Those two idiots are always fighting." He picked up his off-brand tablet which failed to operate. His mouth opened in a silent snarl shaped exactly like the name of his former pupil but then he remembered he'd kicked the idiot out. He tossed it aside then ran through the channels, looking for a new show.

Intervention.

The assembled deities were assembled back in the room at the Blackstone in Chicago, sitting on the edge of their seats as Crane finished his litany of sins against humanity in a fit of tears and snot. He blew his avian nose into a rag.

"So, that's about the end of it. I'm feel egret–"

"Don't you mean regret?" asked Rati.

"Uh, no. I feel . . . remorse . . . For the way I've handled it but, you guys know what it's like. You get lonely. You get weird."

"Thoth, why didn't you come to us?" Lakshmi had defrosted from being a cold, merciless version of herself–far more Kali than Lakshmi–but she still has her arms crossed and she's not buying any of it.

"I think you would have been," Crane looked in the middle distance for the time it takes a stalagmite to grow then be worn down to nothing again, then finished his sentence, "upset," Crane said.

"I would have slapped the unholy shit out of you, Thoth, but we'd all still help you out. We're not bad people." She looked around the room. "We're gods."

The door opened and Herbert leaned into the room. "The car is here."

"Anyhoo," Crane says, standing on his noodlish, knob kneed legs,

"That's me. You guys drop me a line–not a timeline, ha! But seriously, have your people worship with my people and we'll carve out some . . . I was gonna say time, but, ha ha." They all stared at him like he was a dick, which he was.

Ox head snorted. Horseface neighed. Crane left with Herbert who held the door for him then spoke to the driver then got in the back with his boss. They drove through the city then west through the suburbs past the airport where the traffic thinned out. Crane was reading *Birds of North America,* while Herbert poured him another Rat King from their mobile espresso maker.

"So, what are you, like, his butler?" The driver asked. Herbert froze while he was pouring the espresso and looked out of the window of the car across the narrative highway at the author as he said, sotto voce, "Really?" and shook his head as they sailed away into the distance.

Necrophone

The little phone dragged himself out from under the kitchen cabinets of The Narrows, across the galley floor, under the other cabinets to the side of a great box. He looked around and found a couple of cans that had rolled under the counter and a box of sterno. It took all night, but he managed to climb to the top of the box, over the edge, and dropped in.

It was as he remembered. Dead phones—at least thirty of them. Then, way in the corner, he saw a dim glow.

Is that a . . .

He drug himself as fast as he could along the corpses of his brethren toward the light. It was a multi-port charger with short cords dangling off its edge–and it had bars! Nearly half a charge! With his last ounce of strength, he grabbed an iPhone nubbin and shoved it up his outlet. Everything went dark.

A few hours later, he woke shining like a spectral warrior prince. His light illuminated the entire field of dead phones. He dragged the charger behind him as he marched across the electric abattoir to find his old friend, the Moto, selected the right dongle, and shoved it up his dead friend's port. After a minute or two, a dull red light pulsed. It would take a half a day, but his friend would soon rise from the dead to be by his side. He looked at the power cord for the charger, at least two feet long. He knew there was an outlet behind the garbage can by the box. He looked out over the graveyard, reached for the nearest cordless cadaver, and turned it over, looking for a way to plug in.

Grandpa

"Tell us about the ice again, grandpa!" George Junior's middle grandtardigrade larva cried. His other larva crowded around him, pawing his corpulent body with their stylets vibrating joy. George gazed into the rows of eye holes and papillae and smiled. It was a good life.

Long after the End of the Whirl, and immediately after the Rejoining of Waters, George Junior had led his lodge of the Assembled Champions of the Alabaster Sash through several years of prosperity and growth as the Man in the Front in the Big Chair, before moving on to being the District Deputy Guy Who Yells at Everyone In Lodge, and finally to become the Acknowledged Grand Illuminated High Hatted Illustrious Repositor before retiring.

It had been a time of unequaled placidity and joy, the waters of their world having been in near perfect stasis for years. It was only his stories, burnished to a dull bronze, told with a chuckle and melodramatic pauses and long-winded asides that took his audience of fascinated larva down vivid rabbit holes of time travel and frozen deserts and heroic tardigara fighting massive single-celled microflora and managing to escape with their lives and not much else that kept the memory of the Big Chill alive. His grandtardigara couldn't get enough of them.

But he was a tired old tardigrade, and his eight old legs didn't hold him up quite like they used to. Fortunately, the waters were warmer now and the light, though dim, was somehow spiced and exotic. Tropical.

He stood up with the help of his canes, screwed a worn old fez onto his massive, wrinkled mantle, and hobbled off to bed.

Rodney

And in an adjacent, but completely separate timeline, that's happening right now (but elsewhere) Rodney the spider is dangling from a roofbeam in the basketball gym of Northside Elementary. Six other spiders are hanging with him while another spider, older, shaggier, missing the last joint in one of his front legs, slides down a silvery silken thread to dangle at the front of the group.

"My name is Leonard and I've scared an arachnophobe."

The suspended arachnids all mumble together.

"Welcome, Leonard, this is a safe space."

"Would anyone like to start?" The older spider is looking right at Rodney who is oscillating slowly. "Rodney, this is your third meeting and while we don't keep score, I do feel like it's time you shared your motivation for attending Arachnophobe Abusers Anonymous."

"Well, I scared a spider hater, didn't I?" Rodney says.

"Did you?"

"Yeah, I did. Guy had it coming." The rest of the group mumbles their disagreement. One spider slides backward up its thread a little. Leonard sighs quietly. This is part of the process, he remembers.

"Why did the guy have it coming?"

"Cause he hates the eights, is why."

Another spider jiggles on his silk. "Eighter haters!"

"Spiders! This is not why we're here."

"He saw me and just started screaming, and I mean, like, endless. Not the usual shout-and-out, but prolonged howling." Rodney nervously grooms his eyebrows. "I'm sure you've all seen the video."

Everyone tries to appear as if they have no idea what Rodney is talking about except the one spider who snorts. "Classic."

"Well, it didn't feel classic, Gerome. It didn't feel classic at all. It felt bad. What did I do wrong? Huh? What did I do wrong? I introduced myself. That's it. A polite, *good morning sir, lovely day, isn't it?* And this guy re—" Rodney quivers with shame.

"It's ok to use the words that mean the thing you're talking about, Rodney." Leonard says, his spider voice gravelly and warm. "This is a safe space."

"He *recoiled*."

Three spiders zip back up their lines.

The snorting spider has his phone out and it suddenly plays the video. The gym is filled with the tinny horror of a terrified Analyst, echoing and rebounding through the halls. As everyone is staring at the image in the snorter's paw, the double doors at the end of the gym fly open and the women of the Jefferson Park Cozy Mysteries Book club totter in about three steps before they see the circle of dog-sized spiders hanging from the ceiling, the sound of Steve's howling bouncing around. All six of the women scream and run back out into the hall. Laura Jean Harper pees herself.

The snorter puts its phone away.

"You see?" Rodney says, chagrined. "Every time. Every frikkin' time."

the end

About the Author

Born in Birmingham, Alabama in 1964, Christopher "Bull" Garlington is a beloved storyteller whose books have brought readers the joy of highly literate fart jokes, Zombie-based telephone sales, and transglobal non-corporeal skills based guild-societies. He is best known for his travel memoir, *The Full English,* his work as a columnist for various online and print magazines, and for his writing at *All American Whiskey.*

Garlington lives in Chicago with [his attorney] on the far north side where he divides his time between writing and staring at things. These two efforts are often indistinguishable. He is an amateur chef, an ambitious if not exactly gifted gardener, an amiable neighbor, and a bad, though willing, dancer. You can learn more about Garlington by visiting his website: www.bullgarlington.com

Give this book away.

Did you like this book? Well, *thank you.* I was hoping you'd get a kick out of it. If you did, if you laughed out loud or snickered, even *once,* I'd say that's a win for both of us. Finding just a *sliver* of joy in this endless soul crushing madness is a bonus these days. I am overjoyed if I made you laugh.

Maybe I could convince you to pass it on? I mean, look: most people live in an endless rushing river of cold anxiety, bone cracking worry, and endless dread. Making them laugh does more than just bring joy into their life. If a person laughs, even once, it changes their whole demeanor–sometimes for a minute, sometimes for a day.

They walk around the office with a bounce in their stride. They wave at strangers. They smile for no damn reason. There's great value in this. It is, I am convinced, the surest and most effective way to connect people. When people feel connected, they make better decisions, they consider the bigger picture. They grumble less, and they help more, and even just the teensiest little bit of such behavior, even a sliver of kindness, is powerful. It ripples outward from the smile, from the wave, from the returned grocery cart, out into the nearby world, igniting sparks of kindness in others. Smiles are contagious. Laughter is contagious.

What I'm asking you to do, in no small way, is to save the world. I know it sounds ridiculous, but hear me out: *Give this book away.*

You're done with it, right? Hand it to your funniest friend. Give it to a co-worker. Throw it at your most ardent enemy. Hell, hand it to a perfect stranger and say: *I loved this book. I laughed my ass off. Take it. Enjoy it. Pass it on.*

Spread joy.

Save the world.

—Bull Garlington